© 2022 Nicholas John Smith

Neither the vastness of the universe... the cosmic body shall ever become... exploration. The minuteness of matter... observed or measured by man. The profundity of the human body is such that it exceeds human knowledge, which can merely scratch the surface. Life is so complex and diverse that it shall forever be an enigma to man.

A wicked person is born of jealousy. Out of selfishness and anger he complains about supposed "unfairness."
A good person always has compassion in his heart. Free of discontentment and hatred, he sees hardship as joy.
An enlightened person has not any attachment. He quietly observes the people of the world lost in illusion.

He who disregards ordinary sorrows and joys,
A cultivator is he.
He who has no attachment to worldly loss and gain,
An Arhat is he.[1]

---

[1] Zhuan Falun (Volume II) Li Hongzhi English Translation (June 2008)

1.

Twenty-three-year-old Theresa Hogan awakes staring at the pastel pink ceiling to snoring in stereo and initially has little recollection of the previous night. The tantalizingly sexy and beautiful spoilt daughter of an Irish construction tycoon feels sore between her thighs and her ample breasts feel bruised; at least she is at home in her king size bed in the upmarket city center apartment her father rents for her. She turns her head to the left and sees the short cropped afro hair and muscular broad black back and shoulders of Stan Taylor, a twenty-five-year-old up and coming gangster who considers himself an entrepreneur and strongman of the Manchester nightlife scene. She got to know Stan from clubbing and supplying her with cocaine over two years ago when she started to hit the student nightlife scene after moving to Manchester to study at the university. Recalling the previous night she turns her head to the right to see how Jack Jones looks in his slumber, also twenty-five, good looking and, to her knowledge, a playboy come business man running things for his well-known father and often accompanied and minded by Stan. Theresa has been fascinated by the black and white duo since meeting Jack over a year ago but has never been intimate with either, until now. As she gazes Jack stirs.

"Good morning, Theresa, thanks for letting us crash here last night," he whispers so as not to wake Stan.

"The way my pussy feels I think you have a lot more than that to thank me for," Theresa replies in a similar hushed tone while wearing a mischievous smile.

"Shall we begin where we left off?" Jack whispers as he rolls onto his side to face Theresa.

"And where would that be, Jack. I can only remember

taking a taxi back here with you and Stan and having a few drinks here. Then what?" She asks although she has some recollection and a good idea of what transpired the previous night.

"Then you invited us to bed, and from what I remember you seemed to have the best time out of the three of us. I can only hope you are on the pill…"

"What! You didn't wear a condom?" Theresa interrupts.

"Theresa, I didn't even think about it, I had taken an E on top of all the booze we had. I don't know if Stan did but I doubt it, he was in a similar state."

"Yo, man. I think I was in a worse state than the two of you put together if the pain in my head is anything to go by," Stan mumbles into consciousness as he comes out of his slumber and turns to face them.

"Shit!" Jack cannot hide his disappointment at not being able to take soul advantage of Theresa.

"What d' ya mean, bro, am I interrupting something?"

"Well, you could have been if you hadn't woken up just now but a little later."

"Hey, man. Forget I'm here, just carry on, I'm in no fit state to join in anyway," Stan replies and turns his back again.

"I think I've had my fill of you two guys, especially since you didn't wear condoms, so I mean it literally. Fuck knows what I've caught from you!" Theresa exclaims but the real reason she is so agitated is that she is in the middle of her ovulation and does not take the contraceptive pill due to her father's strong Catholic leaning. Before she left for Manchester he informed her that if she ever took contraceptives he would disinherit her. She considered taking them anyway but if her father were to find out, which could easily happen since he makes her use the family's private doctor, she stands to lose a fortune in inheritance plus her current relatively lavish lifestyle she is provided with while she studies property management.

"Hey, where you goin?" Jack asks as Theresa climbs over him to get out of the bed.

"I told you, I've had enough. The only thing you're going to get out of me now is coffee. How do you take it?"

"Black, with no sugar, but not too strong," Jack replies then drools over the sight of the pert, firm naked buttocks as Theresa walks away towards the door.

"If I may, Theresa, could you make mine white with two sugars, please. And if you've got any aspirin, I would really appreciate it, Theresa," Stan says not too loudly, bordering on the obsequious and very uncharacteristically as she leaves the bedroom. Stan and Jack both know the father of Theresa or rather his reputation: a self-made multi-millionaire rumored to have initially gained his construction contracts and wealth through extortion and intimidation with the help of the I.R.A. of which he was a member.

Three weeks later, after missing her period, Theresa finds it almost unbearable to look at the home test result. The bold pink line screams at her and she feels her stomach plunge then breaks out in a cold sweat as the panic attack envelops her.

"Theresa hasn't been in touch for weeks, she never usually goes this long without ordering some gear," Stan mentions to

Jack as they stand at the bar of a pub popular with students and several of Stan's customers.

"She was obviously unimpressed by our performance the other night or maybe she found another dealer," Jack replies nonchalantly.

"What d'ya mean, talk about yourself maybe but I've never left a woman unsatisfied," Stan replies indignantly.

"Why don't you give her a call?"

"What! I never call a customer, it could give them the idea that I'm desperate to push then they'll start thinking about a discount," Stan answers as Jack makes a call to Theresa.

"Shit!" Jack exclaims after a moment and his look turns sour.

"What?"

"Her number is no longer in service."

"So, why so pissed-off?"

"I was hoping to get another night or more with her, but alone. You know, get to know her better."

"Never thought you could be bothered about the loss of a fuck buddy. You really got the hots for her," Stan chuckles then adds, "why don't you go and ask Steph over there with the Harry Potter lookalike? She often hangs out with Theresa, maybe she's got another number for her or knows where she's at," he suggests and to his surprise Jack walks over to Steph.

"Steph, isn't it?" Jack asks the tall slim flat chested academic looking student who is sat at a high table talking to her boyfriend.

"Yes, you're Jack, a friend of Theresa's if I'm not mistaken;" Steph answers and looks at Jack questioningly.

"That's right. I wanted to ask you about Theresa. I just tried calling her and her mobile is out of service. Do you know how I can get hold of her?"

"Yes, but you'll have to go to Dublin first."

"What! She's gone back home?" Jack's disappointment is evident.

"Yes, she left the day before yesterday. Said she had family problems but wouldn't say what. Said she was cancelling her mobile but would let me know her knew number when she gets a replacement in Ireland. I'll let you know it if it's okay with her. Do you want to give me your number?" Steph asks and looks expectantly at Jack.

"Er, no, she has it. It wasn't important. Could you ask her to call me when she gets back, Steph?"

"Sure, but she said she had no idea when that would be."

2.

The icy chill of a particularly cold February morning in Vienna streams in through the open window but has little effect. I perspire profusely as I bear the wheel before me, face bathed in sweat, beading and trickling, so hard to ignore but I must have tolerance, the nausea building. I defy my aching arms in an effort to sustain the stance and retain composure though it is impossible to stop the slight swaying of my body caused alternatively by the forces of yin and yang. The butterflies in my stomach dance with ever increasing urgency; a fluttering of wonderment and great anticipation? Once I would have thought so, but no, now I know it is really the turning of the wheel. The crown of my head alive with an electric, tingling, tickling sensation as it communicates with the vast universe and other entities of myself in other dimensions, another irritation that must be ignored. I can only be on the threshold of some spiritual passage, I am taking a step closer. The light ones appear, two, three even five at once whilst the dark ones hardly take a look in. My hands trace an eerie outline in this foreign worldly dimension I view them as I gradually lower the throbbing wheel to my abdomen. What was that? That's a first, I've never heard that before; I've never heard anything before. Almost inaudible but definitely there, a strange, low incomprehensible muttering, am I experiencing clairaudience? It would be another sign of my level rising. The sensations and nausea overwhelms, I open my eyes as the vomit fills my mouth and only just manage to make it to the bathroom.

As I clean myself up I gaze at my reflection in the mirror; is it a residue of vanity or do I appear healthier, more vibrant, younger, even?

Had I experienced these manifestations earlier in my practice I would have been astonished, bewildered, since it could only have been proof of the existence of the Fa, of which I had initially no fathomable reason to believe in, only some kind of intrigue - no something more than intrigue - a calling more like, an innate knowledge that it was a possible way to find what I look for, an answer to why I exist and why I exist where I exist. Now, after over five years of practice, which I always feel I have not been determined and resolute enough in doing, I feel no excitement, I feel its existence and realize I would not have such experiences if I were to find them sensational. Reality is not sensational, maybe I'm getting closer to it. It's paradoxical, the closer I get, the further I go, the crazier the experiences, dreams and visions, the more mundane I find them, well, perhaps not mundane, simply natural on a journey back. My cultivation level must be rising, nothing else can explain the tranquility of my mind as it observes such phenomena. This I longed for not so long ago, a longing that could only hold me back, but now, now it is merely a trivial step forward. My whole existence is inconceivably trivial, this dimension, this world, all of what I know - trivia - something created by unimaginable beings out of their compassion for us damned to annihilation. One last chance embedded in a multitude of existences to unravel and purify those thoughts and deeds which, out of greed, pride, selfishness, any kind of desire or attachment, even fear, would have otherwise condemned us to oblivion if it was not for this opportunity provided by such compassionate divine beings. A chance to redeem ourselves by purifying the karma we have created over countless lifetimes in the human realm and those beyond and replace it with virtue.

I'm convinced I have found that something indefinable that I was looking for. Some search for it in worldly ambition, achievement and success, others in religion and spirituality, a few look to science, while some lost souls submerge themselves in alcohol and drugs, as I once did, but most just remain oblivious, in infinite ignorance and complacency, struggling, competing to be the best, to earn the most or just to pay off the bills, clothe their kids and take a vacation when the bank balance allows. Never looking further than the next pay check, promotion or salary increase people meander through their lives looking for the easiest way forward in this material malaise they only know of as reality, and are enslaved by it. And they are the lucky ones;

people whose past life sins are not so great as to put them at the bottom of the human pile not to mention the animal realms and those below. The ones privileged by the light density of their karma to be born into a so called developed and westernized society. People who do not have to fear famine, pestilence, war and the elements on a daily basis. The greatest fears most people hold in our societies are those of disease, poverty, failure, misfortune befalling themselves and loved ones; even the down and outs have a soup kitchen or food charity to turn to, they are not going to starve to death living in the midst of such material abundance.

I close the windows and linger as I take in the view of Vienna's skyline. The commanding spire of St. Stephan's Cathedral taking center stage. A huge monument testament to the devotion, subjugation and sacrifice of people and the wealth and power of the Roman Catholic Church. A church that has been by far the most instrumental spiritual influence in the history of Western civilization. A church created when the Roman Empire decided to take on Christianity as its religion in an attempt to control it despite the fact they had crucified its creator over three hundred years previously. A church that tortured and burned people in the name of God for not following it by the likes of the Spanish Inquisition and witch finders worldwide. But it is not a true church of God, it is just a ruling establishment created by the rulers at the time of its inception, which even to this day, taxes its members at source in many countries.

Taking a shower I contemplate my latest exercise experience, my mind drifts back to Tibet; what kind of person would I be now if I had never made that trip? A trip my wife coerced me into since I did not believe capitalist westerners entertaining themselves by gawping at the natives and their lifestyle would be appreciated by such a rural, peasant-like, backward, suppressed people. How wrong was I about them and especially wrong about what they would and would not appreciate. Although I believe that my knowledge now of just how ignorant and egotistical I am in no way makes me a better person than I was before being touched by Buddhism intimately, I begin to understand perceptions can be as great a falsehood as they can an insight. Did I believe in God or a higher being then? I do not know what it is that I believe in now, it is indiscernible, Dafa, the Fa, but I believe in it. I can fully accept God to be Dafa, the creator of all, and even Jesus one of his enlightened beings, a Buddha, not so different to Shakyamuni trying to save souls in a way that people around him might understand. I believe this existence we live is just a dance choreographed by our own ignorant, selfish egos and realized through desires and aversions. Emotions, which define our character and actions and ultimately create our reality in this domain. This understanding first led me to a state of nihilistic despair, which I still sometimes fall into, causing depressions so suicidal that the only thing that keeps me alive is the love of my family and the fear of rebirth in a lower realm and these reasons, aversion and desire, are things I must strive to extinguish. I have to remind myself that pain and suffering, in whatever form it comes, is something to be endured, tolerated and accepted as the righteous fruition of karma; in fact, something to be invited to cleanse oneself. I wonder if some of the more extreme members of Opus Dei, who carry out self-flagellation are expediting themselves along a spiritual path, a kind of short cut to divinity. But, I ask myself, is not the practice of Falun Dafa so different in essence? Apart from the physical discomfort the exercises bring there is far more albeit involuntary suffering, whether mentally or physically, in order to cleanse karma. I desperately hope to cleanse enough of it to render a rebirth somewhere as something that can continue cultivation. This hope, since hope is an attachment, in itself goes against what I try to practice. What is the point? Just what is the point? It's hard to comprehend my feelings, a natural love for and attachment to my wife, child, my whole family but it's not natural because our existence is not true existence, it's a result of selfish desire and the fear of whatever it is we fear during this lifetime and countless ones before. Fear and desire, every attachment is birthed by these parents. So who or what makes us to love and cherish, to hate and fight? Nothing but a chaotic ensemble of contradicting opinions and emotions, desires and fears that make us the human beings we are. Our whole existence in this realm is as a ship sailing a sea of hope and fear, battered by suffering and elated in ecstasy, the mind has no time for refuge or quiet observation because the wind of our karma driving the sails is ceaseless and forever changing, mirroring the thoughts that generate our existence as they ripen into action and hence more karma. I long to make the right decisions and do the right thing with my life but find it so difficult. I perfectly understand wu wei practicing monks who refrain from thought and therefore making decisions and wish I could be in a similar permanent state. But that is impossible in this materialistic secular world in which I live and have to make decisions in the hope they are the right ones, which do not create karma. To envisage making a decision in the extreme I contemplate what would have happened to someone who made a decision to risk their own life to save the life of a drowning boy and that boy turned out to be Adolf Hitler, would that someone create virtue for saving a life or would that someone amass great karma for being responsible for the suffering of millions?

"I'm home Jack! Hope I didn't disturb your daffering?" My contemplation is broken as my wife, Nora, enters the apartment after dropping Tasha, our four year old daughter, off at kindergarten. At least she has reduced her harsh ridicule of my practicing Falun Dafa to a mild form of mockery. Being a staunch Catholic she turns a blind eye and deaf ear to any other religion apart from to denigrate them, despite the fact she is indirectly responsible for the belief I now hold. Call it a religion, practice, philosophy, Falun Dafa encompasses all including science but no scientist could scratch the surface of its reality because scientists are trapped in this dimension they call reality. I realize some studying quantum physics and string theory are looking at the possibilities of other dimensions but they will never see them using scientific means alone. I believe that when the great 19th century inventor the popular electric car was named after, Nikolai Tesla said, 'The day science begins to study non-physical phenomena, it will make more progress in one decade than in all the previous centuries of its existence', was exceptionally accurate. Probably two of the most knowledgeable *scientists* this civilization has seen among people are Jesus Christ and Buddha Shakyamuni. During the initial months of my practice and years after I had acquainted myself with Buddhism, Nora considered it some kind of gimmick I had adopted that I would surely bore of when I realized just how foolish a thing it was to do and an utter waste of time. As time went by and it became clear my *gimmick* was becoming increasingly important to me rather than diminishing so her hostility and irritation toward me grew ever increasingly aggressive. Bitter and pointless arguments ensued, but it was something I could only expect since the Master had stated in his work, Zhuan Falun, this would probably be the case with partners who were not practitioners, and so it was with Nora and myself for a while. But as time went by she noticed a change in me, initially an alien side that was more tolerant, sympathetic and less egotistical; although she would never admit it I could sense it. For this I was thankful.

"No you didn't, I had to cut it short to throw up, dear."

"I'm at a complete loss as to why you bother with that stuff when it makes you ill, you're some kind of masochist."

"You know why. It's proof to me that something is going on, something I cannot explain because I don't exactly know what it is myself, something so real that it is affecting me physically. I would rather get an unpleasant reaction than none at all. Besides, I've had far greater benefits from the practice than I've had discomforts. I've told you, I no longer need laxatives or antacid tablets...'

"Yeah. And you no longer need sex!"

Damn. She has me. It's not that my libido is failing, just my attachment to it. So now I fail my duties as a *normal* healthy husband. Another guilt trip, I have so many I put myself through. The list includes an ever-growing acknowledgement and immense regret of my wrongful deeds against a multitude of sentient beings from animals I killed, considering it sport, to hearts I broke in various ways. Deeds I now feel so bereft of human decency I am left in shame. I even feel an extreme guilt for the way in which I abused my own body through booze and drug fueled nights resulting in hospitalizing accidents, usually car crashes, contracting sexually transmitted diseases, not to mention the inherent dangers involved in the way I made a living involving drug dealing, prostitution and robbery. Nora is ten years younger than I and deserves more from our relationship but the desire just isn't in me any longer. A thing I know my practice is responsible for, something I should be happy with myself about since it means the end of another attachment. The first to go was smoking, from two packs a day I stopped completely within a few months of practicing. It was not something I consciously tried to do, I just lost my taste for cigarettes until I detested the smell of them. My love of alcohol took a little longer but the same scenario. It came to the point where I had no idea why I had been so reliant on it. Typically a couple of bottles of wine and many beers a day plus vodka or cognac. I knew I was an alcoholic in the eyes of society but I never considered myself to be one until I started to lose my taste for it. Initially the vodka and cognac, then my wine consumption declined over a few weeks until I didn't touch it and then I didn't enjoy a beer anymore. Next up was meat, which I ate almost every day in some form or another. Again, without setting out to be a vegetarian, I didn't enjoy salads, fruit and vegetables any more than I had done, I just lost my appetite for meat and only eat it occasionally usually when I make something for Nora. One thing I did not notice abandoning until sometime after I had was my propensity to use vulgar language, I would curse using the most extreme swear words at the drop of a hat, something that irritated Nora immensely. These are developments I am happy about since they were unhealthy attachments and now my desire for them has gone so the attachment has genuinely dissolved but the sex thing I cannot help feeling guilty about and cannot tell Nora why. It would only give her more ammunition to condemn my practice with. This thing that has instilled in me the adamantine belief it is a true way to the salvation of my very being is also leading me down a path which denies me the comfort of being a contented, unquestioning family man and perhaps even a normal human being in the eyes of humanity, as it is widely known. I could not blame her if she strayed. Intelligent, attractive, athletic, tall and blond, looking exceptionally young for her age she would not have to try in the least to find some young stud to entertain her and Vienna is far from short of such people looking for a little excitement.

"Hey, come on, that's not fair. I am over fifty and cannot stand the side effects Viagra gives me!" my defense is not a lie but also not complete.

"Yeah, I know. Forget I mentioned it," Nora's acceptance just makes me feel worse.

"How was Tasha when you dropped her at kindergarten?" I need to change the subject.

How Tasha, our four-year-old daughter, has become a main focal point in my life not only as a daughter I cherish in the way a normal loving father would she also draws me closer to Dafa and Buddhism in general. A strange contradiction since attachment in any form is considered something that should be discarded. But the strength of feeling and unconditional love I have for Tasha is such that it compels me to contemplate having such feelings towards all sentient beings more so than reading literatures that propend this contemplation. But this love is inextricably linked to sorrow since all living things, which we love and cherish in this realm will experience suffering and eventually die. So if we look no further than this realm ultimately all we have to look forward to is dying ourselves causing suffering to those who love us and the ones we love suffering and dying before us.

"The usual. Ran off to join her class. Not even time for a goodbye kiss."

"At least it shows she's happy there."

"Guess so."

"And her German is as good as her English now." Tasha initially spoke only English since that is the language her mother and I converse in.

"She needs it if we are going to stay in Austria for the duration of her education," Nora doesn't try to hide the little exasperation in her reply.

"Now you're a Ph.D. and with your position here, there's not much point in us going to England in the foreseeable future, I'll just have to find something I can do from here." Nora is a university professor and I a software contractor without a contract for the last five and a half years, which I don't really mind since it allows me more time for Dafa albeit at the expense of income but I have few desires for myself only the wellbeing of my family and to progress in cultivation. I met Nora nine years ago while working a contract in Vienna and we married a year later.

"How long do you think we can go on like this? My

income isn't as much as we would like and your savings are being spent."

"Yeah, I know, but I've told you my software knowledge is practically obsolete and I'm not getting anywhere with the UN, I'll just have to do something myself." When I met Nora I was working on a contract for Telekom Austria developing software in a programming language rapidly declining in popularity, but the money was good so I stayed as long as I could and the initial six month contract grew into five years. When the contract finally ended, hard to find work with software in Vienna, I applied to the UN for anything tech based since they have a headquarters here and the working language is English, my German is worse than bad considering how long I have been in Austria.

"You keep saying that but what and when are you going to do it?"

"I don't know, I'm racking my brains and scouring the internet for ideas." My brains are far from racked and I cannot find anything I can trust on the net to make an honest income. Besides, I feel no inclination or motivation to make money as long as there is enough to cover basic living expenses, but Nora doesn't see it that way. Before I became so spiritually inclined towards Buddhism and Falun Dafa I tried a supposed investment guru I found on the net, who actually did have a good proven track record. Despite this I lost quite a large proportion of my savings on the stock markets. I went through hell as I watched my investments turn into liabilities but now I put it down to karma cleansing rather than bad luck, which I now know luck, good or bad, is an illusion, just the product of karma or virtue. This knowledge gives me some kind of closure on the: *woulda, coulda, shoulda,* debates I once held in my mind that produced such mental turmoil and anxiety. I understand that every final outcome to anything will be just. It may not appear so initially: a drug dealer lives a life of opulence and incomparable luxury, a human rights defender is incarcerated, worse still, Falun Dafa practitioners are outlawed and tortured, even rumored to have their vital organs harvested for high paying recipients. There is no shorter waiting list than in China for a desperately needed liver or kidney or whatever - ordered and available within a few weeks.

"If you learnt to speak German better it would help...." The ringing tone of the landline is a welcome interruption. I eagerly retrieve the handset.

"Hello?"

"Hi, Jack, it's Beth."

"How are you sis? Long time no speak." Although I try to keep in touch with my alcoholic, ex-junkie wayward younger sister with the IQ of a genius living in England she rarely answers her phone or emails, this is the first time we've spoken in three months or more.

"I'm fine. You - what are you up to?"

"Yeah, I'm okay. Busy as ever despite not having a job. Tasha keeps me well occupied and there's always something needs doing in the apartments Nora rents out, usually re-decorating or assembling Ikea furniture for new tenants and then there's my Falun Dafa." Two apartments in our building became vacant about eighteen months ago and Nora managed to purchase them with my financial help with deposits at a knock down price because of her relationship with the owners. We look upon them as investments for the future when the mortgages are paid off.

"Still doing your daffy dafa," Beth teases. Although I explained the benefits of the practice to Beth she considers it a topic of great humor and ridicules me in a childish fashion whenever I mention it, not unlike Nora just more comical rather than cynical.

"That's suitably crass for you Beth."

"Listen, Jack, Stan just called me and I gave him your number."

"You what?"

Stan is a character from my dark and distant past and he is the darkest character, literally as well as metaphorically, that I have ever had the misfortune to meet. Stan is of Negro blood having a Jamaican father and Haitian mother he embodies all that one could imagine of a violent, black yardie gangster. Six foot four and powerfully built Stan worked out at the gym most days when he wasn't running his organization of hookers, drug dealers, pimps and plain robbers back when I was involved with him. In my early twenties my lifestyle, outlook and desires could not have been more removed from what they are now, just as I cannot now understand how and why I have morphed into something unrecognizable as the something I once was. This, I can only put down to Falun Dafa. Even after training in software programming, and working in the industry after turning thirty I still had ties with some very dubious characters. It was not until my contract in Vienna that I really let go of my past.

"Come on, Jack. What the fuck was I supposed to do? Tell him I don't know it - do you want to have a crippled or dead sister?" Beth once had an affair with Stan and used to visit him in prison on the occasions he was incarcerated, but that was long ago, before he treated her however he treated her. When she got to know the real Stan she distanced herself as much as possible and has had no contact with him for the last twenty years or more to my knowledge.

"Okay, Beth. Do you know what he wants me for?"

"He heard you are living in Vienna. Maybe he wants free accommodation on a holiday, ha, ha. I don't know, Jack, he just said it would be nice to catch up with you."

"God. It's been a long time. What was he like and how did he get hold of you?"

"The same old Stan the Man but with a shaven head. Probably going gray or bald or both, you know how vain he is, but looked as fit and threatening as ever. He only had to ask around to find out where I live now. I never go down town anymore. I'm content looking after my chickens and ducks and dogs."

"Okay, sis. Guess you couldn't do much else. Are you staying off the gear?"

"Of course. Just drink wine these days. I'm getting too old for the other shit. Stan offered me a bag but I told him I don't do it anymore."

"Good girl…"

"Look, Jack, I'm sorry I gave him your number but at least you're forewarned. Let me know if he calls and what he wants."

"Will do, Beth. If you answer your phone, that is."

"I'm sorry, just haven't felt like talking to anybody lately, but I will pick-up in future. I've got to shoot, the dogs are whining to be walked."

"Okay, Beth, we'll talk later. Bye," I replace the handset and must look concerned.

"What was all that about?" Nora sounds concerned.

"Remember Stan, the black guy I told you about, the one that used to be my minder sometimes?"

"You mean the murderer?"

"It was never proven, just rumored," I reply meekly. During our acquaintance Stan had one of his hookers latch on to a diamond dealer in Antwerp. Stan had connections in Belgium and during one of his many visits there the diamond dealer was found dead in the toilets of a popular bar. He was a heroin user and had shot up some bad gear, which killed him and the cache of diamonds he was carrying disappeared. Interpol stopped Stan when he tried to return to the U.K. but had insufficient evidence to hold him. Since Stan had a lot to do with my life in bygone times I had told Nora this story amongst many others, which usually entailed crime and extreme violence.

"Even so, everything else you told me about him was pretty horrific. And what does he want?"

"I've no idea. Beth just said he heard I was living here now and wanted my number."

"And she gave it to him!"

"Come on, Nora. He knows where she lives. What was she supposed to do?"

"She could have told him she didn't know it."

"Stan knows I'm close to Beth and probably also knows she's been to see us a few times."

"So what will you do if he calls?"

"I dunno. I'll have to wait and see what he wants. Maybe he won't call. His lifestyle is so erratic, well used to be, he might decide to do one thing one day and totally forget about it the next. Especially if something more interesting pops up. I'll just have to wait and see."

"There's no way he's going to come here. I'm not having an animal like that around Tasha."

"Do you think I would allow it? If he comes I'll tell him he'll have to stay at a hotel. You wouldn't have to meet him at all."

"So you would see him?" Nora is exasperated.

"Come on. What do you expect me to do?"

"I don't expect you to go partying with a drug dealing, murdering pimp. You're a father. You've got responsibilities," Nora's exasperation grows.

"Hey, calm down. Like I said, he probably won't even call never mind come visit. Just forget about it for now. We can discuss it if and when he calls. Okay?"

"Just make sure he doesn't come if he calls."

"I'll do my best. Now, what would you like for dinner tonight?" I need closure on the subject.

3.

The calm Caribbean makes fast and easy headway for Esmerelda, one of the fastest production powerboats money can buy. Even so, the speed at which she travels causes her bow to constantly lurch out of the water before crashing back down throwing up a storm of rainbow colored sea spray, which engulfs the two occupants every few seconds.

"Jesus, Moses! Do you have to go so fast? We're nearly there," Branden, the thirty-year-old high paying passenger, asks the boat's owner. It is Branden's first trip of this sort. He is dipping his childlike naive chubby toe into the dark, dangerous world of drug smuggling. He doesn't need to do it out of desperation, he comes from a wealthy middle class family based in New York. He used to work in the family textile business but after hanging out in Little Italy with some of the Mafioso his father had to pay protection to he was enlightened to how lucrative the cocaine business could be. It started when his father sent him to Toni's bar in Mulberry Street with a roll of dollar bills every week to give to Toni who would pass it on to the mob. Soon Branden was giving the money directly to mob members. Stories of the late Pablo Escobar's wealth and power transfixed him. Of small demeanor and chubby appearance Branden had a little man's syndrome but Pablo had made phenomenal wealth and was feared and respected by countless of his Columbian natives as well as international criminals and he was not slim and stood at only five feet five. This gave the inferiority complexed 'would be' macho man Branden great encouragement. When his New York Mafia connections suggested they arrange and finance him to collect a hundred kilos of uncut cocaine from Colombia to be delivered to Barbados he jumped at the chance.

"Look, Branden, the U.S. are supplying the Barbados Defense Force Coast Guard with some pretty fast intercept boats. Fast, but couldn't touch this baby flat out, so we've gotta stay flat out until we get to the drop off if you want to hold on to your merchandise and stay outa jail. And most importantly, I wanna keep my boat. Capisce!" Moses, the tall, greying middle-aged Jamaican boatman flashes a gold toothed smile at Branden, but the threat is tangible.

"Whatever you say, Moses. You're the captain," comes Branden's sheepish reply.

"That's right, boy. Now fetch us another beer. We've just got enough time to sink one before we get there."

Valentina sips on her ice-chilled Kilian vodka as see scans the Caribbean from the terrace of her luxury villa in Holetown, Barbados. A smile creeps across her usually stone expression when she sees the black powerboat heading in her direction in an otherwise vessel free seascape. She enjoys combining business with pleasure but has grown bored of the Caribbean island and is eager to get back to a colder climate and eventually her beloved Nikita. She places her drink on the small glass topped table by her side and pushes herself out of the deep rocking-chair.

"Alexie, Nikolai! I think it's here, you better go down and be ready to offload it fast," she commands in her deep voiced thick Russian accent.

Her two obedient, tall, steroid-enhanced muscle-bound henchmen appear on the terrace behind her almost immediately. She stretches her arms into the air and thrusts out her firm ample breasts that are barely covered by the micro-bikini top she wears, her erect nipples threatening to burst through the fine golden fabric at any moment, her flimsy matching gee-string also leaving little to the imagination. The men have no choice but admire her scantily clad bronzed physic, over six feet in her heeled sandals she clenches her fat-free rock-hard buttocks to emphasize muscle definition then turns to face them. They stand transfixed while she raises her sunglasses and gives them a smile that could never be warm with such ice-blue eyes and sharp but beautifully cold features accentuated by her short cropped platinum hair.

"Should we bring it up here?" Alexie, the forty-five-year-old shaven-headed older but slightly smaller at six foot six, of the two enquires.

"No, stick it in the car. We can leave for the airport soon. There is no point in bringing it up here."

"Nice place your friend's got here, Branden," Moses comments as he maneuvers the boat up against the private quayside. Alexie catches the rope Branden throws and secures the boat. Nikolai jumps aboard, takes two of the four matching Samsonite suitcases and passes them over to Alexie then retrieves the other two, which he places on the quayside then disembarks the boat himself. No word is spoken between the four men during the process. Moses looks out to sea while Branden smiles apprehensively at the two Russians. He has been briefed on what and who to expect at the drop off and there was no mistaking Alexie and Nikolai from who had been described to him.

"Warm friendly guys, huh?" Moses quips as the Russians saunter off with the merchandise.

"Let's get out of here, should they come back," Branden quivers.

"The sooner the better, boy. The sooner the better. Untie us and we're outa here," Moses replies with uncharacteristic concern.

Customs officials paid to turn a blind eye look on as the long range Gulfstream private jet is loaded by Alexie and Nikolai while a cold faced Valentina boards the plane without paying any attention to any of them despite the fact she is the object of the officials interest with her high stilettos, mini-skirt and tight, almost see-through, black halter-neck top; the fact she is braless is very obvious. Once in the cabin, feeling tired, she takes a small vile from her Gucci handbag and sprinkles out cocaine onto the cabin table and prepares herself two generous lines with a custom made two inch engraved silver chopping blade, one for each nostril. Then she retrieves a similarly engraved silver straw from her bag. As she snorts the second line, Simon, her British pilot, comes out of the cockpit.

"We've been cleared for takeoff ma'am. Please let me know as soon as possible when you are ready."

"Don't worry, Simon, the boys will soon be finished." Two minutes later Alexie and Nikolai board the plane and ten minutes later it is air-born on its way to Bratislava.

4.

I open the window and settle my mind in preparation to start my exercises after Nora has left to take Tasha to kindergarten. What now? Just as I begin the phone rings. No one usually calls so early. It's only been a week since Beth called, so I doubt it's her. Please do not let it be Stan. Should I answer? He will not stop trying if I do not. I pick up the handset with great trepidation and listen.

"Yo, is anyone on the other end of this fucking line?" comes Stan's unmistakable voice after about five seconds.

"Hey, Stan, how's it going? Long time no speak," I try to sound composed and relaxed.

"Yo! Jack. I heard you were in Vienna and got your number from Beth. What you do'in over there?"

"Well, not a lot really, Stan. Remember, I got into computers and programming. I finally ended up with a high paying contract in Vienna. It's finished now but I married a university professor and we have a daughter here so I'm just bumming around and taking life easy trying to be as respectable as possible, my daughter takes up a lot of my time with taking her to kindergarten the zoo, you know, kids' stuff," I say in the hope it might dissuade Stan from any idea of visiting.

"Great! So you'll have lots of time to show me around when I come to visit."

"What?" I am deflated.

"I want to come and stay with you for a couple of days max, Jack."

"Stan, no disrespect, but my wife is a very reserved, church-going, private person. She doesn't like having people stay and besides there's no room for guests. I've also changed big times. Believe it or not I've become kind of religious in a strange way. I'm not the guy you used know. I stopped doing the gear before I came to Vienna and since I've been here I've stopped smoking and drinking. If you really want to come over there's plenty of hotels close by, I'll even pay the hotel for old time's sake." I think if I can't stop him coming at least I can stop him staying with us.

"What Jack! You started going to church and shit?"

"No, Stan. I'm not a Christian my wife is, and I do believe in their religion in a certain respect. But I'm closer to being a Buddhist if you want some kind of comparison." I know it would be a waste of time trying to explain Falun Dafa to Stan over the phone and probably even face to face.

"Okay, Jack. Here's what's go'in on. You may have changed but I ain't. I've got some business in Vienna, some serious shit arranged by my friends in Brussels. I've been told not to stay in a hotel since they'll want my passport and register me as staying there. The people I'm doing business with are serious as cancer and they've told me there's to be no trace of me in case anything fucks up. I can't even fly to Vienna, I've gotta get a ferry over and drive down through France, Belgium and Germany, you know there are no border checks while we're in the EU, besides, I'll need a car to bring the merchandise back. Then my connections in Belgium are going to arrange for me to get back across the channel without going through any kind of customs check." I had never heard Stan admit to doing as somebody tells him.

"I can take a guess at what your merchandise is but I don't know who these characters are, Stan, or what exactly they are capable of, but don't you think it's a bit risky? If they want you to leave no traces of where you are and something does go wrong maybe they make you disappear for good and no one will know where to even look for you." After hearing what he said I am desperate to stop his visit.

"Hey Jack, nothing will fuck up, I've just gotta follow their instructions. I'm joining the big league, man, so don't try and stop me," Stan finishes his sentence in a tone that I had heard many times, usually just before somebody got hurt, but he had never used it before when talking to me. I know I have no choice but to let him come and stay if I do not want to put Beth in jeopardy, or risk him just turning up anyway, probably very angry and violent. What the hell am I going tell Nora?

"If it's gonna be like that, Stan, I guess I have no choice. When do you plan on coming and how long will you stay?" I reply despondently.

"Don't be so down, man. I should be with you within ten days. Next Friday or Saturday, if everything goes to plan.

I have a meeting which should happen the following Sunday at some apartment in Vienna city center. Maybe you can show me exactly where it is and how to get there before I have to show up. I'll be gone after the meeting so I'll stay only one or two nights at your place, on a sofa if need be or even the floor," Stan's tone becomes more conciliatory. Maybe I can persuade Nora to take Tasha to visit relatives in Styria during his visit. There's no way I want Stan to get to know my Austrian family.

"It'll have to be the sofa then, Stan," I reply and exhale deeply. There is a sofa bed in the room I use as an office but I want to make Stan's stay as uncomfortable as possible.

"I'm looking forward to it. I'll call you from Brussels next Thursday or Friday. Ciao, Jack," Stan ends the call to my relief and I return to my practice.

During the first four exercises nothing happens, no nausea, no perspiring, no tingling of my crown and no sensation of the turning of the wheel in my lower abdomen, or even between my arms during the second exercise. I am too mentally distracted to exercise and consider calling it a day but then:

I have saved us so many times, why do you risk it happening again? As I begin the fifth exercise what can only be my subconscious soul, my secondary spirit taps into my consciousness while I sit in the full lotus position with my hands slightly held out at waist level, palms down I try to empty my mind, which is difficult after the call from Stan. But it is further proof of my level rising, this coherent communication has never happened before. I feel profound guilt and sorrow humbling me as I am led to relive some of the most horrendous events of my life. Some I have no conscious memory of due to extenuating circumstances such as being stoned but events that now play out. Catapulted out of my convertible - lucky the top was down - as it somersaults down a ploughed field. I watch my body ejected by a mysterious force that pulls it from the driving seat. I am propelled sprawling through the damp ploughed soil and come to rest choking with a mouth full of it. My car is upside down in flames some distance from me. This happened when I was eighteen. I had no conscious recollection of the actual crash. The friend I was racing told me in hospital the next day that I had just gone off the road going at least 120 mph. I was thankful to be alive. A broken arm and leg, plus a very swollen head was a small price to pay for such an accident that my father, whom I worked for at the time, was furious about since I had totaled a very expensive sports car that I had not insured.

I seat myself in a comfortable armchair and demand to be shot up with some heroin out of bombastic, drunken bravado. I hate needles and have only snorted coke and speed, smoked marijuana and dropped ecstasy and LSD tabs. My tone is derogatory and superior although I slur my words. The bouncer whom I forced to give me a lift to the drug den turns to the dealer and whispers in his ear. The dealer disappears into the kitchen and returns a few minutes later with a loaded syringe. I am wearing a tee-shirt which makes it easy for him to find a vein and inject me, then he returns to the kitchen after whispering to the bouncer that I have definitely been infected with AIDS now. I feel a warmth rush through my body then oblivion. I never remembered anything definite of that night after getting a lift from the bouncer when the nightclub closed. I woke up the next morning in bed with an Asian girl who told me I picked her up in Babel's, a sleazy afterhours bar frequented by gangsters and low-lives, which I only used when it was so late everywhere else was closed. I took a cab home where I lived with my girlfriend. I ignored her requests as to where I had spent the night and drew a bath. As I lay in the suds I noticed a syringe mark in my right arm. Very vague and misty flashbacks came to me but I could not be sure. I contacted the bouncer who gave me the lift and demanded to know what had happened. He sounded nervous, but insisted that he dropped me off at Babel's and had taken me nowhere else. Even so I was panicked, at the time AIDS was well publicized as having no cure and basically being a death sentence and the most efficient way of being infected was the use of a contaminated needle. I visited my doctor who confirmed it was a syringe mark and suggested I take an AIDS test in some months since it would not be detectable at that time. I never showed for the test out of fear but a few years later, after my fears had subsided and marrying my first wife, I applied for life insurance, which was rejected on the grounds that my doctor had stated I had not shown up for an AIDS test. Even though I was pretty confident I was not HIV positive I was nervous awaiting the results of the test I then took. I called the clinic where I had taken the test. I knew they were not allowed to divulge results over the telephone but I tried anyway. The doctor who answered was very nonchalant, almost dismissive in the way I'm sure he pretended to shuffle through notes for what seemed an age. He then, matter-of-factly, informed me the test was negative. I now know some people just do not develop HIV after being exposed to it, could it have been my secondary spirit, my guardian angel that stopped me from developing it?

Ex-girlfriends whom I've betrayed appear in my mind's eye and I'm overwhelmed with guilt as they seem to telepathically communicate to me how regretful they are for aborting my child, sometimes children, just because I did not want to be tied down to fatherhood and responsibility, no, I just wanted to screw around and have a good time.

Another serious car crash, my drunken friend, driving at my behest because I did not want to risk my license, hits a lamp post head on at sixty mph, his head smashes through the windshield, but I duck down below the windshield and my body slams into the stowage box and I walk away but my friend dies at the scene. Images and previously not forgotten but unknown to me recollections of my wrongdoings and other violent chaotic events tumble through my mind increasingly intense and vivid until I cannot bare anymore. I open my tearful eyes and begin to sob. How could I have been what I have been and how could I have done what I have done? I believe I am now being warned by an entity, which has saved me so many times, not to return to my old ways. I also believe the warning is in obvious connection with Stan's planned visit. Why else would it come at this time?

I feel wretched, despondent and shameful. This path I've taken is tortuous but what else can I expect if I am to clear the karma produced by my wrongful deeds of this life and those before. What is there to live for but suffering, this is the only way, in whatever shape it comes, mental, physical or materialistic. Everything is falling from me as my attachments loosen, including my humanity. If part of being human is to strive for the best for yourself and cherished ones and to progress in this materialist malaise then I am losing it. Losing my manhood, losing my ambition, I often lose my will to live, am I also losing my mind? If so, it matters not. What matters is that I must endeavor to temper my character and lose my attachments.

The word 'inhuman' is usually used to describe atrocities and people who were architects of them: Adolf Hitler, Mau Zedong, Pol Pot, Stalin, to mention a few without contemplating the countless murderers, rapists and pedophiles who have carried out and carry on among us now with their atrocities. Even greater atrocities were carried out by ruling regimes in earlier times such as the Roman Empire, the Spanish conquest of the Aztecs and the following Inquisition in the name of religion, and then there was the British Empire, probably responsible for more deaths than any other ruling body in the history of our civilization. I contemplate these facts in connection with the word 'inhuman' and realize it was exactly humanity that carried out and carries on with these 'inhuman' deeds and know that I do not need to be part of it, that I cannot be part of it. I need to return to that which I was before I was human, not inhuman but also far from and above human.

5.

"Morning, governor. I got a call last night from one of our informers, Dirty Dave. He said he'd received some info on Stan the Man, you know the drug dealing pimp nigger we've pulled a few times but never been able to put him away for a long stretch," Police Sergeant Andy Price of the Greater Manchester Police Drug Squad informs his superior,

Inspector Roy Collins, as he enters his office.

"Oh, yeah?" The stout balding sixty-year-old Inspector Collins stops reading his gutter press, looks up from his desk and peers over the top of his bifocals with an expression of vague disinterest. Little interests him now, only the prospect of his retirement and a generous pension.

"Well, gov, apparently he's got himself involved with some sort of Russian Mafia," the sergeant replies in earnest after closing the door.

"Okay, take a seat, Andy, and tell me all about it."

"There's not a lot to tell. You know what Dave's like. Won't tell me where the info came from, probably cos he's shitting himself over what the consequences may be from them he informs on, and, of course, he thinks we might bung him some more cash for extra info," Andy answers questioningly. He is thirty-two and very ambitious. Any means, including bribery, to enhance his career is welcome.

"There's no chance of more money for him. Besides, he could be trying to frame Stan to get him off the streets. I've heard Stan's trying to takeover Dave's porno shops instead of just providing protection for them."

"You've got a point but he sounded legit. Said it came from a very strange and unknown source and that Stan was going to take possession of a hundred kilos of uncut coke in Vienna within the next few weeks."

"Russian Mafia? Vienna? This sounds a bit too outlandish for even Dave's imagination. I know Stan has or had connections in Belgium, but Austria?"

"I'm afraid that's all I know, gov."

"I can't see what we can do about it from here. Inform Interpol, I guess, to keep a look out for him at the probable airports and ports and thoroughly check him out if they come across him entering the country. Offer Dave more money for more info and keep your ear to the ground on Stan's movements."

"Will do, gov," the sergeant replies before leaving the office to begin his daily grind of watching, waiting and shaking down the occasional suspected dealer. As he leaves the station he calls Dirty Dave, who has acquired his nickname due to his dealings in pornography.

"Hello, Andy. What can I do for you? I've got nothing new to tell you," Dave says barely above a whisper since he has customers perusing sex toys and DVDs while he stands behind the counter of one of his three seedy little shops.

"Not even for some more dough?"

"No, Andy. I've got nothing else."

"What about the name of who told you about Stan?"

"I don't know it. Some serious looking big white guy that I've never seen before with long black hair and a beard wearing leather trousers and a flying jacket, could have been a biker, came into my shop and told me he wanted a word. I wasn't going to argue with him so took him into the backroom. He told me what I told you about Stan and said I should let the relevant people know, like the boys in blue. I reckoned he could only mean you, that's why I called you," Dave whispers nervously.

"That and the fact you get a nice wad every time you give us some serious info that turns out to be reliable, Dave."

"Yeah, there is that too, Andy. And I think this is reliable. It's too weird not to be."

"Okay, Dave. As always...."

"Yeah, I know, Andy. Keep you informed."

"That's a boy," Andy replies and ends the call.

Since Stan had long been a thorn in his side Andy is excited by the prospect of bringing him down. He believes in white supremacy and almost convulses on the occasions he sees Stan flaunting his wealth driving an exotic sports car or ordering Crystal champagne in the trendiest of establishments with an entourage of beautiful women, albeit not ladies.

6.

Simon places the jet on auto-pilot and leaves the flight cabin in the hands of his young co-pilot nephew momentarily to personally inform Valentina that he will begin the descent in five minutes. She is asleep on a fully reclined chair, Alexie and Nikolai are in barely audible Russian conversation sitting at a table to the rear of the aircraft.

"Ma'am. Excuse me ma'am," Simon stoops and tries to stir Valentina by talking quietly into her ear but the cocaine has worn off and she has taken a sleeping pill so as to be rested when she gets to Vienna. He looks up towards her two henchmen with pleading eyes, which has the desired effect. Alexie joins him and gently shakes Valentina's shoulder while saying something in Russian to her. As she comes round she replies to Alexie also in Russian, then turns to Simon.

"Is there anything wrong?" she asks, a little concerned.

"No, ma'am. Not at all. I just wanted to let you know we are about to start the decent so you can prepare for landing."

"Is that all. Then thank you, Simon. Oh, Simon?" Valentina asks just as he is about to return to the flight cabin.

"Yes, ma'am?"

"Why are we landing in Bratislava and not Vienna?"

"I'm not exactly sure but I think it's because Nikita's people have much better contacts with the ground security and customs here than they do in Vienna. And Bratislava is a much smaller airport than Vienna, much easier to have influence here," Simon replies and gives a knowing smile before returning to the cockpit.

Valentina, invigorated by the cold weather, gets into the front passenger seat of the black Range Rover as Alexie and Nikolai load the luggage into the trunk.

"How long's it going to take to get to Vienna?" Valentina asks Helmut, her Austrian driver, as Alexie and Nikolai seat themselves in the rear of the car.

"The traffic was not too much when I drive here madam, so I think we will be by your villa in Vienna in about one hour if I am to drive quickly," Helmut replies with his best English in a thick German accent.

"Good, Helmut. But there is no rush so do not break the speed limit. We don't want to be stopped by the police, okay?"

"Of course not, madam, I will drive correctly," he replies clinically.

One hour and fifteen minutes later Helmut uses the remote on the key fob to open the electric gates to the high fenced modern villa built on a hillside crest in a very salubrious part of the nineteenth district of Vienna. He then does the same to open the double garage doors as he pulls into the driveway.

"Will you get out here, madam, or should I go into the garage?" Helmut requests.

"Is the alarm activated?"

"I do not know, madam. But the housekeeper was here yesterday to turn the heating up and make sure everything was ready for you. And to bring supplies."

"I had better get out here and go through the front door in case it is on so I can deactivate it. I'll let you all in through the house door to the garage. Alexie, just take our luggage, leave the other stuff in the car, it will be safe enough in the garage and the low temperature is better to store it in," Valentina instructs. She gets out of the car and eagerly retrieves a set of keys from her bag and opens the two locks on the heavy steel reinforced glass door. She enters the high ceilinged hall to see the alarm light blinking and so crosses the hall quickly retrieving the code number from her bag as she does so. Although she finds the dry chill of Vienna refreshing she finds the warmth of the villa comforting. After deactivating the alarm Valentina is eager to see the city for the first time in winter so hurries to the large ultra-modern kitchen at the back of the villa. It has been over six months since her last visit when the temperature was hitting the high thirty-degrees centigrade. The kitchen gives a wonderful panoramic view of Vienna in the snow enhanced by the brilliant sunshine. Her gaze is interrupted by a knock at the door to the garage, Helmut is impatient to get home.

"I am sorry, madam, but my frau is expecting me," he says as Valentina opens the door.

"That's alright, Helmut. Should I order you a taxi?"

"No, madam. My car is not far away," he replies as he

walks towards the front door.

"Would you like a schnapps before you go?"

"Thank you, madam, but I must drive."

"Okay, Helmut. Till next time."

"Will you be needing me again?"

"No, Helmut. Alexie and Nikolai will take care of everything from now until we go back to Moscow."

"As you wish, madam. Auf Wiedersehen," Helmut eagerly lets himself out into the clean crisp air, relieved to get out of the villa and away from the Russians. He will never forget the horrific stories his grandfather told about being a prisoner in Russia, being held doing hard labor in a gulag for ten years after world war two had ended and amazed to have survived it. He resents having to work for them, albeit transitorily, but the money he receives is far too much to turn down, he is putting his three children through higher education.

Nikolai opens the refrigerator to retrieve a bottle then pours out three excessive shots of ultra-cold Stolichnaya vodka on the kitchen bar and gives one to Valentina.

"Nastroyeniye!" Alexie raises his glass to the moment of success in arriving at the villa with the merchandise without any complications.

"Nastroyeniye!" Nikolai raises his. Just as Valentina is about to do likewise her

Smart-phone, resting on the bar, starts ringing. Glass semi-raised she pauses momentarily but decides to finish the toast.

"Nastroyeniye!" Valentina knocks the vodka back in one quick gulp as Alexie and Nikolai do in unison with her.

"Lucas, how are things coming along?" Valentina

answers the mobile in a business-like manner. Lucas operates from Brussels as a kind of middle-man for many business associates, some bordering on legal but most not. He had started his career as a legitimate accountant and soon realized the most profitable clients for him were the ones who asked for special favors in what to do with large amounts of cash that had no legal explanation as to its existence. After gaining their confidence he got closer to their businesses until, after several years, he finally became part of some of them. Bespectacled and balding the almost frail looking sixty-year-old exudes an aura of respectability and authenticity.

"Valentina, how nice to hear your voice again. It has been such a long time. I have arranged for someone to meet you at the apartment we use in the city. I know you do not accept people visiting your villa, with which I quite agree. Shall we say next Sunday? It's best when the city is quieter, I can't be sure on a time yet until I've confirmed it with the courier."

"I am agreeable, Lucas, but please, not too early on Sunday."

"Why so, Valentina? You, of anyone I know, is in need of beauty sleep the least."

"Don't flatter, Lucas. We have business to do."

"And I so wish we had much more than just business together."

"I'm sure Nikita would be interested to know that."

"Valentina, I jest. Don't you think I realize no one could take anything or anyone from Nikita?"

"So long as you know, Lucas. So long as you know. Now who is this person I am to give the cases to?"

"An English black guy called Stan, in his fifties but

very fit, he can handle himself. I know your opinions on blacks but I can vouch for him. I've known him for years. First started when he needed to get rid of some diamonds in a hurry while he was in Belgium. Since then we've kept in touch because he's needed premises for various things in Brussels, mainly sex business, and used me to set up companies to put them in the name of. He's driving from Calais and I've arranged for people in Ostend to put him on a freight ferry to get back to the UK. He'll be with an assignment that will have already been cleared by customs," Lucas explains excitedly.

"I don't care who he is, Lucas, or what color he is, in fact I'm okay with blacks, I find some of them sexy, but Nikita doesn't. So if anything goes wrong you know who's going to pay for it."

"I know, Valentina, that's why I use Stan. Nothing will go wrong, I assure you," Lucas lies. He has tried several contacts in the UK to distribute the contraband but hit brick walls, UK criminals are not in a rush to get involved with the Russian Mafia. Stan is the last resort. Lucas believes Stan will try his utmost and succeed in the distribution but is concerned about his ability or trustworthiness to collect and transfer the capital expected by Nikita. Will the amount of money give Stan ideas of an early retirement in the Caribbean where he could disappear? He already regrets agreeing to the deal despite having done similar things for Nikita involving the German market over several years, but his contacts in Germany have Germanic reliability whereas Stan has no history doing such deals with Lucas.

"I don't give a shit, Lucas, it is Nikita's business, between the two of you. I ran this errand because it fitted in with my holiday and Nikita asked me, nothing more. Now may I get back to relaxing in Vienna?"

"Of course, Valentina. Is it okay if I give you a call next Saturday evening to let you know when Stan should turn up at the apartment?"

"How else would I know, Lucas?"

"Of course, Valentina. Speak to you on Saturday. Have a nice evening. Au revoir."

"Goodbye, Lucas," Valentina ends the call on an abrupt tone.

7.

"Hello, darling, how was your day?" I try to sound upbeat and cheerful as Nora enters the apartment with Tasha.

"Boring. Spent most of it reading theses written by people who pretend to be teachers. How about yours, what did you get up to today apart from daffering?" Nora replies as she takes Tasha's coat and boots off in the hallway.

"Not a lot. I made a cottage pie for dinner. You know that takes me two hours." It is one of Nora's favorite dishes and I need to soften her up before dropping my bombshell.

"Great! That's a nice surprise. When can we eat?" she replies with enthusiasm.

"It's a bit early for dinner but I've only got to finish it off in the oven, which will take about half an hour if you like." I make small talk as I prepare the food then pour out a large glass of a good Barolo, a favorite of hers when eating meat, while I take water. We begin the meal in silence.

"Stan called today," I venture offhandedly after a second mouth full. Nora swallows as she puts down her knife and fork.

"And?"

"Um, he wants to come and visit the end of next week," I say as I make an exaggerated exhalation.

"No! You did tell him NO! Didn't you?" she raises her voice.

"It's only for a couple of days, Nora. I thought you could take Tasha to visit your relatives in Styria while he is here. The mountain air would be good for the both of you and I'll pay for Tasha to take more skiing lessons. You don't work Thursday and Friday and you know Tasha would love it," I pitch my sales talk.

"Why should we leave just because he comes to Vienna? He doesn't need to come to our home, you can meet him wherever he's staying," Nora replies coldly with a face like thunder.

"I was going to suggest he stay in a hotel but he was so excited about seeing me and being shown the sites by me I didn't have the heart to tell him to get a hotel." This is really not good for my karma cleansing.

"And what kind of sights will he be interested in, Jack? The museums quarter, St. Stephan's Dome, Schönbrunn Palace perhaps? Don't bullshit me, Jack," Nora answers in a tone and language she rarely uses in front of Tasha, who is, thankfully, glued to her mother's tablet playing games on the sofa.

"Okay, okay. He has a meet with some people in the city on Sunday next week. I didn't ask what it's about, but we can probably guess it's not legal," I lay my cards on the table.

"So why does he have to stay here and not a hotel or under a bridge for that matter?"

"He has his reasons and I would rather go along with him than risk upsetting him. I've told you what he's capable of. I don't want him turning up and kicking the door in.'

"I would just call the police," Nora stubbornly answers.

"And how long would they take to get here? Besides, I have Beth to think about also. If I don't oblige and he doesn't turn up then he will take it out on her. I'm sorry about my past following me here but can you please let it go this one time?" I beg.

"That's another thing, Jack, What if it's not a one off and he wants to do it on a regular basis? What if whatever he's up to ends up on our doorstep with God knows what consequences?
Police, gangsters, who knows what. If you don't care about me what about Tasha, do you want to expose her to this lowlife world you used to be involved in?"

"You know I never would, Tasha or you. I'll tell Stan that if whatever he's up to is going to be repeated he needs to find elsewhere to stay in the future. I'll find a way to make him listen, but for this time please let him come once." My mind is already full of ideas as I finish the sentence. Maybe I could tell him I have a problem with a neighbor who is color prejudiced and wants to call the police to see if he is registered as staying here.

"I'm not happy, Jack, but, because I love you, just this one time. If he tries it again you can tell him I'll call the police and tell them he is harassing us. Okay?" Stan is not someone who believes a word a woman said was to be taken seriously but at least I had a way out.

"Okay, and thank you." This is much easier than I

expected but shame on me, only down to Nora's devotion.

8.

"I need something very reliable and very ordinary, not too flash, maybe a four wheel drive Volvo or something like that. But it's got to be completely legit, nothing stolen, I'm going abroad with it so I don't want any problems because then you'll have a big problem," Stan threatens Eric, the second hand car dealer he occasionally does business with and not just involving cars.

"Sure, Stan. When do you need it by?" Eric asks obligingly. Although not a feeble man he knows not to upset Stan.

"Like yesterday, I wanna make sure it's good before I go. Got it?"

"I've got a Nissan X-Trail on the lot right now. It might be just what you need. Do you want to look at it?"

"Show me," Stan answers with a semblance of interest.

"Two years old. It's a kosha motor, Stan. Previous and only owner looked after it really well. It has a full service history and low mileage for its age. Do you want to take it for a spin?" Eric gushes as he opens the driver's door.

"Sure. But what about the price?"

"Take no notice of the price label, Stan. For you there's a ten-per-cent discount," Eric says as he looks at Stan's increasingly contemptuous stare, "okay, Stan, okay, twenty-per-cent?" he offers after Stan's expression grows ever more menacing.

"Twenty-five," Stan growls.

"Sure, Stan. That's what I meant to say," Eric caves

in despite the fact he will take a loss on the car if Stan decides to buy it. He gives the key fob to him and explains the rudiments of the car's operation.

Stan stows away the Nissan in his warehouse on a large industrial estate on the outskirts of town, he doesn't want anyone to connect him with the car, especially any nosey passing police, and he much prefers his Porsche anyway, which he has left in the warehouse. As he makes his way home through the rush hour traffic he gets a call, when he sees it is Lucas he puts his phone in hands free mode, the last thing he wants is to be stopped by the police.

"Yo, my man, what's happening?"

"Hi, Stan. Everything is going as planned. Have you made the necessary arrangements your end?" Lucas asks flatly.

"Sure, I've just picked up a car to make the journey. I've only got to book the ferry and I'm all set," Stan replies.

"What about accommodation, you know the Russians don't want you to stay at hotels."

"I'm sorted. I'll stay with one of my ex-bitches in Brussels on the way over, Manchester to Vienna is too far for one trip no matter how much coke you take," Stan jokes.

"What about Vienna?" Lucas's tone is serious.

"I had a stroke of luck there. An old friend of mine actually lives there. I can stay with him."

"Who is this friend, Stan?" Lucas does not try to hide his concern. If Stan's friend is like Stan he could be a problem.

"We go back a long way. Haven't been in touch with him for years. Found out on the grapevine he's in Vienna."

"What's he doing there, Stan? Is he a criminal, is he involved in your sort of business?" Lucas comes straight to the point, he is worried Stan's friend might be known to the police. What if this so-called friend was even talking to the police? Lucas is extremely wary by nature. He has to be in his line of business.

"Chill, Lucas. This guy is totally straight. He went to work in Vienna as a computer programmer. He's married to a professor, he's even had a kid with her. Believe it or not he told me he's turned religious, doesn't even drink anymore. I know what you're thinking but this guy won't bring any interest from the law down on us," Stan tries to reassure Lucas.

"If this guy is so straight, how come he's a friend of yours, Stan?" Lucas isn't reassured.

"It's a long story, Lucas," Stan doesn't want to go into details.

"I've got plenty of time, Stan. Shoot!"

"I met Jack when I was about twenty in a wine bar he was fronting, we're the same age. His father, who I used to do some debt collecting for, introduced us. As well as the wine bar they had night clubs and betting shops and were well connected with some of the older, well known gangsters and so they made a good connection for me. Jack started buying ecstasy and coke from me, which the doormen in the clubs would push. He even got me to let him use some of my girls for his and his father's business contacts. We also did some fraud together but those details are too long to go into, Jack knew how to screw big companies over. I'd go out with Jack and look after him, sometimes he'd get so smashed I'd have to carry him home…"

"So how come he ended up being a religious programmer in Vienna? It doesn't make much sense, Stan," Lucas interrupts.

"Let me finish. The family business went bust and Jack disappeared from the scene, moved out of town cos he had to, no dough. His wife divorced him, he even lost his car. Lived in some village where the rent was low. I visited him once and took him out on the town for old time sake, but that was when we were about thirty. Never saw him since but heard he got a contract on good money in Vienna after learning how to program in some government sponsored tuition for the jobless. When I called him in Vienna a few days ago he told me how he was a different person to the one I knew. I had to put a bit of pressure on him but he's agreed to let me stay at his place for the time I'm there before I meet with the Russians. He'll cause no problems. He'll just want me gone asap," Stan finishes.

"Okay, Stan. I'll go along with it. Does your friend, Jack, know why you will be in Vienna?"

"I've told him I have some serious business. He knows better not to ask but he'll know it's not legal."

"Keep it like that and keep in touch with me on your progress. Let me know when you get to Brussels. I'm going to call the Russians on the Saturday to let them know when you will meet them. If everything goes well you can pick the stuff up on Sunday. Then you drive to me in Brussels. You can sleep over at my place before I take you to the boat, if I'm unable to arrange anybody else to, that will get you back to the UK. Hope to hear from you next Thursday at the latest, Stan," Lucas ends the call.

Stan returns to his relatively modest living quarters considering the amount of cash he turns over, a modern studio that is worth about twice as much as his car. His ego does not allow for anything he cannot present and he cannot afford a home he considers presentable so spends his money on a flash car.

"Hey, Lizzy, wanna go out to eat at that fancy new French place?" he asks his current live-in girlfriend who lies sprawled out on the bed wearing a pink track-suit watching TV. He usually tires of them after a few months then forces them to hook for him but Lizzy is different. She is the closest thing to a lady Stan has ever encountered. Thirty-five-years-old, tall with a mass of wavy red hair that tumbles to her hips, large firm breasts and well-toned body she strikes an imposing but elegant figure. Stan met her at the upmarket gym he is a member of and where she works as a fitness instructress. Stan melted when he first set eyes on her. He needed no instruction on working-out but paid for a course with her anyway. Although she comes from a working class family, Lizzy educated herself as well as she could since her state schooling was very poor, she had even managed to rid herself of the Mancunian accent. She normally dates respectable professionals such as a doctors and solicitors but is turned on by power and black guys and especially the danger Stan exudes. She sits up, pulls her legs in and places her arms around them. Her come to bed large emerald eyes and the smile that creeps across her full ruby lips make Stan want to strip off immediately.

"It's super expensive. What's the occasion, stud, won the lottery or something?" Lizzy answers slowly.

"Let's just say I'm expecting a windfall when I get

back from Europe," Stan replies as he takes his coat off.

"Europe! When are you going to Europe?" Lizzy exclaims as the smile vanishes from her face to be replaced by a look of utter confusion. She is used to Stan disappearing for a night or two on very short notice but he has never left her longer than that and has never left the country over the six months they have been together.

"Next Thursday or Friday. I've got some business to do. I'll only be gone three or four nights," Stan answers as he takes his shoes off.

"Oh, can I come with you?" Lizzy is worried Stan might be taking some other female to keep him entertained on his trip.

"I wish you could but I've got to do this alone. I'll treat you big times afterwards," Stan answers as he seats himself on the edge of the bed.

"Is it dangerous?" genuine concern is apparent in Lizzy's question and she knows better than to ask Stan exactly what kind of business he will be doing in Europe.

"No, no more dangerous than anything else I've done," Stan lies since he is not sure himself as he tries to reassure Lizzy.

"Will you call me?"

"Every day, sugar," Stan replies as he puts his arms around her and starts to kiss her neck in a prelude to something more erotic.

9.

The silver Jaguar sports coupe slowly pulls into the drive of a housing association terraced house for abused single women. Jason, the president of Hells Angels England, gets out of the car and rings the doorbell. Forty-five years old, clean-cut, of average height, stature and looks, short cropped brown hair, crystal blue eyes and a dazzling smile the only giveaway to Jason's call in life are the colors sewed on the back of his black leather jacket and a the few small badges on the front including one that reads 'President'. He loves his Harley to the point where he keeps it in his living room during the winter, dressing it up with tinsel during Christmas, and only rides it when duty calls, besides, his Jaguar makes a much more comfortable mode of transport in the inclement winter weather.

"You timed that well, Jay. The vindaloo is ready and the rice is almost done," Beth says on opening the door.

"Great, I'm starving," Jason replies enthusiastically.

"Wipe your feet, darling, I've just cleaned the floor," Beth asks and passionately kisses Jason on the lips.

"Whoa. Let's eat first!" Jason exclaims as Beth tries to undo his belt.

"I've made it super spicy. Would you like a naan bread too?" Beth enquires as Jason makes himself comfortable at the small table in the dinning kitchen.

"Sure. And have you got a beer?"

"Silly question, Jay," Beth replies as she opens the fridge which is half-filled with cans of Budweiser. It used to be cider but since starting an affair with Jason, over three months ago, she has acquired a taste for Budweiser, Jason's favorite beer. Although some years younger than Beth he has become a kind of guru figure to her. She is in awe of his position and impressed by his intellect. He, in turn, finds mature, experienced and intelligent women a big turn-on although he takes advantage of many young Hells Angel groupies on the side.

"Heard anything more from the nigger?" he asks as he opens a can.

"No. Nothing."

"What about your brother?"

"No. Him neither. I'm sure he'll let me know when he hears from Stan," Beth responds as she places the pot of curry on the table.

"Give him a call."

"What! Now?" Beth is indignant.

"It wasn't a request! I want to know if the nigger's been in touch," Jason raises his voice.

"Okay, okay."

I am viewing the BBC World News on my PC when the landline rings out. I consider not answering it since Nora is giving Tasha a bath and I do not want to get involved in some boring small talk conversation with one of her friends who usually calls around this time in the evening. Whenever I answer the phone to one of them it would be relentless: How was I? What was I doing? How was Tasha? What did I think of ….whatever? I believe they just want to practice speaking English.

"Will you please get that!" Nora shouts from the bathroom when the phone keeps ringing for an inordinate length of time.

"Hello," I answer with a kind of irritated disinterest.

"Hi, Jack, it's me, Beth."

"Hi sis, to what do I owe the occasion? Two calls in less than as many weeks, I'm honored," I am surprised to hear from her so soon again. I never thought she would really be bothered by what Stan was up to and I did not want to bother her with it.

"I just wanted to know if Stan got in touch and what he wanted," Beth shows an uncharacteristic concern.

"Afraid so. He's gonna come and stay with me for a night or two at the end of next week."

"What's he going to Vienna for, surely not a holiday? Stan is about as cultural as a house brick! He's reggae and techno music not Beethoven and Mozart," Beth laughs.

"Cos' he's not coming for pleasure, Beth. You know Stan better than I. He's got some business in the city and doesn't want to stay in a hotel because of being registered as being here. He said he had to take something back with him and it can only be something that's very valuable and probably stolen or, more likely, it's drugs," I reply and sigh.

"Shit! How's Nora reacted?"

"Surprisingly calmly. She was really annoyed when I first told her but has agreed to take Tasha to go and stay with relatives while he is here. But she made it clear that it's not going to happen again, whatever it is he's up to."

"I don't blame her, but she's never met Stan, has she?"

"No, but I've told her about him in the past. I wished I hadn't, it would make things a lot easier for me now," I say dejectedly.

"Cheer up, bro. It'll soon be over. And as you tell me, Falun Dafa says whatever happens is the result of our own behavior in this life or ones before, so, you can't complain can you? You're just repaying your karma debt so be happy as you profess to me you should be when shit happens," Beth expounds glibly; she enjoys this opportunity to point out that according to my belief I should be welcoming the aggravation.

"Guess so, Beth. But the suffering is a pain in the ass no matter how I try and look at it. I'd much rather go through physical suffering than have this worry about my family hanging over my head."

"I feel for you, Jack, and thanks for the info on Stan. I'm sorry that he's turning up now you have got yourself nice and respectable, but I couldn't do much about it. I don't have to tell you what may have happened to me if I didn't cooperate with him."

"Hey, it's not your fault, just forget about it."

"Okay, and thanks again, Jack. I've got to shoot, I've got naan bread burning in the oven. Call me when Stan has left and stay lucky if you can't stay legal. Ciao for now," Beth ends the call.

"So when's he going?" Jason asks as the call ends.

"Next week, end of. He's gonna stay with my brother for one or a couple of nights," Beth replies and looks at Jason with deep contemplation in her eyes.

"Good. So he could be back with the stuff in the UK in less than two weeks, if everything goes to plan for him, that is," Jason retorts and smiles to himself.

"What do you have in mind, Jay, taking it off him?"

"Time will tell, Beth, only time will tell, now let's eat."

As I replace the receiver Nora enters the room carrying Tasha wrapped in a bath towel.

"Who was it?" She asks.

"Beth. She wanted to know if Stan had been in

touch," I reply although I don't want to bring his name up I know Nora would ask anyway.

"And did you tell her what he's forced you to do and that I've got to leave with Tasha while he's here?" Nora says bitterly.

"I told her everything and she was very sorry for everything even though she couldn't really do anything about it," I say in defense of my sister.

"I suppose you're right. It's just so annoying, that's all," Nora loosens up.

"It'll soon be over and you have the skiing to look forward to," I try to placate further.

10.

Scruffily dressed in faded jeans, trainers, black polo-neck jumper and scuffed brown leather jacket, Sergeant Andy Price, with his shoulder length greasy light brown hair and a five day growth of stubble, tries his utmost to look the part of a lowlife junkie. He sits alone with a bottle of strong German beer at a small table in a sheltered corner of The Moon Underwater. A large traditional popular pub in the city center frequented by businessmen and the professional class such as lawyers and real-estate agents during the day but at night drug dealers, low class prostitutes and prospective clientele consisting of a very multi-cultural crowd, frequent it. It is early evening and quiet, the transitional period. Andy is waiting for Roger Facey, a fairly major black drug dealer in the city who has only kept himself out of prison by providing Andy with reliable information on other dealers and various other criminals and their nefarious activities.

"What took you so fucking long?" Andy growls in a

low voice as the six foot seven dreadlocked Rastafarian Roger wearing dark glasses sits himself opposite and places his large rum and coke on the table. He is a formidable sight in his almost ankle-length black leather coat although his frame is slim and far from muscular.

"Chill, man. I had some shit with my bitch. Today was the first time I got home in three days and she wasn't happy when I told her I had to go for a meet. I had to sooth her the only way I know how and it takes a little time even for a stud like me," Roger replies in similar hushed tones.

"Okay. So why did you call the meet, have you got anything on the Man?" Andy lightens up.

"I dunno for sure but he asked for a meet yesterday. I thought it was strange since although we're not enemies we are competitors. I went along with some back up just in case he had ideas about knocking this competition out," Roger says and makes a pistol with his hand pointed at his temple.

"And....? Come on Roger I haven' got all night, cut the dramatics," Andy interrupts after Roger pauses too long with his finger.

"He told me that he had an assignment of uncut coke coming in the next week or so that was too big for him to get rid of alone in the time he needs to, which is kinda strange for Stan to admit anything is too big for him. He even went further and said whatever amount I could take he could provide, and the craziest part is he said he would even provide it on credit! Now Stan knows I'll take on five, maybe ten k's max, which I pay upfront for and my pushers get rid of it within however long," Roger doesn't want to give Andy an idea of what he is earning on the streets, "so for him to offer me coke on credit, and cheap coke too, he must have or is going to get a hell of a lot of it, don't you think?" Roger finishes and looks around apprehensively.

"Did he say where it's coming from or who's supplying it?"

"Get real, Andy."

"Okay, Roger, I want you to go along with it. Set up a deal where you can put your hands on as much as he'll allow with cash and credit. I'll talk to my governor about boosting your cash reserves for the deal. I want as much gear around as possible when I bust that bastard," Andy says with a glint in his eyes.

"Sure thing, Andy, but I dunno how long it'll take and I wanna know about my protection. We're probably talking about anything up to twenty or thirty k's or even more. Stan ain't gonna be the only one involved, he's gonna have muscle with him and probably a shooter or shooters. We're talking heavy shit, man. This stuff is worth a lot of dough!"

"So why didn't you go for the deal if it's so good, why are you informing me?"

"I figure if he has got so much stuff to get rid of I'm one of the last people he'll contact unless it really is a fucking lot. He'll flood Manchester and farther with the gear and the price is going to crash so how much profit will I end up with unless I can move it somewhere else, which could prove complicated? That and because you'll probably find out about the abundance of shit on the street and you'll come after me to find out why and where from. I know you keep tabs on me, Andy," Roger replies quietly although there is no one in earshot.

"Of cause I watch you, Roger. Why else would I have nicked you in the first place with a kilo on you? You know that's worth a long time in jail and we both know that's the reason you tell me things, up to a point. And what do you mean by 'protection'? I thought you had your own. You told me you took back up yesterday to meet him."

"I don't mean Stan. If he's prepared to give me the gear on credit he doesn't think I'm going to try and steal it. He reckons he's got too much muscle for me to dare cross him. I mean you guys. If you bust him he could very well try and shoot his way out so you guys are gonna start shootin back and if I'm around I don't wanna get caught in the crossfire," Roger answers with an expression of what planet do you come from man?

"Okay, Roger, most of my guys know who you are and the ones that don't will be informed, it's not like you're the inconspicuous type, is it. If anything goes off just try and keep a very low profile. Try and do a runner if you can."

"Yeah, sure. I come running past you guys and you all just look the other way while Stan and his guys are taking pot shots at you and you are returning fire? Do me a favor, Andy, how am I gonna live it down, that is if I manage to live long after it at all. It's gonna be obvious I set Stan up and if you put him away he's got an older brother in London who's kinda retired but he was bigger than Stan in his day and that was in London and Jamaica. And I know he's still very protective when it comes to family. I would be as good as dead as soon as he got the word," Roger does not try to disguise his fear.

"Point taken. So what do you suggest? We could nick him before you even show at the meet, when and wherever it's gonna be, as long as he has the gear with him, that's all that matters," Andy replies thoughtfully. He knows this suggestion is not a good one for Roger but he does not care what happens to Roger. In fact, Andy would consider it killing two birds with one stone if anything fatal happened to Roger, he's too useful to send to jail while he's alive but Andy would welcome the demise of another black drug dealer.

"That'll point the finger at me even more, Andy. And he might not have the gear on him when we meet. We could meet and then he drives me somewhere blindfolded, gives me the gear then takes me back to wherever blindfolded, we've gotta think this thing through."

"We can't start doing that until we have all the details like when and where the meet will be and how much stuff he'll let you have on credit. Call me as soon as you know the arrangements, okay?"

"Sure thing, man," Roger replies before knocking back his drink in one and leaving.

11.

It is Friday, 17:00 CET and Stan disembarks the P&O ferry at Calais. After leaving the port he pulls over to make a call to Lucas, he needs all his faculties free when driving on the opposite side of the road to the one which he is accustomed to.

"Hi, Stan, where are you?" Lucas answers quickly.

"Just got off the ferry, so I should be in Brussels by about seven-thirty. Do you want to meet for a drink? I know I've got everything I need to know but I don't want to spend the whole evening with Chrissie, she bores the shit outa me," Stan replies. Chrissie used to hook for Stan years ago, when she was young and naive and although she has now moved on to older and wealthier clients with which she deals without an intermediary such as Stan, she has a soft spot for him because he protected her well, only passing on clean kind clients to her and even took her as a temporary lover. Chrissie is physically sexy and attractive and knows how to please men physically but intellectually she is not so gifted.

"Sure, Stan. Where do you want to meet?"

"What's the Monk Bar like these days?"

"Still the same, but a bit loud when there's live music on. But I think that's just Saturday and Sunday, so it should be okay tonight."

"Great, see you there around seven-thirty," Stan says enthusiastically.

"Looking forward to it," Lucas replies.

Stan scans the bar on entering and sees Lucas sat in a corner on a bench seat at a small table. He smiles and waves to get Lucas's attention then goes to the bar and orders a Duvel beer.

"How was your trip so far?" Lucas asks as Stan shuffles in besides him.

"Sweet, no hassle and the crossing was smooth. Worst part of the trip was driving from Manchester to Dover. The M6 and M25 are a fucking nightmare, man. Good job I bought an open ended ticket. Got there later than I expected," Stan replies and takes a swig of the beer from the bottle.

"The Russians have agreed to the meet on Sunday, but not too early," Lucas says in a serious tone.

"What's too early?" Stan asks.

"Knowing Valentina, I'd say before midday.'

"What's she like, this Valentina?" Stan has a glint in

his eye as his face breaks into a cheeky grin.

"Don't even think about it, Stan. She would eat you for breakfast then spit you out. Besides she'll have Alexie and Nikolai with her."

"And?" Stan asks incredulously as his grin is replaced by a look of contempt, "Should I be worried?"

"They are two of Nikita's best and Nikita is the one running the show. I know you're fit and experienced but you couldn't handle one of them, never mind two, you'll get the picture when you see them. Forget about trying to get friendly with Valentina. Collect the merchandise and come straight back here. Okay?"

"Okay, Lucas, okay," Stan complies.

"I know I've asked a thousand times but are you sure you can sell the stuff in time and deposit the agreed amount into the account by the date we have decided on?"

"Sure. What I can't get rid of myself through my dealers I can kick over to other guys who have connections," Stan replies but Lucas senses a touch of apprehension in Stan's voice.

"Can you trust these 'other guys'?"

"Lucas, you can't trust anyone in this game, you should know better than me. The only thing you can put trust in is the fear you instill and with these 'other guys' I make sure it's instilled my man, so stop fretting," Stan assures.

"Okay, so long as you know that if anything fucks up you're the one responsible for the gear and the proceeds from it. You know the Russians will not tolerate any deviation from what we have agreed," Lucas lies. He knows that he will be the first and probably only port of call if Nikita is not satisfied with the outcome of the transaction.

"Cool it, Lucas. Stop being so fucking paranoid, man. Think positive. I've just gotta pick the shit up take it back with me and everything is gonna be sweet."

"For your sake, I hope it is, Stan…"

"Wow my soul! Just take a look at what just walked in," Stan interrupts Lucas on seeing a twentysomething brunette enter the bar wearing a very expensive looking almost ankle length brown and silver fur sable coat. Stan doesn't know what animal it comes from or even if it is real, he is consumed by the wearer. Her long voluminous wavy dark hair tumbles over her shoulders and halfway down her back, her elfin face perfectly made-up, long eyelashes accentuating her large dark almond shaped eyes which Stan thinks he will drown in. On noticing his obvious gawping interest she flashes him an inviting smile, her luscious ruby lips parting to display a perfect set of dazzlingly white teeth. He watches transfixed as an attentive waiter helps her out of the coat. Around five ten in her flat calf-length boots, which match her coat, she exudes an air of wealth and sophistication despite the fact she is wearing jeans, albeit skin-tight designers. Although her white silk blouse is quite loose fitting as she extracts herself from the coat it is obvious she is braless, the outline of her firm pert breasts and nipples plainly visible especially as she maneuvers her shoulders out of the coat. Stan's excitement peaks as she gives him a little wave and a wink then turns to face the waiter who ushers her away to a high table where a middle aged, overweight balding man wearing a black Versace suit is perched on a high stool.

"You can forget that one too, Stan," Lucas says through a chuckle.

"Whad'ya mean? She seems interested."

"She's only playing with you. You don't have to be a millionaire to get Elise's interest, no, you have to be a multi-millionaire or preferably a billionaire. If you haven't got a jet and a yacht you're not worth looking at unless she's bored then she might tease just to see you grovel. A smile is as much as you'll get, forget about a spoken word. See the guy she's with, Emmanuel Salazar, hedge fund manager. He earns more a year than you will during your whole lifetime, even if you live to be a hundred," Lucas is enjoying himself.

"You never know, Lucas. This Russian connection you have set up with me could be the start of something big," Stan says in all seriousness.

"Yes, you might get some repeat performances as long as you carry out this operation to the letter and there's no fuck ups," Lucas jumps on the opportunity to remind Stan.

"Jesus, man. How many times I gotta tell ya, nothing will fuck up!"

"Okay, I'll give it to you, if this operation goes smooth there's going to be more without a doubt," Lucas encourages the successful outcome of the deal, "but, even so, you're never going to join the income league of hedge fund managers, my friend. Be content with your Chrissies and whatever else you've got there back in the UK. Don't go boxing above your weight, it will only end in tears. Take my advice, Stan. No offence but I've advised a lot older and wiser men."

"Point taken, Lucas, point taken, but there's no harm in looking," Stan replies.

"Just don't look too hard. Salazar is very rich and powerful. You do not want him as an enemy. He appears to be a respectable businessman, but I've heard stories about how he got where he is and they are not pretty," Lucas warns and then tries to change the subject, "You must be hungry and I haven't eaten yet. There's a great Chinese around the corner. Do you want to try it?"

"Why not," Stan answers as he takes a long lingering look in the direction of Elise.

"I'll settle our tabs," Lucas replies and hurries to the bar and close to where Elise is sitting. He does not want Stan to get the opportunity to try and communicate with her. He motions to the bar tender and drops a note on the bar then hurries back to where Stan sits. "Okay, let's move."

After gorging on a selection of Chinese dishes Stan's mobile rings.

"Hi, honey. I've just finished eating so you shouldn't have. I'll be with you in half an hour, okay?" Stan sighs as he ends the call.

"Chrissie?" Lucas enquires.

"Who else. She's prepared some dinner for me and I couldn't eat another grain of rice after all that. Best Chinese I've eaten, and they do some pretty good ones in Manchester. Thanks, Lucas."

"Don't mention it. You can treat me if ever I find myself in Manchester, God forbid."

"Hey, don't knock it, man. We've got one of the best football teams in the world. And the nightlife is kick'in. Brussels is like a retirement home compared. You all drive around at thirty miles an hour."

"You have still made money out of the city, one way or another. Whatever you think of Brussels it's treated you well and you've had some good times here. And you weren't so keen to leave the Monk bar earlier, but Elise was out of the question."

"You're really talking about the diamond thing. That was just a piece of luck that came my way. I never set it up, I didn't even know the guy was carrying around such valuable merchandise, if I had I would've set it up. I was just lucky Chrissie was with him when he croaked and out of loyalty she brought the diamonds back to me. Running the girls over here was too much like hard work compared to what I do back home. And when you found a buyer for the gems I was happy to let the hookers in Brussels go their own way since I wasn't so desperate for the cash anymore," Stan speaks in a matter of fact fashion.

"Out of loyalty? Come on, Stan, Chrissie couldn't tell a diamond from a marble. The luck that came your way was that she liked the bag they were in when she found him unconscious in the toilets. And that she left him there and went running to you," Lucas replies.

"You do have a point, Lucas. But Chrissie can tell the time and if I want a bed tonight I had better go."

"You know you're going to get more than a bed, Stan. Au revoir and sweet dreams," Lucas comments as Stan stands to leave the table.

"I'll keep you updated on my progress and look forward to seeing you on Sunday night."

"Safe journey, Stan," Lucas remarks as Stan turns to leave.

12.
I delve as deeply as I can into my consciousness without going so far as to let it slip away while I hold the wheel

before me. I am a practitioner and must remain in the moment otherwise my secondary soul will be the major beneficiary of my efforts and I myself, my true soul, will be left with little if anything from my practice. I must try to remain in a state of wu wei, uncommitted, free of attachment whether fear or desire and neutral but pure in thought. It is so difficult. Am I doing the right thing by allowing Stan's visit? But what else can I do? Should I believe this is just a one off occurrence never to be repeated? If it is some sort of stolen goods he is coming to pick up, be it gems, artwork, precious metals or even plain cash then it could be a one off. But knowing Stan, it is more likely to be drugs he's coming to collect. And if it is drugs then he's found a new supplier and the supply is going to carry on as long as the supplier keeps supplying. How can I stop him in the future? He'll always threaten me with Beth's welfare, perhaps not overtly but he knows I know what he's capable of. Beth confided in me many years ago that he raped her after she had stopped her relationship with him. How so distraught it made me. When I needed muscle to call on, that muscle was Stan. I was in a complete dilemma, going to the law was out of the question considering the company I kept and the environment in which I lived. Police were considered filth and anyone who conversed and consulted with them even worse. Beth redeemed me a little by urging me to do nothing and never ever mention it to Stan and then I discovered she even had more intimate liaisons with him, I wondered if she lied about the rape or if it was not exactly a rape. Even so I felt weak and inadequate as a brother but fortunately my financial downfall came soon after, which brought little, then no contact with Stan. I force the thoughts from my mind and replace them with nothing, I am only aware that I am practicing. I am already perspiring from the exercise of opening my chakras but little else. Now the familiar nausea starts building. I have not eaten since yesterday, some twenty-two hours ago and just after my last practice. I am finding it easier to cope with nausea when there is little in my stomach to vomit and therefore have started a new dining regime whereby I only eat easily digestible food shortly after practicing. This sits okay with Nora since she prefers to keep meat consumption down and eats at least one meal a day from which I abstain, but at this time that is of little consequence since she is skiing in Styria with Tasha. Thankfully the butterfly sensation in my lower abdomen, as the wheel makes its presence felt, supplants the nausea to such a degree that I feel confident my exercise will be completed without being cut short by a necessary visit to the bathroom. The throbbing sensation between my arms has such force as never before, I wonder how I am keeping them stationary. The crown of my head also alive with an intensity I find almost unbearable, but I must have tolerance, the basis of Falun Dafa, and without Falun Dafa there is nothing in store for me but blind oblivion and despair, as is the case for the great majority of lives and life forms on this planet.

I feel free from anxiety as I assume the lotus and maneuver my buttocks into the most comfortable position possible, which is still excruciatingly uncomfortable. I close my eyes and almost immediately visions flash before me as I perform the mudras in communication to I know not what only that my message is being received. A vibrant dazzlingly colorful barrage of light plays out before me in whatever dimension I am witnessing. Hues of red, blue, yellow, green, violet interspersed by faces, some of intriguing beauty, others quite comical and yet others which appear hideous, but none are human. The white ones appear, points of light in varying shapes and sizes, and stay longer than they have done in the past. As with the faces I sense they are intelligent beings looking in on me, evaluating my progress. I believe the longer they stay the more acceptable my company and therefore the higher my level. They appear to me only momentarily, but a second or less in our earthly dimension may well be hours or even days in the dimensions of the visiting entities. I complete the mudras and hold out my hands palms down at waist height as I try to keep my mind empty but alert. Almost immediately the familiar sensations in my palms and fingers begin. An inexplicable but undeniably physical force, which pulsates giving a similar feeling as to that of the field generated between two magnets placed close to each other with their poles as to repel one another. The sensation becomes so strong that I have to force my hands down to counteract it and keep them level. Perhaps one day the force will become so great as to cause me to levitate, but I should never aspire to it since that would be a desire, an attachment that could only hold me back so I put it from my mind as though it is just a minor natural occurrence, which, I guess, it really is on my journey back.

The silence of the apartment and the still of my mind is broken by the ringing of the landline. I could ignore it and really want to because it is probably Stan and I don't want to talk to him more than I have to. He text me yesterday to let me know he was in Brussels and would set out for Vienna early today. No matter how early he set out or how fast he drives he cannot be due here for at least another four or five hours. It is midday and the drive will take about ten hours if he's fast. But it could be Nora, so I guess I've got no choice but to interrupt my exercise and gradually form the conjoining of hands before breaking off my practice. I see it is a UK number calling and it's not Beth so I guess it's probably Stan.

"Hello?" I enquire nonchalantly.

"Yo, Jack. It's me," Stan answers enthusiastically.

"Who?" I am so adverse I cannot resist it.

"Me, Stan. How many other nigger brothers talking nigger talk you got?"

"Oh, Stan. I didn't expect to hear from you yet. I thought you'd be on your way down."

"Yeah, I am, passed Nuremberg half hour ago. I've stopped to get some fuel and they are selling all kinds of booze at the station. They've got Finlandia Vodka, I remember you loved that…"

"Stan, I told you I don't drink anymore," I interrupt.

"Hey, come on, Jack. What about a bottle of Hennessy X.O? I know that was your favorite," Stan persists.

"Yes, it was, Stan, it was. But not anymore. You liked cognac too as I remember. So feel free to bring a bottle for yourself. I've only got some chardonnay white wine that Nora drinks and mineral water, so you had better bring whatever you want to drink," I reply flatly.

"Okay, bro. Maybe you change your mind when I get there. The satnav says it'll take about four and half hours to get to you. Will you be at home?"

"I'll be waiting, Stan. Let me know when you're here. I'll come down and let you into the carpark where you can use our space since Nora is out of town with the car for the weekend. It's almost impossible to find a free spot on the street, and besides, you need a pass to park on the street. What car will you be in?"

"It's a black Nissan X-trail, why?"

"Just so I know what to look for when you get here and also the parking spaces are not very generous. You'd have a problem with a Hummer, but you'll be okay in an X-trail. See you by around five then, Stan, ciao," I reply and end the call, close the windows and make something to eat.

As I munch on scrambled egg and toast I contemplate meeting Stan. Should I take him out on the town? I'm sure he'll expect it no matter how much booze he brings along. There's no way I can take him to one of my local bars or restaurants where clients and owners know me well from the days I used to drink excessively and I don't think I've ever seen a negro in one of them. At best Stan would draw uncomfortable stares and worse, may well be refused entry, and I know only too well how Stan reacts to anyone he considers is being disrespectful or prejudiced. I could take him to the Bermuda Triangle, an area in the next district only three underground stops away or a short taxi ride. Made up of a few pedestrianized streets lined with bars and restaurants catering for all tastes, age groups and cultures, it is also full of tourists. On a Saturday it is at its busiest and we could blend into the crowds quite inconspicuously and there is very little chance of me bumping into someone I know. Yes, I will take him to the Triangle.

Just after five the phone goes and I know it can only be Stan. I wearily lift the receiver and wait for the inevitable.

"Yo, bro. I'm here, in this little one-way side street. I

am just outside your entrance, you comin down?"

13.

Alexie presses the doorbell to the Feuervogel (Fire Bird) nightclub in a mainly residential part of the first district of Vienna, the first district being in the center and by far the most expensive. The Feuervogel is a very exclusive members' only place where potential members have to be introduced by existing members and then acceptance is not guaranteed. One or two guests of members are occasionally allowed as long as they look the part i.e. sexy and beautiful if a female and well dressed, wealthy and of obvious means if a male. Drinks are served at an extortionate rate by the bottle only, whether it be champagne, wine, vodka or any other spirit, the only exception being exotic cocktails. Beer is not served. After some seconds Alexie presses the bell again and leaves his finger on it as he impatiently glares up at the CCTV camera above the door, which opens in a few seconds. A tall, broad, forty-something well-dressed shaven-headed doorman opens the door wide and beckons Valentina and her bodyguards then bows as he greets them in Russian on their entrance to the luxuriously decorated establishment. Deep red flock wallpaper adorned with various classic Russian paintings of the aristocracy in pre Lenin times subtly illuminated by a huge chandelier hanging above the reception area. A second security man takes Valentina's coat while Alexie and Nikolai remove theirs and hand them to pretty blond in a little black dress at the cloaks desk. Valentina does not have to be a member to receive the most hospital treatment in the Feuervogel. It is owned by Vadim, a Russian entrepreneur and racketeer who is only too aware of Nikita's influence.

The trio are shown to a low circular corner table and make themselves comfortable in the large traditional Westbury leather upholstered armchairs, of which there are four.

"Should I remove this?" the waiter enquires as he takes hold of the back of the heavy empty chair. Valentina shakes her head.

"No, you don't have to bother. Just bring us a Dom Pérignon and a large plate of beluga blini," she asks casually.

"Would that be a magnum, madam?" the waiter asks as he takes in the proportions of the two men.

"Alexie, Nikolai?" Valentina queries her minders.

"Stolichnaya," Alexie replies timidly.

"You get that?" Valentina turns to the waiter.

"One bottle of Dom Pérignon, a bottle of Stolichnaya and a large plate of blini, madam, and, I presume, two tumbler glasses and a champagne glass," the waiter replies in perfect English with only a hint of a Hungarian accent.

"Perfect," Valentina smiles, as she reclines into the soft leather upholstery happy to be in the Feuervogel recalling memories of when Nikita first took her there three years ago, now made so vivid by the background music: Marvin Gaye's Sexual Healing, the exact song that played when she initially visited the place those three years ago.

Joe Violet, a wealthy American businessman sitting on a barstool mistakes Valentina's inviting smile to be an invitation to him since she is inadvertently looking in his direction. But she is not looking anywhere since her mind is focused on a vision of Nikita and she is momentarily oblivious to her immediate surroundings only her gaze belies the lust she is feeling.

Despite being sixty Joe is physically fit and attractive, often likened to George Clooney by his obsequious admirers and underlings back home, but Joe is far from as attractive as he thinks he is. A typical all American boy though no longer a boy, Joe considers himself a woman's dream. He knocks back his glass of Jack Daniels and casually takes the half empty bottle from the bar in his other hand before vacating the stool and sauntering over towards Valentina's table. He assumes Alexie and Nikolai, sat each side of Valentina, to be what they are, bodyguards.

"Hey there, lady. Do you mind if I join you?" Joe almost shouts in his Texas accent as he looks directly at Valentina avoiding eye contact with her two henchmen who glare at him but make no movement or comment.

"Sorry, er, what?" Valentina snaps out of her pleasure trip with Nikita and looks quizzically at Joe as he places his glass and bottle on the table opposite her. Alexie and Nikolai look to her for instruction.

"Would you mind if I take this seat here?" Joe asks as he pulls back the heavy chair.

"You can take that seat anywhere, just as long as it's not at my table," Valentina replies icily, her expression one of utter contempt. But Joe is already making himself comfortable.

"Sorry?" he feigns not to have heard.

"Alexie, Nikolai!" Valentina commands and the two men take great pleasure in rising with smiles on their faces. As they approach Joe from each side he attempts to stand. Nikolai forcefully pushes him back down into the deep seat and motions him with an index finger to stay put. Alexie takes the opposite arm of the chair from Nikolai in both hands and nods to Nikolai who immediately gets the idea and does likewise with the arm he stands by. Joe takes on an anxious expression of disbelief and is unsure of what to do next but before he can make a decision his chair is violently hoisted shoulder height into the air and the men's shoulders are higher than most. Alexie and Nikolai carry the chair with Joe in it to the center of the small dance floor scattering the handful of people on it. There they drop the chair from waist height. It hits the floor hard while Joe clings to the armrests in an effort to stable himself. Nikolai retrieves the bottle of Jack Daniels from the table and pours it over the shocked Joe while he is still in the chair, dropping the empty bottle into Joe's lap then returns to the table with Alexie leaving Joe traumatized, whiskey sodden and quite stationary.

"Is there a problem, madam?" the waiter asks as he arrives at the table with a large tray holding the champagne and vodka in ice buckets plus the glasses and caviar to find Alexie and Nikolai stood straightening their jackets and notices the previously vacant chair has disappeared.

"Not with you or the service. But, I'm afraid your clientele leave a lot to be desired. I've lost my appetite and thirst but tell Vadim to bill Nikita for what I ordered," Valentina replies as she gets to her feet.

"That won't be necessary, madam. I'm sorry you are displeased. Please let me know if there is anything I can do to improve your situation," the waiter asks anxiously. He knows Vadim will be furious when he hears one of Nikita's people were unhappy.

"Just order me a taxi, and don't worry, I won't mention it to Nikita," Valentina says as she gets to her feet and Nikolai pulls the seat back for her.

I motion Stan to the entrance of the carpark and unlock the gate then guide him to our parking space. After turning off the engine he jumps out of the car and gives me a bear hug.

"Yo, Jack, long time no see!" he enthuses as I feel the air being forced out of my lungs. I tap his shoulders since I cannot speak properly.

"Good to see you, Stan," I exhale as he releases me.

"Come on, give us a hand. I bought some great booze, Finlandia, Hennessey and I also got six bottles of a pricey chardonnay for your woman. You said she drinks that stuff, right?"

"That's thoughtful of you, Stan, but she's not here, I told you." Stan's generosity disturbs me, is he trying to bribe his way into making this a regular thing?

"I know, bro. But I thought it would be a token of my gratitude. From what you said I kinda got the impression I wasn't welcome, especially by your woman. She's even left because I'm coming I'm sure," Stan takes on a melancholic expression that actually makes me feel a little sorry for him.

"It's nothing personal, Stan. I told you she's a very private person," I lie to try and make him feel a little more at ease but I'm glad he's got the message about not being welcome. I take a box full of bottles from him and he follows me with his Louis Vuitton luggage bag. We make awkward small talk in the slow elevator on the way up to the penthouse apartment I managed to afford at the time of my employment. I ask him about his trip over and he comments on the difficulty of navigating the Viennese road system even with the aid of his sat nav. I comment on his luggage bag and he tells me it's counterfeit.

"Wow! Looks like you really made it, Jack," Stan exclaims as he enters the high ceilinged apartment furnished in Nora's impeccable taste. Most walls in the open plan living and dining area are hung with old and very valuable Austrian oil paintings handed down from Nora's family. The huge wall where the open staircase ascends to the bathroom, bedrooms and doorway to the terrace is decorated with several artifacts collected on our many trips abroad. A large dream catcher from Canada, a blowpipe from Peru, a mask from Venice, an effigy of Ganesha from India, a dungchen horn from Tibet and, of course, a prayer wheel affixed to the wall to name but a few.

"I just got lucky, Stan. They paid us a fortune at Telekom Austria, where I worked, and Nora found this place which was being renovated by a builder who was about to go bust so we got it really cheap compared to what it's worth," I reply as Stan takes his three quarter length black leather coat off. The acute definition of his ripped torso plainly visible under his flimsy white silk shirt as he twists to hang it on the coat stand. If anything he is more muscular now than he was over twenty years ago. I go into the kitchen and place the box on a work surface by the fridge.

"Let's crack the cognac, the vodka's too warm," Stan says as he makes himself comfortable on the soft padded leather sofa.

"How many times do have to tell you, Stan..."

"Yeah, yeah, I know. You don't drink anymore. I just thought, maybe, just maybe, for old time's sake we could enjoy a drink together?" Stan smiles at me, feet resting on the coffee-table and hands clasped behind his head exemplifying his lats as I walk out of the kitchen. Thank the Lord or Dafa Nora is not here to see this. She would be more than displeased with anyone entering the apartment in shoes and as for someone to rest their feet on a table, shoes or not, she would be more than livid. I contemplate sharing a drink with him, I won't enjoy it and drinking alcohol goes against Falun Dafa teachings, but under these circumstances and just for one night perhaps it would not set me back so far.

"Sorry, Stan. You go ahead and drink what you want, but I'm not touching it," Dafa gets the better of me.

"You sorry son of a bitch, if you're not gonna drink with me then at least take me somewhere there are people, especially ladies, that do drink, hey bro?" Stan replies and smiles at me to let me know it's a friendly request with no threat behind it.

"Okay, Stan. There's a place not far away that I think you'll like, it' only a couple of stops on the underground, or we can take a taxi if you like," I answer.

"Taxi, underground, I don't give a shit, man. Does this place have plenty of pussy?"

"It's not exactly a single place, Stan, it's an area. They call it the Bermuda Triangle, and yeah, when you've drunk enough, you can easily get lost there. It's just full of discos, bars, clubs and it's full of all sorts of people, including pussy," I smile back.

"So what are we waiting for, bro?"

Alexie pays the driver and gets out of the taxi front passenger seat to open the rear door for Valentina while Nikolai gets out of the other rear seat.

"I'm sorry I can go no closer, it is only for walking

there. The nearest entrance to the Triangle is fifty meters by your right," the driver summons his best English to tell Valentina as she gets out of the car. He suggested the Triangle when Valentina asked for a fun place to go. The trio walk briskly in the direction they were instructed, Valentina a little up front with Alexie and Nikolai flanking her. They turn right into the pedestrianized Rabenstieg. Valentina surveys the multitude of bars that surround her and decides on the Roter Engel(Red Angel) to her right and points to the door. Alexie goes forth and opens the door for her, she walks in and glares at the dark-skinned slim built, thirty-something doorman, perhaps of Turkish or Egyptian origin.

"Do you speak English?" she asks as Alexie and Nikolai flank her in the small reception area.

"Of course, madam. Can I show you to a table?" he replies in an indiscernible but thick accent.

"Show me, as far away from the music as you can," Valentia replies aloofly as she enters the large bar come disco. The interior, to a degree, lives up to its name, red walls, red furniture and red carpet, even red lighting but several scantily clad females of all ages and colors gyrating on the dancefloor to loud techno music on her right do not meet the criteria of angel although Valentina does not find them displeasing and she is fascinated by the three mini-skirted girls actually dancing on the long bar, which stretches most of the room's length up to dancefloor. Mainly drooling men crowd the three areas of the bar where the girls are dancing, transfixed by the erotic motions of their shapely thighs and especially what lies above, G-strings or nothing. Valentina motions with her left hand for the doorman to proceed to find her a table. Although it is very warm it is obvious the place has no cloakroom so Valentina does not bother to ask, she finds it quite refreshing to be surrounded by the common but bohemian people. The doorman takes them to a corner furthest from the dancefloor where two effeminate, gay looking men in their twenties are sitting on high stools at a drinks table.

"Geh weg!" he commands and the gays take one look at the Russians, pick up their cocktails and vacate the table without saying a word. The doorman picks up a vacant stool and places it next to the table to make three and beckons to a waiter. Nikolai pulls out the center stool while Alexie takes Valentina's coat then places it over the backrest. The two men do the same with their own coats and perch themselves either side of Valentina whose attention is fully taken by the three dancing girls on the bar but a waiter soon distracts her.

"English," the doorman says to the waiter before returning to the door.

"What can I get you?" the waiter asks in a similar accent to the doorman and not knowing whom to address he looks to each of the three while doing so.

"Do you have any Dom Pérignon?" Valentina asks.

"What, madam?" the waiter has no idea.

"Champagne!" Valentina shouts over the music.

"Oh, sorry, madam we only have Moet & Chandon but we do have some very good sekt. The Austrian version of champagne if you like," the waiter offers.

"As the saying goes, 'when in Rome', why not. Bring me a bottle of your best medium dry sekt and a bottle of Stolichnaya. You do have Stolichnaya, don't you?"

"Of course, madam. Our best-selling vodka. Anything else?"

"No, that's all, just make sure the drinks are well chilled," Valentina could see the establishment did not provide food and the energy she felt in the place subdued her appetite.

"One more thing, madam. How many glasses should I bring for each bottle?"

"One sekt, two vodka," Valentina replies as she holds up fingers signaling her instruction to make sure the waiter gets it.

We walk in the cold night air from my apartment building to a nearby taxi rank where I tell the driver to take us to Schwedenplatz. I avoid saying the Bermuda Triangle because of past experiences when I found only the most experienced taxi drivers knew where I meant because it is not an officially named place but Schwedenplatz is and the Triangle starts there.

"This place is kickin, man," Stan remarks as we walk along the cobbled pedestrianized area surrounded by the bars, clubs and discos. Blaring music, some live, changing in beat and style as we pass by one establishment and near the next.

"Which one do you want to try first?" I casually ask.

"I dunno, you're the expert here, Jack," Stan replies and looks at me quizzically.

"You hungry?"

"Maybe a little, and I guess it's a good idea if I'm gonna be drinking. Especially with the business I've got on tomorrow," Stan mentions the reason for his visit for the first time since arriving.

"And what business would that be, Stan?" I venture.

"Ah, you don't want to know the details, Jack. And,

besides, what you don't know can't hurt ya," Stan is giving nothing away.

"Let's try the Bermuda Bräu. It's similar to a regular pub only it has a dancefloor downstairs, lots of tasty ladies used it in my drinking years and the food was pretty good too. Bräu means brewery so they make their own beer, which is good, well it used to be when I drank here. It's just around the corner," I say as we make a right turn. The place is busy but we are lucky. As we enter I notice a couple vacate their table and I quickly make my way over to it and take a seat leaving Stan to follow.

"Nice one, Jack," Stan says as he takes the other seat and sees there are no other free tables.

"This place has always been popular, a lot of tourists come in plus the natives too, mainly for the beer," I remark as I hold my hand up to get the attention of a busy waiter who is unable to come straight away but acknowledges my request with a nod.

"Yo, they even do burgers here," Stan thinks aloud as he peruses one of the menus left on the table.

"Yeah, I told you it's like pub grub. Why don't you try the spare ribs?"

"Why spare ribs?"

"Because they're not like back in England or from a Chinese takeaway back home. You get a whole rack of ribs from a piglet marinated and slowly roasted. Taste great and they come with chips, salad and dips and we can order a large portion, two racks, to share," I suggest since I'm not that hungry and don't want to eat much in preparation of the following day's Falun Dafa exercises. I remember Stan has a big appetite and know he won't comment on however little I consume.

"Sounds good to me," Stan replies just as the waiter gets to our table. I order the ribs and two beers for us. I figure if I'm going to have to stay out with Stan a few beers will act as a kind of anesthetic even though I don't actually enjoy drinking the stuff these days and its low in alcohol compared with cognac or vodka and so hopefully it won't have much of an impact on my practice. The foaming beers arrive quickly and the waiter tells us the ribs will be twenty minutes.

"So, what do you think?" I ask after Stan empties half the half liter glass in a few gulps.

"Great beer; Jack. It really hits the spot," Stan grins broadly and wipes the foam from his top lip with the back of his hand. We reminisce and I actually begin to enjoy the conversation interspersed by pangs of guilt since we are discussing past events that could hardly be more incongruent with my current beliefs. The ribs arrive on a large wooden platter, three racks of them atop a mountain of French fries surrounded by salad, chopped onion and three small dishes containing various dips. I order more beer.

"When you said it would be enough for two, Jack, I had my doubts but this is enough for three, how we gonna manage it?"

"I'm sure you will, Stan," I answer and twenty minutes later he had done. I probably managed twenty percent of it, mainly fries and salad.

"Okay, where next?" Stan asks as he finishes his fourth beer and I my third.

"Do you want to take a look downstairs? I thought you wanted to meet some females..." my sentence is cut short by the ringing tone of Stan's mobile, which is lying on the table.

"Hi, sugar. Sorry I haven't called. Just been too busy," Stan answers to Lizzy.

"Where are you? I can hear a lot of people and music," Lizzy is paranoid about Stan's fidelity.

"I just had dinner with an old friend, I'm staying at his place. I'll pass you over to him," Stan gives me the phone and tells me to explain to Lizzy who I am, where we are and that we have no female company.

"Hi, Lizzy. I'm an old friend of Stan's. We go back a long way, so long in fact that you have probably never heard of me, I'm Jack. I understand your concern. He was quite the Casanova when I mixed with him," Stan gives me a mock angry glare, "but I can assure you he's being a good boy. We have just had something to eat and I will soon take him back to my place and tuck him up in bed or probably the sofa," I try to humor. Stan takes the phone from me.

"You happy now, sugar?" Stan says triumphantly.

"Yes, but you said that you would call every day!"

"I'm sorry but I was just busy with an old friend today. I'll call you tomorrow night and the day after before I come back to you," Stan says apologetically.

"You better," Lizzy replies and ends the call.

"Sounds like you've got yourself quite an attached lady back home, Stan," I mock.

"Yeah, but she's something else. Never had a girl like her in my life. Maybe she is the real thing, you know, someone to spend the rest of my life with," Stan turns serious.

"So why are you still playing around?"

"What d'ya mean?"

"Tonight for instance. You said you wanted to go somewhere where there's pussy," I reply incredulously.

"Come off it, Jack. Variety is the spice of life and when I play around with other women it makes Lizzy all the more desirable. Have you forgotten about the way you used to treat women in your life? Especially the ones you had long term relationships with," it is Stan's turn to be incredulous. Again I feel guilt and shame.

"Okay, point taken. So do you want to go downstairs?" I feel embarrassed and want to change the subject, who the hell am I to attempt to be so righteous.

"Lead the way, bro. Let's take a look," Stan smiles. I get up and walk towards the downstairs entrance at the back of the pub-like area. We tramp down the stairs to the ever increasing volume of 'Start Me Up' by the Stones.

"Best rock band ever," I comment as we approach the entrance to the disco.

"I'm getting turned-off before I have a chance of getting turned-on my man, I can't jive with this shit. We maybe old but I can't be this kind of old, get my drift?"

"Okay. Stan. Let's go somewhere else." I should have known that Stan would not be into the Stones, but how should I have known it was that kind of music playing that night. We turn and ascend the stairs. As we step outside I take a look around and the Casablanca to the right catches my eye. Another place I used to frequent a long time ago where live music is performed. But as we walk towards it passing the Kra Kra bar Stan stops in his tracks.

"Let's take a look in here." His attention has been taken by something or probably someone inside. There are plain glass windows at the front and it is possible to survey most of the interior from the outside due to the harsh bright electric lighting in the bar.

"Stan, that's the Kra Kra, mainly locals use it, and not many female locals and the ones that do are usually not the kind to interest you, look more like horses than women," my words fall on deaf ears as Stan opens the door. I am not just worrying about what Stan will think of the clientele but more so what the clientele will think of Stan, 'nigger' is not considered an offensive word in Austria. As we enter Aha's 'Take On Me' is playing but not so loud as to interfere with conversation. I immediately zoom in on the bar staff, I had a drunken one night liaison with one of them many years ago and I am relieved to see she is not behind the bar, probably too old to pull the customers now. But I do see what caught Stan's attention. He takes a seat at the bar next to three very attractive Austrian girls in their twenties obviously on a fun night out, two long-haired blonds and a bobbed brunette all fully made up and dressed to tease. The two blonds sitting while the brunette stands in between them relaying her day's events at a spa. I can roughly guess that she is describing various male genitalia she has observed in the sauna area on her visit to the spa and when they burst out in raucous laughter I become quite sure.

"What's so funny?" Stan leans over and whispers to me with his back towards the girls.

"They're just talking about small dicks in the sauna," I reply in similar hushed tones.

"What?"

"She was at a spa today and the spas have unisex saunas here where everyone is naked," I explain.

"You mean men and women go naked together in the

sauna?"

"It's normal here. I'll never forget the first time I went in one. I was with an Austrian work colleague and he took me to this gym. After the workout it was time for a sauna, so we showered got changed into dressing gowns and went down to the sauna taking towels with us. I was surprised to see lots of naked ladies on loungers and chairs as well as men but didn't say anything so as not to appear ignorant and to hide my embarrassed surprise. We entered a large sauna and I sat by the feet of a very sexy woman in her twenties with long black hair, there was nowhere else to sit. She was lying on her back with her hands under her head and smiled at me. I didn't know where to look so made small talk with my colleague who sat on the other side of me. When she heard me speaking English she asked where I was from in a German accent. I had no choice but to turn and answer her between her open legs. I couldn't help noticing her very well trimmed pussy and it was hard for me to keep my attention on her face. She was a real turn-on and I had to channel my thoughts so as not to make a spectacle of myself, if you know what I mean," I reply quietly.

"Man, I couldn't do much business here if you don't have to pay for that sort of shit! Did you fuck her?" Stan asks.

"Shush, Stan, not so loud. No, I didn't. It's like talking to someone in a pub. She was just interested because I spoke English, she was from Berlin and wanted to know what I was doing in Vienna when she heard me speaking in English," again I reply quietly.

"Crazy place. No wonder you decided to stay here,"
"It's not that different, Stan. There are still plenty of

brothels and lap dancing places. You did business in Brussels, wasn't that the same?" I query.

"No, no it's not normal. You can find it if you look and pay like you can in the UK but it's far from normal," Stan replies also quietly this time.

"Zum! Zum! Zum! Zum! Zum!" the three girls shout loudly completely taking our attention.

"What the fuck!" Stan says as the girls knock back schnapps shots in unison and slam their empty glasses on the bar so hard it is surprising that they do not shatter.

"It's an Austrian thing," I shrug my shoulders. The girls take their coats from the nearby stand and bid farewell to the bar staff. Stan looks forlorn.

"Still want to drink here?" I ask although I know the answer. The remaining customers are mainly working class Austrian men and a few far from attractive Austrian women in all shapes, sizes and guises. I shake my head when a barmaid asks what we want and Stan shakes his as he gets off the barstool. We leave the Kra Kra without having consumed anything. I take us to the Casablanca next door. Stan shakes his head before the door is fully opened to us when he hears a very bad rendition of George Michael's 'I Want Your Sex'. We both turn around and the door closes behind us.

"Now, you choose, Stan," I say wearily. He looks around at the various bars opposite us since the Casablanca is the last one on our side of the walkway. He wanders over to Excess, I think the electronic dance music blaring out from the place he quite likes and I join him by the entrance.

"This looks okay," he comments. It's been some time since I was in the Excess but even then I thought I was far too old for the place but maybe Stan is into girls under twenty. We enter and I pay the doorman the token ten euros for both of us to enter and he gives us a smile that can easily be interpreted as 'you dirty old men'. We descend the stairs into the warm, damp and clingy atmosphere of the dance club. Stan stops four or five steps before the bottom to survey the scene and I stop with him.

"Jesus, Jack. Most of these can't be legal," he says in disbelief taking in the sight of frenetic dancing bodies of teenagers on the dancefloor then turns to go back. I am a little mystified since I had never known Stan display such morals ever since I had known him. I turn and follow him. The doorman looks at us quizzically and I just wave my hand and he opens the door for us to leave.

"Where's our next port of call?" I ask, and as we walk into the pedestrian area Stan sees two smartly dressed black guys leave the Roter Engel. The first Negroes we have seen all evening and so he is intrigued to see why they used the place. I knew I didn't have to ask.

"What's that place?" he says pointing to the Roter Engel about thirty meters away to our left.

"It's called the Red Angle in English. Big variety of customers, many from Vienna, real Bohemian types but also a lot of tourists. The music varies but it's pretty much modern stuff, well it was the few times I used it in the past. Shall we?"

"Sure, let's take a look," Stan replies a little more enthusiastic than he was in the Excess. The doorman gives us a cursory glance and is satisfied we are not falling down drunk or worse and beckons us in.

"Now that's more like it, Stan remarks while looking at the girls dancing on the bar and begins to make his way towards it. I follow but stop short of the bar at a rare vacant high drinks table although there are no stools around it it's better than standing with a drink in your hand. Stan pushes himself to the bar and turns to see where I am.

"I'll have a bottle of Bud," I shout to him although I know his reason for going to the bar is not to get the drinks but he nods and smiles anyway before turning his gaze up to the girls and especially their thighs performing directly in front and above him. I lean against the table and take a look around the place. It hasn't changed since the last time I was in before I met Nora. The same mixed Bohemian type crowd and crowded it is, I take my jacket off and hang it on a hook affixed to the underside of the table, a common Austrian gimmick found in many establishments that proves to be very practical. The dim red lighting and half naked dancing girls on the bar and floor wouldn't be out of place in a lap dancing joint but the girls are dancing for fun not money. A point which I found a real turn-on in the days I used to get turned on. It takes a while to get served at the bar but Stan takes an inordinate amount of time to come back with two bottles of Budweiser.

"Now this place was worth coming out for, those girls are something else," Stan enthuses.

"Yeah, and they know it. They compete with each other on who can reveal the most. If they have enough to drink their tops come off," I explain through a grin.

Valentina empties the last glass of sekt and Alexie stands in anticipation of fetching her another bottle, the waiters are so busy that it is quicker to go directly to the bar. Valentina tells him in Russian to sit down and that she will go herself and gets off her stool, takes the ice-bucket holding the empty sekt bottle and sets off towards the bar. On seeing her the mainly male customers stand aside to let her through to the bar where she sets the bucket down.

"Noch einmal?" the bartender asks her as soon as she does so ignoring many who were waiting before.

"What was that?" Valentina doesn't understand German.

"Ah, English. Sorry, miss. Would you like another bottle?"

"Please," Valentina asks politely and while the bartender goes to fetch the sekt Valentina watches the dancers on the bar, which makes her feel a little competitive and cocaine and sekt have made her feel fearless. She taps the shoulder of an athletic good looking young Austrian man sitting on a stool at the bar. He is irritated by whoever it is taking his attention from the dancers. He turns aggressively with a look of anger on his face but his face lights up when he sees Valentina. She points to herself and then to the dancers. He happily gets off his stool and helps Valentina climb onto it, which is made a little awkward due to the height of her stilettos, from where she steps on to the bar greeted by whistles, whoops and cheers from the onlookers. Alexie and Nikolai look on from the table wearing big grins, confident in the belief they could handle anything if things got out of hand in any way. The other girls on the bar look a little disconcerted, one climbs down but the other two are not going to be outdone and increase their tempo and the eroticism of their movements. Valentina joins in the gyrating and is soon outperforming them despite the fact she shows less flesh, she wears skin tight black nappa leather trousers and matching halter top and it is obvious she has the far superior physique.

We lean on the table almost shoulder to shoulder so we don't have to talk too loudly to be heard over the music, sipping at our ice-chilled Budweiser from the bottles and talking about what happened to us both since I left the scene.

"Now tell me you would roll over that to get out of bed," Stan says to me when he sees a truly gorgeous platinum blond with short cropped hair wearing black leather climb onto the bar.

"Yes, she is something special, especially if you've got a leather fetish" I dryly reply.

"Come off it, Jack, in the old days no one would have kept you off her," Stan says excitedly.

"Like you say; Stan, that was the old days. I told you, I'm a changed man," I reply thoughtfully.

"Yeah, I can tell since being with you, but the weird thing is, man, I kinda feel different being in your company. You make me feel strange, not in bad way, but I feel bad about the way I am. Are you doing some sort of voodoo shit on me?" Stan passes me a look full of consternation. I laugh.

"You're the one with a mum from Haiti. Don't you think I should be the one to be worried about voodoo?"

"Seriously, Jack, the longer I'm with you, and it's only been a matter of hours, the stranger I'm feeling," Stan takes on a melancholic expression. A vision of his disgust at the under-aged in the Excess flashes in my mind. Is it possible my gong energy is not as weak as I believe? Perhaps it has the strength to affect Stan while he is in my presence. This I am not allowed to even contemplate and surely not take any sort of satisfaction from since it would be a form of attachment only serving to reduce my level of attainment.

"Would you like me to tell you about Falun Dafa?"

"What?"

"Falun Dafa. The thing I do. Remember I told you I had become religious in a way when you first called me?"

"In the morning, hey, Jack? There's too much going on here right now," Stan replies and diverts his attention back the dancing platinum blond on the bar. We spend about half an hour over the beers mainly watching the scenes and enjoying the music.

"Shall I get replacements?" I ask Stan after our bottles have been empty for five minutes and I am actually enjoying the beer to my surprise, but not as much as Stan is the action on the dancefloor and especially the bar.

"No, no, I'll get'em in. It's the least I can do, you're putting me up," Stan lies as he gets to his feet, he knows we both know the lady in leather is the real reason he is so eager to get to the bar. He never offered to pay the taxi or the entrance to Excess and we shared the bill in the Bermuda Bräu, but I guess he did get the first beers in the Roter Engel, but then there were also girls on the bar. I just smile and nod as I give him my empty bottle. He joins the crowd at the bar and, uncharacteristically for Stan, politely waits his turn instead of shouldering his way through. I am not sure if he's being polite, wary of being in a foreign environment or just wants an excuse to be closer to the bar and the action on top of it for as long as possible, but I lean towards the latter. I look on as he slowly makes progress towards the bar nearest to the lady in leather, his attention consumed in his gaze up at her, I cannot see but I imagine he has a huge grin on his face. To my surprise, if I have not got the angle wrong, which I sure I have not, the lady in question appears to take an interest in Stan. She focuses on him and directs her movements towards him and then even bends down and rubs his head. I am a little confused. Stan is attractive in a menacing way but why would she be interested in a black guy? Austria does not have a colonial history such as France or the U.K. where many Negroes became citizens. The only other girls I've seen with black guys in Vienna have been so aesthetically challenged that they obviously find it hard to get a guy at all but most of the black guys in Vienna are refugees and are happy to latch onto any female who will give them a bed, a meal, anything. So why is this gorgeous woman showing an interest? It must be a fetish of hers. Stan gets served soon after receiving the dancer's attention but still lingers awhile before returning with the drinks.

"Did you see that, Jack?" Stan places the bottles of Bud on the table beaming with pride.

"Yeah, she probably feels sorry for an old bald black guy in Vienna," I joke.

"Is it the light or have you turned green, Jack?" Stan counters.

"Well, just in case anything does happen with her, I hope you brought your Viagra with you," I cannot help myself.

"What, Jack? Don't tell me you need that stuff to perform, do you? You had no problem doing it anywhere, train toilets, you had that stewardess on the way to Spain just so you could join the mile high club and I'll never forget the night you took that barmaid over the pool table when the place was packed, just for a bet. What happened to you boy?" Stan sounds genuinely surprised. I hate to think what he would say if he knew I could not or just did not, Viagra or not.

"Let's not go there, Stan. Let's just say I'm older and hopefully wiser, now." I have no idea how else to respond. Stan just smiles takes a swig of Bud and turns his attention back towards the bar.

Satisfied with herself taking the great majority of attention from the ogling clientele in the place Valentina is helped down from the bar by the same Austrian who helped her up. She takes the ice bucket holding the sekt and makes her way back to Alexie and Nikolai. On her way she notices Stan who is staring at her like a lovesick puppy, if ever Stan could be described as something so vulnerable as a puppy, especially by the way he appears. She makes a detour towards him.

"Do you speak English?" she asks a dumbstruck Stan. I immediately go on the alert when I hear this beautiful platinum blond talk in a thick Russian accent. I had a brief affair with a Russian not long after I arrived in Vienna. I soon discovered her lifestyle and wealth could not be accounted for in a conventional way and, I was sure, not a legal one. She had an Italian passport which allowed her to reside in Vienna but she could not speak a word of Italian. I decided it was in my own interest to severe the contact since I was now a law abiding big earning individual.

"I hope so, I am English," Stan replies quite mesmerized.

"Ah, interesting. Do you mind if I join you?" she asks and smiles at Stan seductively.

"Sure, but we have no seats," Stan replies as a waiter turns up at the table with one, which he places behind Valentina who asks him for a sekt glass. Alexie and Nikolai look on unperturbed, confident Valentina will not put herself in any uncompromising situation and even more so that they could sort it out if ever she were to do so, but then Alexie's phone rings.

"So what is such a sexy Englishman doing in Vienna?" She asks and looks at Stan with come to bed eyes.

"Just visiting an old friend," he replies and tilts his head sideways towards me. But before this Russian femme fatale answers a huge bull like man with a shaven head appears behind her, leans over her ignoring Stan and me and says,

"Nikita!" as he hands a mobile phone to her. Her confident seductive expression is immediately replaced by one of consternation. She gets up, takes the phone and hurriedly walks away towards the far corner of the room. The bull takes the sekt from the table, not even glancing at us, and follows her.

"Well, that was short and sweet," I chuckle.

"Maybe she'll come back," Stan hopes aloud.

"In your dreams, man, in your dreams. Did you see the size of that guy? And non of it was fat. I know you can handle yourself, Stan. But I know who my money would be on," I try and talk some sense into him.

"But he wasn't her guy," Stan is not giving up hope.

"No, or he would have probably knocked you out when he saw you drooling over her at the bar and she wouldn't have patted your head," I concede.

"She didn't pat it, she rubbed it. It was obviously a come on, an invite to something more," Stan won't be discouraged.

"Even so she is now talking to someone called Nikita,

who is probably her boyfriend if not her husband," I reply dryly.

"Nikita! Isn't that a girl's name? I remember Elton John did a song about a girl called Nikita. Maybe it's her sister or mother," Stan grasps at straws.

"Didn't you learn anything at school? Surely you have heard of John F Kennedy?"

"Of course, he was assassinated," Stan answers.

"But before he was assassinated, Stan, there was the Cuban missile crisis, which I'm not going to go into but it meant a lot of discussion between Kennedy and the leader of the Russian communist party who was called Nikita Sergeyevich Khrushchev, and he wasn't a woman, and, besides, Elton John is gay so how do you know he wasn't singing about a guy?" I explain.

"Okay, okay, shall we go back to your place? I guess I shouldn't stay up most of the night drinking when I have to drive tomorrow," Stan replies forlornly and I am relieved he has given up pursuing the Russian.

14.

Sunday morning Beth tries to coach Jason into some early bedtime frolics.

"Come off it, woman, didn't you get enough last night? You're some nympho you know," he murmurs coming out of his slumber.

"Would you like me any different?"

"No, but I'm tired. If you have so much energy fix me some breakfast and call your brother," he replies wearily.

"What do you want me to call Jack for?" Beth is alarmed.

"I wanna know exactly when the nigger is expected back in the UK," Jason replies.

"Jay, if I call him about Stan again so soon he's gonna get suspicious, he'll want to know why I'm so interested. He was surprised last time I called him. Why do you need to know so urgently?" Beth tries to get out of making the call.

"Don't question me, Beth," he flashes her a serious glare.

"I wished I never told you anything about this shit. Why the fuck did Stan have to tell me what he was up to?" she replies thinking out loud.

"Because he's an egotistical loser and the only person I know dumb enough to do business with the Russian Mafia, I can't believe they're using him. Probably couldn't find anyone else. He wanted to impress you, maybe even hoped to get back in your knickers. And you know you had to tell me about it because you need my protection against the nigger," Jason answers coldly.

"Why didn't you let me tell Jack why Stan wanted to visit him?"

"Because I don't know your brother. And maybe, if he knew in advance the reason for the visit he may have found a way to stop it, which I didn't want him to do."

"Why not?" Beth is confused.

"Okay, I'll give it to you straight. I don't want Stan flooding Manchester with cheap coke, the Angels are doing a deal right now to get a regular supply sorted in Manchester but if the price goes down it's going to cut into our profits. To stop him I need to keep tabs on him and that is much easier if you can find out where he is until he actually gets here with the stuff," Jason explains.

"Why don't you just take it off him when he gets here or is that what you plan to do?"

"No, I thought about it but I want him off the streets. If we rob him he could well get more next month, next week, whenever. But the main reason we don't want to rob him is because we're worried about what might happen to us if we do," Jason is uncharacteristically reticent.

"What! The mighty Hells Angels are scared of a black pimp?" Beth is very confused.

"I credited you with more intelligence, woman. Who did Stan tell you was his supplier?"

"Okay, got it. Russian Mafia," Beth answers after a long pause.

"Thank you very much, Einstein. We even considered taking him out but if we do that and he hasn't paid the Russians then we're in the same boat. They'll think we killed and robbed him and then they'll come after us. We've been in touch with the Moscow Chapter of Angels and they said we should stay away not just because of possible repercussions from the mafia but because they do a lot of business with them and they don't want any bad feelings caused by what we do, so we have decided the best solution to this problem is if we can get him put away and if the law catches him with a hundred k's of coke he'll be put away for a long, long time. We manipulate the price of coke on the streets and the Russians have no one to blame, and hopefully no one else to sell it for them," Jason answers reluctantly since he hates to concede he has to comply with things above his control.

"So what will you do when he gets back, Jay, grass

him up to the drugs squad? I never dreamed I would ever see the day the Angels got into bed with the law, you shock me," Beth's bewilderment is evident.

"We have no choice. We can sit back, do nothing and watch our profits turn into loses. We could hit Stan and have a war with the Russians, which we would probably lose one way or another, like me being made dead. Or, we can get Stan arrested, taken out of the picture and leave the Russians with no one to sell their shit and no one to blame for it. Now, in all your wisdom, what do you think we should do?"

"I'm sorry, Jay. It's just, you know, the whole rat thing. It just seems so incredibly not the Angels. You know what I mean?"

"Of course I do, but I think the notion of the rat thing died completely when John Gotti was put inside all those years ago. Now please call Jack and try and find out when Stan is due back in Manchester," Jason requests. Beth resigns herself to making the call and puts her imagination into overdrive as she descends the stairs to do so.

I wake just after seven on Sunday morning, which is early considering I didn't get to bed until two after leaving Stan to his own devices watching MTV with the bottle of Hennessy he brought along at his disposal. I hear him snoring loudly downstairs. I guess this is as a good a time as any the day will afford me to practice. By the time Stan wakes and leaves, Nora could be arriving so I climb out of bed and assume the position to begin opening my chakras. I know the exercises start well due to the warmth that envelopes me and the bright white entities which appear in my mind's eye, the nausea is apparent but not overwhelming and the crown of my head begins to tingle. This is a great relief to me since I was anxious what detrimental effects consuming alcohol the previous night might have on my practice.

After opening my chakras I hold the wheel before me. The throbbing sensation between my arms soon begins, at first hardly noticeable but the pulsating gradually grows in momentum to the point where I have to forcefully hold my arms still. It makes me want to laugh out of sheer glee that this phenomena shows itself to me so strongly, but I have to fight this attachment otherwise the phenomena might cease and my attainment recede. After about ten minutes I lower the wheel to my abdomen and it feels like my insides are spinning, again I have to calm this mental stimulation caused by the physical experience and focus on zhen, shan, ren: truth, compassion and tolerance, the basis of Falun Dafa. After a similar period I raise the wheel to envelop my head which gives the sensation of blood rushing to it as though I were hanging upside down. After another ten minutes or so, I've learned to judge the time over my years of practice, I lower my hands to the sides of my head dividing the wheel in two, each one rotating between my palms and ears.

"What the fuck?" Stan asks as I end the exercise and open my eyes. He is standing in the bedroom doorway.

"How long have you been there?" I ask a little surprised since Stan had been so quiet in ascending the stairs and I did not notice the cessation of snoring, but I wouldn't while practicing.

"Since just before you stopped doing those funny arm movements and stretching," Stan replies.

"That was to open my chakras and free the energy flows. So you have been stood there watching me for well over half an hour?" I point out as I wipe the sweat from my brow.

"Yeah, I guess so, but I didn't want to interrupt. You seemed so serene, there was a kind of light around you and spinning between your arms. It's faded now but it was a sort of blue or purple color surrounding you and a reddish light spinning between your arms, first in one direction then in the opposite, constantly alternating after every rotation. Is this the thing you told me about, your sort of religion?"

"Part of it, Stan, only part of it, but if you could see the aura and the wheel you must have a fundamentally good foundation. I can't believe it knowing what you are, you must have been a holy saint in your last life, I can only feel the wheel not see it," I answer a matter-of-factly but I am astonished by what he tells me.

"You mean you haven't finished?" Stan is only interested in there being another light show.

"No, I haven't finished the exercises. There are five and you just saw two of them. But Falun Dafa is not just about exercises. The main features of it are to build a decent character, become a better person and first and foremost, discard all attachments," I explain as plainly as I can.

"What do you mean, attachments?"

"In your case, Stan, I would say physical strength, looks, sex, money and power but also your fear of not having them or losing them. They're just examples that reveal how attached you are to this human existence," as I finish the sentence I realize Stan is never going to become a practitioner though I believe he must have some deeply buried potential if he is capable of witnessing what he said he did. If his karma had been so heavy he would not have been able to see my aura and especially not the spinning of the wheel.

"But what is life all about? The more money you have the better you can live and the more power you've got the less likely someone is going to try and take it off you," Stan replies a little perplexed.

"Stan, that's just it. You believe only in this reality, this existence. You believe this, here and now, is all there is. I believe we're here by mistake. By our own mistakes made over countless lifetimes, not just on this planet in this dimension but many before. Mistakes of greed, selfishness, jealousy, every kind of failing that is born out of attachment. I first started believing this after going to Tibet and learning about Buddhism. Then I discovered Falun Dafa, which I believe is the best and probably only way for me to strive for enlightenment as seen by Buddhism but I'm pretty sure I won't attain it in this lifetime despite the fact I've been doing it for several years," I try to explain but doubt Stan gets the point.

"This lifetime, man, what else is there?"

"That's a perfect example of your attachment to this existence, Stan. You measure time by how long you live here. I have a different perspective on time. I'll try and give you an idea so try and think about this. There was once a Buddhist monk who went to a master for a teaching on the understanding of time. The master agreed to give it but first told the monk they would drink some tea. As the cup touched the monk's lips he was transported to a beautiful lake and in the lake he saw a beautiful woman swimming. He waited until she came out of the water and introduced himself. There was mutual attraction and they married sometime later, some

Tibetan Buddhist monks are allowed to marry. Time went by and they were deliriously happy, and when the wife gave birth to a son their happiness only increased. One day the wife got the terrible news her father had died. This also upset the monk because he had become very close to her family over the years. Soon after her mother committed suicide by drowning herself in the lake because she couldn't bear the loss of her husband. They both became very depressed but had to carry on with life for the sake of their son. A few years later tragedy struck again when the son became ill and died. This was too much for the wife and she followed her mother by drowning herself in the lake. Now the monk had lost all he thought he had to live for and decided to follow the way of his wife. He walked into the lake and the water got deeper and deeper, he closed his eyes and just as the water reached his lips he took a sip of tea. He opened his eyes to see the master smiling at him. The monk smiled back realizing that time here is irrelevant because this dimension is pretty much irrelevant, just as the one he experienced spanning many years but only a second in this dimension, which is a window to a last chance of redemption. The master had placed him in another dimension just to give an example of time's flexibility and what seems like a lifetime is really nothing if not used wisely and what we consider here on earth to be a second could be a lifetime in some other dimension. Our existence in this life is also nothing but a fleeting moment of our real existence. If we don't try and do anything about our situation during this lifetime, probably the last chance we'll get before being reborn as an animal, a plant, even a rock, then we are destined for destruction," I conclude on a somber note.

"Shit, Jack. You know I can't get my head around this stuff, but I can't deny you're having some weird effect on me. The light I just saw around you was unreal, man, I've never seen anything so beautiful and it made me feel so quiet and still. I could have watched you forever. Why don't you go to the TV and demonstrate this stuff?"

"Stan, if I ever tried to do such a thing it would never happen in public and it probably wouldn't happen to me again in private. It is showing-off and showing-off means you have a great attachment to fame and fortune fueled by vanity and arrogance. This attachment would destroy what I have cultivated and it wouldn't happen to me again, at least not for a long time. The only reason you saw it was because I was not aware you were watching and I'm sure the great majority of people would not be able to see it anyway because they are too encased in karma. The only way I can progress in my practice, faith, religion, whatever you want to call it is to abandon attachments. The exercises you saw me doing are just a way to make me healthy and more spiritually aware and they actually reduce the black karma I have accrued over many existences, which is priceless. Due to the reduction of my karma I can hopefully live longer to continue with my practicing and get closer to my goal," I try and explain.

"Goal? What is your goal, Jack?"

"To get away from this planet, this existence, this dimension. You're not a practitioner, Stan, so you can't understand. I am fighting to understand it myself and I've been trying for years. Attachments I have to rid myself of even include the people I cherish most because cherishing someone or something is an attachment. Well, I don't get rid

103

of the people but the act of cherishing them. I should feel compassion towards everyone and everything and tolerate everything. It makes this lifetime something of a burden, but for some reason I have no idea of, I just feel it is the most truthful thing in existence I have come across," I find it impossible to tell Stan in an understandable way since I do not understand it myself.

"You're dead right, I don't understand it, Jack. And what I can't understand even more is that you are following this religion, or whatever it is. What about your family? Are you just going to blank them out of your feelings? I can't understand why you want to prolong your life if you want to leave it. Why don't you just top yourself?" Stan is agitated but not in an aggressive way.

"Because I have to get as close as I can to my ascension, if you like, by practicing as long as I live and the longer I live the closer I'll get, I hope. If I commit suicide I cut it short and have to start again in the next life, and then only if I would be fortunate enough to be reborn as a human in an environment whereby I could practice. Otherwise I may be reborn as something else and be put countless lifetimes away from being able to practice again, if ever at all. As for my family, the compassion I feel for them I try to duplicate towards the rest of humanity, but it's amazingly difficult. This life I believe is a piece of shit. Whether you're the president of the USA or homeless living in the street, there is less than a hair's breadth between the two existences because the existence of humanity itself is so trivial and wretched. We only perceive the difference as enormous because we are trapped in this tiny existence. So how can anything we perceive to be so enormous be constricted by something so trivial and unimportant in the grand scale of existence? Simply because what we perceive is so much more miniscule itself," I say to myself as much as I do to Stan.

"Whoa, Jack, whoa. You're losing me. But I am seriously impressed after I saw you in that beautiful light. Can't you simply enjoy pleasure, success, power and money at the same time as following your religion?"

"Look, Stan. Although you're not a practitioner you must still be able to understand the fundamentals of spiritual life. Look at nuns and monks for instance. What do you think they think of personal success, power and personal indulgence? Look at the Muslims, they don't even drink alcohol. The reasons for these abstentions and abandonments is that their faiths don't allow it if they want to truthfully follow the path they have chosen. Falun Dafa is no different. I believe Christianity, Judaism, Islam and obviously Buddhism plus many other religions are just different ways to show the people how to be released from this existence permanently and be freed from reincarnation here or total destruction. A way for people to find their heaven if you like. As Jesus said, 'It would be easier for a camel to pass through the eye of a needle than for a rich man to enter the Kingdom of God'. This is because a rich man is far too attached to his wealth to let himself be freed from it and effectively leave this place we call the Earth and its existence, he will constantly be reborn here and he will carry on life after life in search of that which enslaves him, because that is his nature. When I say there is little difference between a homeless and the President of the USA, in fact the homeless is probably far better off. He has little to be attached to and also has to physically suffer during his miserable life, but in his next one on this Earth, he will probably be far better off than the US President in his next one because he has repaid more of his karma since he suffered more whereby the president enjoyed a life of power and opulence. I believe Falun Dafa is the most effective and fastest way to find a release from this cesspit we live in, and it's a cesspit full of shit like us," I explain the best way I can to Stan.

"Okay, I'm getting it and guess it's nothing I'm going to get involved with since I only believe in the here and now, magic too, but magic in the here and now. What I saw you doing just proved to me that there's something beyond what everyday people believe in but it's something I'm not willing to give up my lifestyle for in the hope I will find heaven or whatever because I think I'm just too bad to make the grade. Besides, I've heard stories about these strange religions ripping their followers off, taking all their money and possessions. How much do you have to give to be part of what you're involved in?"

"Nothing, Stan," I reply.

"What?"

"Nothing. Not one single penny. The only money generated in Falun Dafa is used to print books and information to spread the word. I just get everything from the net completely free. A lot of followers join others to do the exercises together in parks and such places but you can also do it alone at home as I do," I try to encourage Stan.

"No kidding. You got any breakfast in here?" Stan replies but has a look of deep contemplation on his face. I believe he changes the subject to digest the fact that Falun Dafa could be a genuine movement.

"Sure, Stan, but it's only continental stuff, I can't fix

you an English breakfast, you can't get hold of bacon here but I've got a good selection of hams and cheeses, plus a baguette," I reply.

"Jack, you're forgetting I spent a lot of time in Brussels, I'm fine with ham and cheese. You got coffee?"

"The best you'll ever taste," I answer as we make our way down the stairs. The Austrians love their coffee like the Italians and Nora installed a coffee bean machine as soon as we moved in. I make the coffee and prepare a continental breakfast for Stan, I have no appetite and need to finish my exercises, if I get the opportunity, on an empty stomach.

"So, whatever it is you're doing, Stan, it's not going to happen again, is it?" I venture as we sit at the breakfast bar.

"What do you mean?"

"I mean you needing to stay at my place again," I say wearing the most serious look of disdain on my face I can muster.

"Why? It would only be for a day or two like this time and not for a couple of months or so. I told you I can't get registered as staying here," Stan queries.

"It can't happen, Stan. I don't think a black guy has ever been seen in this apartment building and the people living here take an unhealthy interest in people if they are not Caucasian. Get my drift?" I need to nip Stan's idea of another visit in the bud.

"What! You mean they're prejudiced?"

"Sorry, Stan, but Vienna is not like Brussels, Hitler lived here for a while and some people here don't object to his legacy to this day. If people living in the building, which incidentally happened to be built to house high ranked SS at the end of the war, catch a glimpse of you on more than one occasion they may well go to the law and ask if you're registered here, just because they don't want you here. That will bring a load of aggravation down on me and you will have to account for yourself, why you're here, where you're going etc. Besides that, Stan, I'm a completely different man to the one you knew all those years ago. You wouldn't be able to comprehend how bad I feel about the way I used to be. The people I hurt and abused, the drugs we peddled, the unborn babies I had killed, the frauds we committed. You are still in that world, Stan, and I can't be near anything associated with it anymore," I explain slowly in the most serious tone I am capable of.

"Shit! Could you help me find somewhere else I could stay in the future?" Stan seems to accept the situation, which I am pleasantly surprised by.

"So you understand the situation?" I have to confirm it to myself, this is not the Stan I knew.

"I told you, you make me feel different. You even make me question myself. Before I got here I felt great, big new deal, new connections, the sky was the limit. But now, after being with you for a while, I'm not so sure. The reason I'm here, Jack, is to take collection of a hundred k's of uncut coke, I did tell Beth about it. Although I told her not to tell you I thought she may have done but obviously not. This would probably turn into a repeat business every time I got rid of a consignment I'd come back for more. I even intended to bring you in on it just like the old days but I now realize you're not the Jack from the old days and you almost make me feel ashamed of what I am, since I'm still Stan from the old days. I'm not even sure if I want to do this stuff again,"

Stan wears a look of confused dismay.

"Why don't you stop it now before you start?"

"I can't."

"Why?"

"I'm collecting the stuff from the Russian Mafia. How do you think they will react?"

"Enough said. They probably have a more feared reputation here than they do in the UK, now I understand what you meant when you said 'as serious as cancer'. But why did you ask if I could find you somewhere else to stay next time if you're not sure there will be a next time?"

"Just in case. I don't seem to know myself all of a sudden. Maybe I'll change my mind and want to do it, after I get away from you and your influence. Or maybe the Russians will make me do it. I hate to ask you, and understand if you can't, but could you find me somewhere if I do it?" Stan asks with an unfamiliar look of pleading in his eyes.

"Sorry, Stan. Not only is this business you're doing completely against my principles my wife would crucify me if she knew I was mixed up in it in any way. She would probably divorce me after first informing the police of what you're up to and I cannot lie, that's also against my religion. Look, Vienna is full of hookers, maybe you can find one to shack up with if you need to in future." I am shocked by Stan's passivity in comparison with how I knew him to react when he was refused anything but his apparent attitude now emboldens me to tell him straight out that he cannot stay again or involve me in any way where he might stay.

"Okay, Jack, whatever I decide to do or am forced to do, I won't involve you," Stan almost looks sad.

"Thanks, Stan, I appreciate..." my sentence is cut short by the ringing tone of the landline. I lift the receiver attached to the wall behind where we are sitting without looking at the display thinking it is Nora calling to tell me when she will arrive.

"Hi, Jack?" comes Beth's loud and enthusiastic voice.

"Hi, sis. What's up?" I blurt out not thinking it is probably a stupid thing to do in Stan's presence but it is a knee-jerk reaction at hearing from her again so soon. I assume something urgent is afoot.

"Is that really Beth?" Stan says inappropriately loudly as he points to the phone. I just nod, there is no point in denying it.

"Is that Stan I heard?" Beth's enthusiasm evaporates as she asks almost in a whisper. I immediately wonder if there is any connection between her call and Stan being here.

"Yes, would you like to speak with him?" I do not conceal my intrigue and feel betrayed by the fact she never told me the real reason Stan wanted my phone number, although I cannot really blame her for not divulging it since Stan's retribution would not have been pleasant for her.

"No, no, er, can I call you back..." is all I hear before Stan takes the phone from my hand.

"Yo, Beth! I'm here. Just like I said I was gonna be. Don't worry, I've told Jack everything so you don't have to feel guilty about not telling him anymore. Should be back in Manchester Monday night as the main man in town, baby. Should I drop by to give you a taste?" Stan is back to his old self. I do not know what she replies but I guess it is in the negative by the way Stan's expression drops as he passes the phone back to me.

"Beth," I say disappointedly.

"I'm sorry, Jack, but I don't have to tell you what Stan's like. That's the reason I've called so often lately, I've been worried about you," the perfect excuse for the call has been forced upon Beth plus she has the information Jason wants, she feels quite pleased with herself.

15.

Valentina opens her eyes after Alexie has been gently shaking her shoulder and trying to rouse her for over two minutes in Russian. As she does so he puts her mobile into her hand.

"Yes?" she speaks wearily into it.

"Finally, Valentina, you are awake…"

"And why are you waking me so early, Lucas? I thought I told you!"

"Valentina, I'm sorry, but it is eleven and I've arranged for Stan to collect the merchandise at twelve, which you said was okay," Lucas grovels.

"Ah, shit. Yes, okay. We will be there to pass it over. A fifty-something year old fit looking tall English black guy with a bald head, right?"

"Yes, he will ring the buzzer of the apartment in the city and say that he is Stan sent by Lucas. You don't even have to meet him. Alexei and Nikolai can put the merchandise in his car," Lucas explains worrying about any approaches Stan might make on Valentina.

"No, no. I must be there. Nikita has entrusted me with this errand so I have to make sure it is carried out to the end, you need everything to run as smoothly as possible more than I do, Lucas," Valentina reminds him of his precarious position.

"Of course, Valentina, of course, I am happy that you put so much importance on it," comes Lucas's obsequious reply.

"For Nikita, Lucas, for Nikita," she reminds Lucas how unimportant he is to her.

"I understand, and wish you a safe journey home," Lucas replies forlornly before ending the call.

"What's wrong with Beth? She has turned into some kind of hermit since you left town," Stan asks me after I end the call with her. I do not know what to think or how to answer, it has been such a long time ago since I left that life. I do not know if it is that I forgive him for raping my sister, if he ever did, or if Beth's reconciliation and further dalliances with Stan nullify what he did to her in my mind.

"Stan, that was a lifetime ago, why do you even think about it now?"

"I dunno, it's your fault," Stan's reply shocks me.

"You what?"

"I never treated her very well and I feel guilty about it. I would just like her to know that I'm sorry for the way I was," Stan answers quietly in a serious tone.

"So why is it my fault?"

"How many times do I have to tell you, you have a weird effect on me? Do you really think I would feel guilty about anything I do or have done? It's only since I have been around you that I have started to think about things. Things I don't want to think about. Apart from the fact you can perform light shows without electricity you give off something that makes me think about what I do and the effects I might cause people. You know, my working girls, my pushers, even the people that take the stuff I supply. You're giving me a conscious, Jack, and I don't want one." Stan is obviously in quite some emotional turmoil, maybe it is possible he could become a practitioner after all. Since he is affected in such a way his karma cannot be so dense as to completely block out his true self, which can see right from wrong and good from bad.

"It is believed in our practice that the effects of Falun Dafa can resonate within someone who is not a practitioner but is simply within close proximity to one who is. I never dreamed that my level was so advanced that it must be rubbing off on you, Stan," I say and chuckle. It is yet more proof my cultivation level is rising.

"Don't laugh, this is serious, Jack. I don't think I would want to stay with you again if you begged me. You're turning my life upside down. Thank God it's time for me to go before I change my mind, Russian Mafia or not, I'm beginning to have serious doubts where my life is going." Stan looks seriously concerned and confused as he leaves the breakfast bar.

"Hey, Stan, I dreaded you coming over here. But you've done me a big favor. You have been a gauge for me to measure my practice, which I think is more advanced than I could have dreamed of. You actually saw the spinning of the wheel and you have been greatly affected merely by my physical presence," I tell him through the open car window as he is about to leave.

"Well, I'm pleased that you got something out of it, Jack, despite the fact that you have kinda fucked me up. I really don't know what I want anymore," Stan answers and shakes his head.

"If there was any way I could persuade you to follow Falun Dafa I would. Your sensitivity towards me and the fact you saw the wheel and my aura means that you're not doomed yet. For your soul's sake, look it up on the net and read about it, that's how I started," I ask out of great sincerity.

"Maybe I will, Jack. It depends how I'm feeling when I get back. But if I do and find it worth following I'll give you a call."

"And that is the only call I will take from you Stan. No more visits or calls about visiting. Now make sure you don't forget that," I reply as Stan raises the window.

Before going up to the penthouse Alexei pays the concierge at the entrance door to the luxury apartment building in the center of Vienna to temporarily turn off the security CCTV until they have carried out their business and left the building. After doing so he beckons Valentina who enters the reception hall followed by Nikolai. She nods in acknowledgement to the concierge as they wait for the lift.

Some ten minutes later Stan parks on the opposite side of the road to the entrance. He is uncomfortable with how he feels a mixture of apprehension and wrongdoing although he feels no fear. He presses the buzzer to the apartment marked only by the label 'Top 30' and notices all the other buzzers are labeled with names, Herr this, Dr. that.

"Yes?" comes Alexei's harsh voice.

"It's Stan, sent by Lucas," Stan replies and looks up to the CCTV camera unaware it is turned off.

"Take the lift to the top floor, turn left. The door is

three meters on your right," Alexei instructs in his deep Russian accent and presses the door release button. Stan enters the building and sees a uniformed concierge reading a newspaper behind a high desk at the back of the large reception hall directly in front of him. The concierge looks up and waves his right hand towards the lift on Stan's left. Stan nods and presses the lift button. He exits the lift and presses the bell button to the aforementioned apartment. Within moments he notices the spy hole in the door blackens, someone is checking him out. Alexei recognizes Stan immediately from the previous night in the Roter Engel and briskly opens the door. On seeing Alexei Stan's face lights up, could the super sexy blond dancing on the bar last night be the mysterious Valentina?

"Hello, pleased to meet you," Stan holds out his hand but Alexei ignores it and points at Stan.

"Last night in the bar, it was you, no?" Stan smiles and nods his head.

"Was that Valentina?" he asks unable to conceal his enthusiasm.

"Come," is all Alexei replies and Stan follows him through the spacious but sparsely furnished entrance hall with various doors leading off from it. Stan sees the four large suitcases standing against the wall to his right and correctly presumes he will be taking them with him. Alexei opens a door close to the cases and ushers Stan into a study type room where Valentina is sat at a desk, Nikolai standing to her right.

"We meet again my sexy Englishman. You told me you were here to visit a friend," she asks and gives Stan a very seductive smile. Alexei hovers at his left shoulder.

"What else could I say?"

"You could have said you were on the lookout for some sexy blond Russian lady for the night," Valentina is enjoying herself.

"If only I had known. What a waste," Stan doesn't hide his disappointment.

"Maybe next time, Englishman, if there is a next time," Valentina suggests.

"If everything goes well why shouldn't there be?" The thought of getting to know Valentina better has eradicated Stan's newly developed conscience and feelings of guilt.

"That's up to Nikita," Valentina replies flippantly.

"Who is this Nikita?"

"The one who runs the show and the less you know about Nikita the better for you, my sexy Englishman. Now, let's get this thing done. Where is your transport?" Valentina returns to her ice-cold businesslike persona.

"Parked on the opposite side of the road to the entrance. A black Nissan X-Trail," Stan replies, a little confused by Valentina's apparent instantaneous change of attitude.

"Good! Alexei and Nikolai will follow you out with the goods. I wish you a safe and trouble free journey. Goodbye," Valentina gets to her feet and shakes Stan's hand, which confuses him even more, he wonders if she is bi-polar. Alexei opens the door for Stan, Nikolai and himself to leave the room. As Alexei and Nikolai pick up the suitcases in the hall Stan opens the apartment door for them to leave. They enter the lift and Stan presses the ground floor button and a low volume alarm sounds. Nikolai curses in Russian leaves the cases and exits the lift. Alexei chuckles.

"We are too heavy for the lift and he is the most heavy, so he must take the stairs," he grins at Stan who finds himself quite liking Alexei.

16.

Dirty Dave calls Sergeant Andy Price on Sunday afternoon who is in his local pub enjoying a beer with drinking friends from the pub.

"This had better be good, Dave, disturbing me on a Sunday!" Andy answers the call irritated as he walks out of the pub into the beer garden, which is empty due to the cold wet weather, to get some privacy.

"I just got a call from the big guy who came into my shop to tell me about Stan. He said that Stan will be back in town by tomorrow night with the coke," Dave explains.

"Did he say anything else, like where and what time?"

"No, he just said, 'An update for the boys in blue. Stan will be back in town tomorrow night with the gear. Tell them to look out for him.' And then he ended the call," Dave says expectantly in the hope Andy will reimburse him for the information.

"Okay, Dave. I'll get on to it. If anything comes of it I'll let you know," Andy answers casually, he doesn't want Dave feeling important but is mildly excited Stan may be entering Manchester with a substantial amount of cocaine.

"Andy, er…"

"Yes, Dave, you'll get a bung if anything comes of it, okay?"

"Thanks, Andy. Speak to you soon…" Andy ends the

call before Dave finishes.

Although tempted, Stan does not examine the contents of the cases. His state of mind has become quiet and calm again after the rush of excitement he felt on meeting Valentina and believing that she probably fancies him. But now he can't help thinking about the effect Jack seemed to have on him since he still feels it to an extent. He enters the information into the satnav to go to Brussels and calls Marcus.

"Hi, Stan, great to hear from you. Everything okay?" Marcus answers enthusiastically.

"Everything is cool, Marcus. I've got the gear with me and will be with you in about ten hours according to the satnav and barring any fuck ups," Stan answers impartially. Marcus is a little mystified as to Stan's coolness but considers it can only be a good sign that Stan is handling the situation so comfortably.

"Great! You stay at my place tonight and early, I mean like five-thirty in the morning, an articulated lorry will pick you and your car up from my place, it will be carrying pharmaceuticals, quite apt I thought. He'll take you to Ostend where he will get on a ferry to Ramsgate where you can drive away without any customs checks after he leaves the port. I'll fill you in with more details when you get here. And, Stan…"

"Yes?"

"Drive carefully and don't break any speed limits before you get to me and after, you should be in Manchester by early evening so there's no rush. If we lose the stuff, we're in deep shit," Marcus cannot help but remind Stan that he is responsible for the merchandise in the hope Stan might take better care of it.

"Chill, Marcus, everything's gonna be fine, I'll see you about ten-thirty. Shall we meet in the Monk bar?"

"Can't you be serious about anything, Stan? You're carrying a multi-million euro load in the back of your car. Are you just going to park it in the street?"

"So I come straight to your place?"

"Please, Stan. You know I've got secure underground parking. If you must you can go out after you have left your car here, but I'd rather you didn't. You've got an early start tomorrow. If you want a drink I'm well stocked. I've even got a bottle of Louis the thirteenth cognac, it costs over three thousand euros a bottle. If you stay in I'll let you try it, what do you say?"

"How much of the brandy will you give me?"

"Two measures," Marcus bribes.

"Large ones!" Stan insists. He knows of the cognac by browsing it in airport duty free shops and wishing the day would come he could afford to blow so much money on a bottle of cognac.

"That is hundreds of your British pounds, but if it means you'll stay in, okay," Marcus relents.

"I'll call you when I get to your place so you can open the garage for me, ciao!" Stan ends the call.

By the time he gets to Brussels Stan feels exhausted and is happy Marcus refused to meet in a bar, all he wants to do is sleep, that is, after he has had the cognac Marcus promised. He pulls into the sloping driveway, which descends under Marcus's town house and stops at the electronically operated steel garage shutters where he calls Marcus to open them. They make hardly any noise as they raise into their housing. Stan pulls into the large brightly illuminated garage and parks next to Marcus's Bentley. As Stan gets out of the car Marcus appears from a door to the rear which connects to the house.

"You made good time, I didn't expect you for another half-hour at least," he says as he walks over to check that the shutters have lowered and locked themselves correctly.

"Yeah, I never stopped for a break, only to take a piss and refuel, and the traffic moved quickly. I was eager to try the cognac you promised," Stan reminds Marcus.

"It's waiting for you, Stan. Let's go in," Marcus replies as he enables the garage alarm.

"Wow, you've made some alterations since I was last here," Stan comments on entering the lounge of Marcus's house.

"It's been a long time since you were here, Stan. And Marie is always changing her mind about how she wants things. Soon after she stopped drinking she made me get rid of the bar, so now we have this dainty little drinks cupboard," Marcus says with a hint of disdain in his voice, he misses his bar, as he motions towards an exquisite antique mahogany drinks cabinet.

"Where is she tonight?"

"Visiting her sister in Ghent. I told her you would be coming over and she doesn't want to be around when I'm doing business," Marcus explains.

"Be honest, Marcus, what you really mean is she doesn't want to be around when you have a drug dealing, gangster, nigger, pimp here," Stan comes to the uncomfortably sharp point for Marcus.

"Stan, it's nothing to do with your color or what you do for a living. Marie knows what I do and the business associates I have. And she knows that it is not all above board, shall we put it, so she prefers to distance herself as much as she can from the people who actually provide her with a very comfortable lifestyle," Marcus points out.

"Since I'm one of the comfortable lifestyle providers, where's my cognac you promised?" Stan goads.

"Where else but my pretty little drinks cupboard," Marcus replies sarcastically as he opens the cabinet doors. He takes out the cognac and two gold fish bowl brandy glasses then pours out a large measure for Stan and a smaller one for himself.

"Some fancy glasses for a fancy drink," Stan remarks.

"Let's sit," Marcus says and carries the drinks to a large marble coffee table with brass legs where he takes a seat in one of the four antique French exquisitely upholstered low chairs surrounding the table. Stan takes the seat opposite and Marcus slides the glass towards him.

"This is a defining moment for me," Stan says as he takes the glass and swirls the contents around. Marcus looks on as Stan first deeply inhales the rich aroma, which he finds intoxicatingly delicious, and then takes a small expectant sip from the glass.

"And?" Marcus asks after Stan finally swallows the cognac.

"Wow! Obviously the best brandy I've tasted. But, Marcus, I'm still a long way from considering spending three grand on a bottle of brandy worth it," Stan answers.

"You never know, Stan. If you complete this business well for the Russians as they expect you to, you may have a very prosperous time ahead of you, when you won't consider three thousand so much," Marcus jumps at the opportunity to encourage Stan to carry out the distribution and collect payment for the narcotics as agreed with Nikita's people.

"When I met Valentina today, it wasn't the first time," Stan smiles to himself.

"Where the hell have you met her before?" Marcus does not hide his fierce curiosity, he cannot believe Stan would be in a place where he could meet Valentina.

"In a bar last night. She wanted to get to know me better but her minder came over with a phone, Nikita was calling so she left to take the call, I presume. Who is this Nikita anyway, her boyfriend, husband, who?"

"So she didn't tell you?"

"Only that he ran the show and that I didn't need to know anything more," Stan answers and takes another sip of the cognac.

"Disappointing, then you know only as much as I do. Nikita has never contacted me directly. But I'm assured that he must be a very heavy character, even in the eyes of the Russian Mafia, by the people who do business on his behalf. I'm surprised I even know the name since I only speak to a couple of Russian guys in Moscow and Valentina, of course. They first contacted me after learning of the kind of business I do through a Russian businessman who wanted me to find a buyer for some very valuable stolen art work, which I did quite quickly. At first I just set up companies for Nikita's people to launder money. As time went by I was introduced to Valentina and asked to get involved with some of the practices that produced the money, which needed laundering," Marcus finds himself telling Stan more than he normally would but needs to stay as close to him as possible, at least until the business is completed, which could take over a month depending on Stan's ability to move it. Marcus has no concern for repeat business, which would be done between Valentina and Stan directly, he is just worrying about this initial transaction, which he is responsible for.

"Do you ever think about what you do is wrong?" Stan asks out of the blue.

"Do you?" Marcus counters.

"I never did. I never gave it a thought. It was just life to me. Joining a gang and dealing drugs at fourteen, looking up to my brother, who was far worse than me. Not that long ago I would have said far better. As I got older robbery, protection and pimping entered my CV, but now I begin to think about what I've done, especially what I've done to other people. I kinda feel guilty," Stan answers in a mysteriously sad tone and takes another sip from his glass.

"Stan, are you alright? We do what we do in this world to make things as comfortable as possible for us and those we love. We have had no choice but to do what we've done and to carry on doing what we need to do to bring us the things we want. We're not doctors, we're not lawyers, we're not stockbrokers. We were never given the opportunity to be led in those directions so we do the best we can with what we know. I can't believe that you are questioning your very own existence," Marcus becomes extremely anxious by the way Stan is talking. Could it be possible Stan has second thoughts about the Russian drug deal, about everything they hold in common?

"That may be true for me, Marcus, but you're a qualified accountant. You could make a decent living legally, what makes you get involved in the stuff you do?"

"Look at me, Stan. I didn't look much better twenty

years ago. Now do you think someone like Marie would look at me twice if I were some pencil pushing obedient little slave working for some international conglomerate?"

"So you do it to get prestige, respect," Stan replies.

"I mainly do it for the money, Stan. That's where we are different. I know you like the money but your first need is celebrity. You want to be known and feared for what you do whereas I need to keep as low a profile as possible. You want fame and I want obscurity up to a point, my name is only mentioned in certain closed circles. That's why you puzzle me now talking about the way we make our living as if it were wrong and you suddenly have a conscience. What makes you talk like this?"

"I guess it started when I stayed with Jack, you know the English guy I knew from way long ago?"

"Yes, and?"

"If you remember, I told you he had become kind of religious, he follows something called Falun Dafa. I saw him this morning making these weird movements, hc didn't know I was watching because he had his eyes closed. A beautiful light was shining from him and a kind of ball of red light rotated between his arms. It made me feel like a child seeing a rainbow for the first time. I felt clean and good in the moment but afterwards I question myself. I'm not clean and I'm certainly not good. I thought I would forget about it but it just keeps bugging me every time I drop into my usual character mode, the drug dealing gangster and worse," Stan falls silent in his reflective emotion and takes a long slow sip from his glass, almost emptying it.

"Falun Dafa! I've heard of it. It's a sect that the Chinese outlawed years ago, the guy who started it all in

China started to take it abroad and never returned staying in the US, probably to stay out of jail in China. Forget about it, Stan. If you get involved it will probably cost you everything you've got, like some Scientology thing," Lucas tries his utmost to discourage Stan.

"That's where you're wrong, Lucas. It doesn't cost a penny. Jack told me and he's been doing it for years," Stan replies with something Lucas does not want to hear.

"There's got to be some kind of catch behind it. Maybe its leader gets a kick out of so many people following him, maybe he's a power freak, maybe he just likes the fame," Lucas tries to find reasons behind the creation of Falun Dafa. He remembers reading an article on it many years ago and being very intrigued.

"So many people? How many and how do you know there are so many?" Stan's interest only grows.

"I read something about the Chinese government banning it because it had such a big following and they felt threatened, because the numbers of Falun Dafa practitioners grew bigger than the members of the Chinese communist party," Marcus tells Stan about the exact point that had intrigued him those many years ago.

"So what's wrong with that, Marcus? You're defeating your own point. If so many people in China took it up then there must be something real behind it, don't you think?" Stan answers.

"If it is so great why doesn't anyone know about it in Europe for instance? If you mention it people ask what you're talking about. It's not part of our world, Stan, it's an Asian thing. You don't have time for it, you want wealth and success as well as your fame, don't you?"

"I guess so. But I just can't seem to shake this feeling, almost like guilt. I hope it goes by the time I get back to Manchester," Stan sighs.

"I'm sure it will. Let me give you that refill I promised," Marcus offers in the hope the cognac will loosen Stan up and take his mind off Falun Dafa and picks up Stan's glass from the table.

17.

"Got a call from Dirty Dave yesterday, gov," Sergeant Andy Price informs his superior, Inspector Roy Collins, after entering his office.

"You had better take a seat then, Andy, and tell me all about it," the Inspector shows more interest than usual since he believes capturing a huge consignment of cocaine would be a nice feather in his cap before retirement and he has received news from Interpol that Stan took a P & O ferry from Dover to Calais, so the information from Dave may well be correct and catching Stan would prove he put in his best effort right to the end of his career.

"He received a call from the guy who first told him about Stan and the coke from Vienna. He was told Stan would be coming back to Manchester tonight with the drugs but doesn't know where or exactly when he gets in," Andy explains.

"Interpol are looking for him at airports and ports. If he comes in by any conventional entry method they should get him. But if he's smuggling a hundred kilos of coke he's not going to use a conventional method and if he does he's not gonna have that much coke on him, if any," Roy points out.

"We can still use Roger Facey if we don't get him earlier," Andy replies.

"Only as a last resort. I don't want things to get messy and the less people involved the less messy it will be, that's why I'm not going to authorize any cash for him to make the deal. Besides, we don't know how much of the original consignment will be with Stan, if any, at the meeting he has with Facey, and can you trust Facey?"

"I think so. He knows I can close down his operations immediately and put him behind bars if he doesn't conform, and he still thinks I can reactivate his possession with intent charge," Andy answers.

"Okay, but we still need to try and nick Stan beforehand with all of the stuff. Stake out the warehouse he's got although he probably thinks we might know about it and won't take the gear there, but it's the only place we know about so stake it out anyway. He's definitely not going to take it home with him because we've paid him visits there before. Get in touch with Facey and tell him to call Stan and ask about the meet and to try and find out as much as possible about what Stan is up to with the coke before he meets Facey, and keep me informed on everything," Roy instructs.

"Will do, gov," Andy says as he gets to his feet.

At just before 13:30, half-an-hour after disembarking the freight ferry at Ramsgate, the lorry comes to a halt in a quiet layby and a moment later the hydraulic rear door opens providing a ramp to the road surface. Stan starts the car and slowly reverses down the ramp as the driver guides him out.

"Thanks, mate," Stan says through the open window.

The driver does not acknowledge, just looks to the ground, his English is very poor unbeknown to Stan who ignores the apparent ignorance and waits until the driver has raised the tailgate and returned to the cabin of the lorry then gets out of the car to take a desperately need piss, sighing as he does so. The lorry leaves as Stan finishes. Although it is not raining the sky looks heavy, grey and miserable matching his mood Stan reflects. He enters the required information into the satnav to get him to the secure self-storage unit he has hired on the outskirts of Manchester purely to store the cocaine then sets off on the final leg of the drug importation operation. Less than an hour into the journey Stan's mobile, which is lying on the front passenger seat, rings out. He looks down to it and sees that it is Roger Facey calling.

"Yo, Roger, what's up?"

"Hey, Stan! You have any idea yet when you wanna deal?"

"Soon, Roger, soon. Just wait until I have everything in place and I will call you, okay?"

"Do you have it yet?"

"What's your problem? I told you I'll call when I'm ready," Stan becomes suspicious but knows not of what, surely Roger fears him too much to do anything that might piss him off.

"It's just that I've got my pushers geared up to sell big time and they are eager," Roger lies.

"You'll just have to tell em to wait until I let you know, which will be in a couple of days, okay?" Stan relaxes a little but wants to see what he can initially push himself before going to Roger.

"Okay, Stan, I'll wait for your call," Roger replies

despondently and ends the conversation.

After securing the cases at the self-storage company Stan drives to his warehouse to change cars. Andy sits in his car in the darkness parked amongst vans on the parking area to the adjacent but one warehouse completely unnoticed by Stan. Sat next to him is Brian Roberts better known as Brian the Burglar, a craftsman at lock picking and breaking and entering. Andy has brought him along for this specific purpose, another criminal at Andy's disposal due to what Andy knows about Brian's past activities that he hasn't been convicted of.

"Okay, let's move," Andy says to Brian as Stan drives away in his Porsche after locking the warehouse. Brian easily gains access to the premises with a few tools of his trade. Stan flips the switch to the bright lighting and goes to the car. He tries the driver's door and finds it open, which doesn't please him since he considers it is a sign there is nothing in the car worth hiding.

"It looks like Stan did bring something back with him if he needed so much luggage space for such a short break," Andy comments to himself on examining the interior of the X-Trail, "shame there's nothing in it now," he adds thinking to himself that a hundred kilos of cocaine would be way too much to hide in the door panels. Brian just looks on while Andy searches the warehouse, which he completes quickly since there is obviously nothing there of interest: a Honda Fireblade motorcycle, a Mazda MX5 soft top sports car. There is a large quantity of cigarettes and alcohol, obviously bought across the channel in France where the tax on such items is minimal compared to the UK and can be re-sold in the UK at a generous profit, but Andy has no interest in taking Stan to court over smuggled tobacco and alcohol. They leave the warehouse as they found it.

Stan silently lets himself into his flat at just after 22:00. Lizzy is nude, in anticipation of Stan's arrival, on her stomach, sprawled across the bed watching TV. When he sees her he quietly undresses himself and quickly positions himself over her.

"What the fuck!" Lizzy tenses in her initial shock.

"Relax, honey," Stan whispers in her ear as he readies himself to mount her from behind. Her relief on knowing it is Stan behind her is short lived as he aggressively takes her in the fashion he usually does. She whimpers and Stan holds back.

"I'm sorry, sugar, did I hurt you?" Stan says as he pulls away feeling disgusted with himself.

"Not really, honey," Lizzy is shocked by Stan's uncharacteristic behavior, she is used to him becoming more aggressive as she becomes more submissive and is not adverse to it, in fact she sometimes exaggerates her discomfort and pain to encourage Stan's aggression.

"You sure?"

"Yeah, what's up?" Lizzy asks as she feels Stan rapidly going flaccid between her thighs.

"Um, I was just worried that I hurt you," Stan answers not knowing what is up with him.

"What's wrong, did you betray me in Europe, were you with someone else?" Lizzy asks grasping at straws since she can think of no other reason Stan would suddenly lose his desire for her body apart from guilt despite the fact she knows that would be close on a miracle, but what else could it be?

"Lizzy, you know I wouldn't tell you if I had been because it would have meant nothing to me but would hurt you, so I wouldn't bother letting you know if I had, which I haven't. You know I stayed with an old friend, you even spoke to him," Stan tries to calm Lizzy's anxiety.

"So what is wrong with you, you never had a problem getting it up before, is it me?" Lizzy dreads Stan tiring of her.

"Don't be silly, sugar. You're the best thing that ever happened to me," Stan reassures as he lies unto his side putting his arms around her and pulling Lizzy close to his chest.

"So are you worried about something, something that happened over there?" Lizzy asks out of sincere concern.

"No, that's the weird thing. I thought I would be or should be worried about what I'm doing but I don't give a shit, and I don't know why," Stan replies with an unfamiliar look of bewilderment on his face.

"So, can I ask you what you were doing over there?"

"I collected a hundred kilos of uncut coke from the Russian Mafia in Vienna, they expect me to move it in two months max. I can probably get rid of it, especially at the prices I can sell it for, but I'm not sure if I can collect all the dough for it on time, and I don't really care. If you want to know what's wrong with me I guess that's another symptom of whatever it is," Stan nonchalantly replies. Lizzy abruptly turns onto her other side to face Stan.

"Are you out of your mind, have you heard the stories about the Russian Mafia? If you don't deliver, you're a dead man. I know you do illegal stuff, I'd be blind and deaf not to and truth be told it does excite and attract me, but, Stan, don't you think you're getting in a little too deep?"

"Probably, especially now the way I have come to feel about what I do for a living. How it affects other people. The way I have treated people. It all started with that friend of mine I stayed with in Vienna, Jack. When I knew him years ago he was as badass as me but now he follows some kind of weird religion and he's changed big time," Stan nods as he finishes the sentence and recollects Jack's appearance in the aura and holding the wheel.

"What sort of religion and why does it bother you?" Lizzy is mystified.

"It's called Falun Dafa and is something to do with Buddhism, have you heard of it?"

"Of course I've of heard of Buddhism but I've no idea what Falun Dafa is, I've never heard of it," Lizzy is no wiser.

"I've heard of Buddhism although I know nothing about it apart from a fat guy laughing, but what I saw Jack doing was really strange, and not just what I saw but how it made me feel, and how just being with him made me feel," Stan says slowly and calmly.

"And how did he make you feel?"

"I had and still have a strange mixture of feelings about Jack or whatever it is that Jack does. Sort of calm and quiet but also guilty for how I carry out my life. The feelings were strongest when I saw him doing some kind of ritual. He didn't know I was watching and he was surrounded by a beautiful light. During the ritual, or whatever it was, he formed a circle with his arms and in between them was a kind of rotating red light. I'll never forget it. This peacefulness I felt and still feel to a degree kind of drowns my ambition and my fear of anything, the Russians, losing everything I have, money, power, anything," Stan looks into Lizzy's eyes for some kind of explanation.

"Are you sure he wasn't just putting on a show to try and get you to join some cult?" Lizzy asks derogatorily.

"No way, like I said, he didn't know I was watching and it wasn't just what I saw that affected me but the way that I felt and feel now. I really don't want to push these drugs, Lizzy, but don't know what else I can do," Stan answers with unfamiliar despair in his voice, which is not caused by the Russians.

"Like I said, you're in too deep. But the problem is you're in that deep you can't get out. You should have called it off before picking the stuff up. What could the Russians have done if you never collected?"

"I didn't want to go through with it after staying with Jack and him having this crazy effect on me but I thought it was just a passing phase I was going through and would regret not doing the deal when I got back here. The problem is I regret doing it now that I am here. I feel like I'm in some kind of limbo. I don't want to push the stuff but what's going to happen if I don't?"

"Exactly, Stan, what's going to happen? You can't give it back to the Russians. They're gonna want payment for a hundred kilos of coke and I don't want to even think about how much they want from you for that much, it's got to be millions. You've got no choice but to sell it and pay them by whatever means you've arranged, which is how?"

"They've given me the bank details of some offshore company. I have to make cash payments into a Lloyds branch of no less than a hundred grand a time and they want a total of two million paid in over the next two months. That means

I get it for less than half of what I pay when I buy it by the kilo here. I know you're a smart girl so do the math. Even if I get rid of it at half street value after it is cut, I'll make a million easy. That is why I got involved," Stan explains.

"Wow! You'll be able to get rid of it more than easy at such low prices. What are you worrying about? Two million in two months!" Lizzy is blinded by the prospect of Stan making so much money that her concerns about the Russian Mafia evaporate.

"I told you, I'm not worried, I just don't feel good about it. Is this what life is all about, money?"

"Hey, what if it's true that you only live once, then you've got to make the best out of what you can, honey. Think of the place you could buy to live in. You always said this is too small," Lizzy is mentally spending the money Stan has not made yet as she gets off the bed to pour some red wine for the both of them.

"What happened to me being in too deep and that I should have called it off?" Stan is irritated by Lizzy's apparent avarice.

"That was before I knew what an amazing deal you have done. You've got nothing to worry about with the prices you're talking. You'll get rid of it in no time, no wonder you said you'll treat me big time when you got back," Lizzy cannot resist reminding Stan of what he told her before he left for Vienna as she passes him a glass and sits on the edge of the bed.

"Lizzy, it won't be so easy to do it so quickly. If I try and do it too fast the price is going to go through the floor because it will cause a price war and on top of that it's going to bring a lot of heat down from the law. But since my heart is not into it I guess I won't go about moving it with the enthusiasm I normally would, which is the most sensible thing to do anyway. I know I've got to carry this thing through since I've gone too far with it now but I sure ain't gonna do it again," Stan tells Lizzy and consoles himself with the fact as he maneuvers to sit next to her on the bed.

"You mean you could do it again?" Lizzy is ecstatic at the thought Stan could replicate the deal and the money that it brings.

"If this goes okay, it could become a regular thing, sure. Why?"

"What do you mean, why? Stan, if you do this three or four times you'll be made for life in a big way. Don't you want that?"

"To be quite honest, Lizzy, I don't know what I want anymore but I do know what I don't want," Stan replies in a defiant, determined tone.

"Which is?"

"Haven't you been listening, sugar? I don't feel good about doing what I do. I begin to hate myself for who I am and what I've been. I feel like losing myself on some island where I have no contact with humanity, where I can just be with no interference from anything or anybody," Stan reacts angrily.

"Hey, honey, does that mean you don't want to see me either?"

"Of course I want to see you. I'm just trying to get you to realize how I feel. Maybe I'll get back to my old self and carry on this business for as long as it lasts or until I end up in prison for a long stretch. I just don't know, Lizzy," Stan exhales audibly.

"You have never mentioned the fact that what you do could land you in prison before, why does it bother you now?"

"It doesn't bother me, Lizzy, I just look at things from a kind of detached perspective now. Before I went to Vienna the only thing I looked at was me. The me no one dares touch. The me far too clever for the police. The me who's gonna make a fortune and rule Manchester. But the way I feel right now none of that is me," Stan replies and knocks back the wine.

"Here, drink some more, it'll help you sleep," Lizzy sees great fatigue in Stan's expression as she tops up his glass and is eager to get him to sleep and hopefully wake up back the old Stan she knows.

18.

I awake feeling so hot as I never have before and look at the clock on my bedside table, which reads 03:15 and the temperature is 20°C. What's going on, am I sick? Nora is sleeping soundly under the quilt which I have obviously uncovered myself from in my sleep. I lie naked, burning up and have no choice but to go outside onto the terrace. The four inch covering of crisp snow looks so inviting, glistening in the moonlight. I do not bother with slippers and quietly let myself out. I lie down on my stomach as to let the snow cool me at the place I feel is hottest, my lower abdomen where the wheel turns. I've only ever done this before after directly leaving a particularly hot sauna but now the relief is not so great since it is not an external source that is causing me to feel so unbelievably hot. I roll around, flattening and melting the snow with my body and come to rest on my back looking up to the stars, galaxies and constellations in a cloudless, moonlit still night and silently curse the city's light pollution. The night sky looks so much more wondrous in remote parts of the world enabling me to better visualize and contemplate what heavens, paradises, perhaps even one that was once home to me before my descent, lie out there.

Could my current physical condition be a result of energy transference and build up that I have learned of from reading Zhuan Falun. I hope so, it would be yet another sign of my gong increasing. What better a time to practice? I assume the lotus position in the snow, close my eyes and, as gracefully as possible, perform the mudras then extend my hands out at just above waist level, palms down. The familiar magnetic field sensation in my hands soon begins, first softly but the intensity quickly increases to the extent that I find it amusing since it is hard to keep them stationary, they begin to wobble slightly. I recompose my mind and ignore the sensations to the best of my ability going into a trance-like state being only aware that I am practicing. When the pain in my legs and feet and all sensation below my waist desist I am conscious of nothing else but the fact I am practicing. I fall into a deep state of wu wei still only aware of nothing but the fact that I am practicing. No good thoughts, no bad thoughts, no desires, no fears, just being and it feels so tranquil. I have never fallen so deeply into this state before. I have no idea how long I have been in the position since the depth of my detachment has been such that my sense of time is completely out of focus but what does come into focus is my vision despite the fact I have not opened my eyes. I have never had to fight a normal human response so strongly as now as I see well above the terrace wall, which is four feet high, across the skyline of Vienna. I must be levitating about three feet from the terrace floor, my third eye open, albeit at a low level since I can only see this physical realm and nothing higher. I change hand positions, my left hand, palm facing down just under my chin and my right palm facing up an inch away from my navel. My vision becomes cloudy and is replaced by a vision of Stan's face and upper body. He appears agitated and troubled. I have no choice since my state of wu wei is now broken.

"What's the matter, Stan?" I telepathize. He looks directly at me.

"Jack, Jack, what's happening to me?" he asks out of some kind of mild desperation.

"I don't know, Stan, I really don't," is the only answer I can truly give.

"I just had a real bad dream, man. I mean the worst nightmare you can imagine, and it was so real, just like I'm talking to you now…" is Stan projecting to me in a dream or am I dreaming, hallucinating? Nothing would surprise me now.

"So what did you dream about, Stan?" I telepathize out of deep fascination, I am eager to know exactly what is going on myself.

"I don't really know. It started with like rapid video clips of my life, just the bad shit I've done in my life and the misery I've caused people, I guess there's not much good shit I ever did anyway," Stan answers in a tone of dismay. His account reminds me so much of what I recently experienced once during my practice and my intrigue grows.

"Why does it bother you so much, you never regretted or thought about what you did or were doing at the time,

Stan? It's only a kind of replay, showing you your history," I speak from experience.

"But why? I don't want to regret it, I don't want to feel bad about the things I've done. It's only started to happen to me since I met you. What did you do to me?"

"I haven't done anything to you, Stan. I really don't know what's happening to you, or me for that matter. As far as I know you might just be like a dream to me. A figment of my imagination," I decide to tell him or his image in my consciousness I am practicing in an effort to find out more for myself.

"What do mean, a figment of your imagination? I'm fucking here, talking to you for fuck's sake," Stan becomes agitated by my response now.

"Stan, remember when you saw me surrounded by a beautiful light at my place in Vienna?"

"Sure, you were making strange movements and stuff and had a kind of spinning ball of light in your arms. Has that affected me in some way?"

"No, I don't think it affected you. I think the effect came from you. I would never have believed it considering the character I know you to have been. I am practicing, or trying to, right now, Stan, that is why I don't know if I'm communicating with you or just your image being played out by my consciousness. If it is really you I'm speaking to, please realize that you have great potential to free yourself from this hell we live in, a great foundation." Stan takes on an expression like he has just realized he is dead. He lifts his arms and looks around but I am unable to see at what.

"What do you mean? I'm just beginning to hit the big time, things are going to be great in future," Stan does not accept the fact that I am communicating with him telepathically or I am unable to distinguish between real telepathic communication and dreaming.

"I'm going to talk like it's really you I'm talking to. Now, you said yourself that I had a strange effect on you. You were even capable of seeing the aura and the wheel when you saw me practicing, even my wife can't see that and she is very religious in the catholic sense, but that is just another road to the same destination. All this makes me believe that you have not strayed that far away from your true self, maybe not even as much as I have, and it's possible that you could return, even sooner than I can," I inform myself as much as I do Stan.

"Shit, Jack! I admit you had a strange effect on me, and I can't say it was enjoyable. I don't enjoy feeling responsible and guilty. But what is this crap you're telling me now?"

"It's not crap, Stan. In fact it's probably the most crapless thing you will ever hear in your entire life here on planet earth. You are living this life now because you screwed up where you lived before…"

"You know where I lived before, it was a shit hole and I was glad to get out of it. What the fuck are you talking, man?" Stan interrupts me.

"Stan, let me speak. I don't mean where you lived before in this life, I mean where you were present in another life, one before this one, or more probably many more before this one. Your true home, heaven if you like, where you were an angel. You have obviously been successful at what you do here on earth and enjoy life because your good karma or virtue as we call it is sustaining you, but you are using it up fast and replacing it with bad karma due to the way you live, behave and treat other people. You're going to have to pay it all back one day and the only way you pay it back is by suffering, and if not in this lifetime then ones to follow," I try to find a way of explaining what I believe is happening to Stan as simply as I can.

"Have I got this right, you think my luck is gonna run out?"

"Luck is an illusion, Stan, there is only cause and effect. The saying 'you make your own luck' is completely true, but it's not luck it's karma or virtue. If you can go through life free of desires, attachments and the fears related to them, you will be on your way back to where you came from and little will stand in your way and without the desire you will be happy since you will feel no pain in not having that which you desire. Things like avarice, jealousy, greed and the dishonesty caused by it evaporates since there is nothing for it to feed on. I hope I am communicating with you and not a figment of my imagination or concoction of my consciousness. Please get in touch with me if you recall this communication between us since I can sense you fading away," I manage just before the vision of Stan dissolves and is replaced by darkness. I gracefully reverse my hand positions, so my left hand is at my navel and my right hand under my chin. I gladly return to a state of wu wei and manage to let the brief experience pass into the past and out of my mind.

"Jack, Jack, are you okay?" Nora is shouting at me quite hysterically. I look around to see the snow has melted within a two feet radius of where I sit in the lotus position. I have no idea of the time but the sun has not risen, which does not say much since it is mid-winter.

"Calm down, I'm fine. I woke up and felt like practicing, that's all," I answer in a rather confused state.

"Are you crazy? I thought you'd gone into some kind of coma or frozen to death. You must be freezing. Come in now before you get pneumonia." Nora's anger cannot hide her relief that I seem okay. I get to my feet and smile at her.

"Feel, I'm warm," I say as I take her hand and place it on my chest.

"But you've been out there for hours," Nora looks at me in disbelief.

"What time is it?"

"After six-thirty. I briefly woke at three-thirty and thought you were in the bathroom or the kitchen getting a drink or something, so I went back to sleep. Have you been out here all this time?"

"Yes, I woke at three-fifteen and was burning up.so much that I lay in the snow on the terrace, I didn't want to disturb you. Whether you dismiss it as usual or not I believe the heat I felt had something to do with Dafa, a kind of energy transference to me. I've read about such happenings. I started to practice and did so until you just brought me out of it. It was by far the most profound thing I've experienced with Falun Dafa. I know your opinion so I won't bother explaining what happened except that I'm fine," I reply as we walk back into the apartment.

"You better take a hot shower to thaw you out," Nora mothers me.

"I told you I'm fine. If anything it is too warm in here for me. Do you want a coffee?" I ask as I go down the stairs. I need a little time to think on my experience and reflect.

"Yes, please. I'll take a shower while you make it and before Tasha wakes," Nora replies to my satisfaction. As I prepare the coffee I wonder if Stan will call. I shouldn't hope that he does or fear that he does not, no matter how I feel, it is so hard to follow Dafa, I can only wait.

19.

Lizzy gets out of bed as carefully and quietly as she can so as not to wake Stan since he woke her several times during the night due to his disturbed sleep, in which he tossed and turned sometimes muttering undefinable words, other times screaming profanities. She considers he needs as much sleep as possible now that he is in a calm slumber.

"Hey, Lizzy, it is light, what time is it?" Stan wakes as Lizzy finishes dressing.

"Nine-thirty. You had such a restless night, I thought you needed as much sleep as possible so I didn't wake you, but now you're awake should I get you anything, coffee?"

"You're not kidding, I had the most crazy realistic dreams and even dreams within dreams. Unbelievable, just un-fucking-believable," Stan sits up in bed wearing an expression that makes Lizzy believe he has still not woken up as the old Stan she used to know.

"Should I get you a coffee or anything?" Lizzy has an idea that his dreams are probably related to the way he has been behaving since he got back from Vienna and she does not want her fears confirmed.

"No, wait. Listen to me. I've got to tell you about them," Stan says as Lizzy is about to make a hasty retreat to the kitchen.

"Okay, but remember they are only dreams," Lizzy

replies in an effort to diminish the importance of whatever these dreams are about, even before Stan describes them, and sits on the edge of the bed.

"At first I went through a replay of my life, well, basically the things I've done wrong in my life. You know when people have a near fatal event and say they saw their lives flash before them, it was like that but seemed not so much as a flash but a lifetime. It made me feel really bad about myself. Then, when that dream finished I thought I met up with Jack, you know the guy I stayed with in Vienna. I started to tell him about the dream because I thought I was really with him. He told me that I wasn't with him and that he was doing his practicing stuff like he did when I saw him in the strange beautiful light. He said he wasn't sure if I was just a dream of his and to call him if I remembered my dream. Don't you think that is crazy? I better call him," Stan excitedly explains.

"Hold on, Stan. Er, don't you think your friend is going to think you've gone nuts?" Lizzy even begins to wonder herself.

"No, I'm sure he won't, not even if it was all just my dream and he knows nothing about it. He's very understanding and accepting. Not the guy I used to know," Stan says as he gets out of bed.

"So what are you going to say to him - 'did you dream of me last night?' - don't you think that sounds a bit kinky?" Lizzy asks, as Stan dresses, in a further attempt to discourage him from making the call and embarrassing himself, as she believes he will.

"No, he won't think so. I told you that he has become very accepting. I'll put him on loudspeaker so you can listen and see for yourself," Stan says as he sits on the bed and calls Jack.

"Hi, Stan, is this about our little chat in the early hours today?" Jack answers and Lizzy's jaw drops.

"Yo, Jack. So it wasn't just a dream I was having. My lady friend here thought I was going nuts when I told her about it," Stan's face breaks into a broad grin.

"You can tell your lady friend that if you're going nuts then so I am and we are doing it telepathically. Like I said, I was practicing when a vision of you appeared in my mind. You were pretty upset over what you had seen in your dream before seeing me. Do you remember everything I told you?"

"Of course, why shouldn't I? It was more real than real, man!" Stan enthuses as Lizzy looks on, speechless.

"And how do you feel about what I told you?"

"I don't know. Worried, I guess. If what you say is right then if I don't change my ways I'm in for a shit time, and even shit lifetimes. But what if you're wrong, Jack? What if we only live once and I go and get religious and stop doing what I do and at the end of it I die after living a miserable life and that's it, oblivion after giving everything up?" Stan makes a point that gives Lizzy some encouragement.

"This is something only you can decide, Stan. If you're not ready, you're not ready and nothing I can do or say will convince you. Maybe you need to fall further before something in you tells you all is not right. That is what happened to me before I found Falun Dafa. I was searching for something more to life for years until I became acquainted with Buddhism, which I thought could be my answer. Through Buddhism I discovered Falun Dafa and for some unknown reason I knew it was my answer. With this knowledge I have no choice but to follow it. If you have doubts about it there is no point in practicing it. Why don't you take a look at it on the web and read some of Zhuan Falun, that's a book written by Li Hongzhi, the founder of the practice. Although this kind of knowledge has been passed to only a select few disciples, even in past civilizations, he revealed Dafa to everyday people and the book explains some of it, but only as much of it that we mere humans can understand. Reading the book convinced me it is a true way to some kind of salvation, if not in this lifetime then in one to come." As Jack finishes Lizzy looks at Stan who appears deep in contemplation.

"I guess the only thing I can do is take a look at this book or get my lady to and see if it has any effect on me," Stan answers after a long pause.

"Good. Just google falundafa.org and you will find the home page plus much more. And Stan, think about the proof you have that there must be something to it. Your saw the light around me and the wheel in my arms and what more proof do you need than the way we had a conversation while you were asleep over a thousand miles away and I was practicing?"

"Yeah, I know, Jack, but crazier things happen that have nothing to do with Falun Dafa. You should hear some of the stories my mum told me about what voodoo doctors performed in Haiti when she was young, and it wasn't just sticking pins in dolls and stuff, they did a lot of good spells too that worked. What I'm trying to say is that I believe in magic and telepathy, but I don't know if I believe in reincarnation," Stan replies, which surprises and also impresses Jack who had no idea Stan believed in anything beyond materialism. Lizzy smiles on hearing Stan's reply.

"Like I said, it's up to you, Stan. Just give me a call if you want to know anything from me. Good luck in whatever you do, as long as it doesn't harm anyone. And I guess that includes most of what you do."

"Thanks for everything, Jack, apart from maybe the way you have made me feel, which is kinda uncomfortable. I'll be in touch if I need to. Ciao," Stan ends the call to Lizzy's relief.

"Does this mean you're back to normal now, honey?" Lizzy asks Stan in a tone that reflects her relief.

"I dunno, I really don't know. In a way I feel stronger and a lot more confident than I did before I met up with Jack, but I still feel bad about what I do and who I am. I'll just have to see how I feel after I've moved the stuff and paid off the Russians. I can't see what else is left open for me without getting myself into a very dangerous position. If the way I feel doesn't change after I've completed this business maybe I'll seriously look at this Falun Dafa thing Jack follows."

"I can do that for you. I'll research it and give you the bare bones facts on it before you go wasting your time, if you like," Lizzy offers with the intention of putting her own personal spin on it, which Stan is immediately aware of.

"You do that, sugar, you do that," he humors her.

"Great, I'll start on it tonight. Are you going to come to the gym with me?"

"No chance, I'm going to be too busy for the gym today, I've got to shift a hundred k's remember. Oh, but you can take my car if you want."

"You worried about being followed?"

"It's better to be safe than sorry and your Fiesta is, well, a Fiesta."

"But it's good enough for you today. Okay, I guess I'll slum it in your Porsche. I'll be back before six. Is there any food you want me to bring back?"

"No, I don't know when I'll be back. I'll call you when I've finished doing what I've got to do."

"Okay, good luck. And be careful, my love," Lizzy says and kisses Stan passionately on the lips before taking his car key from a bowl they use for keys and leaves for her shift at the gym. After she has gone Stan makes several calls in code arranging to meet his pushers and leaves to pick up one of the cases from the secure storage unit taking several diversions and often doubling back on himself to be sure he is not followed. After he is satisfied there is no tail he picks up the case and drives to an old red-brick derelict factory on the city outskirts.

Pulling into the carpark at the rear of the factory Stan is relieved to see an inconspicuous silver Ford Mondeo parked; Carlton, his most trusted dealer, has carried out Stan's orders and hired a car for the pick-up. Stan parks next to it and takes the case out of the trunk of the Fiesta and looks up to an office window from which Carlton waves. Stan enters the dilapidated building through the surprisingly functional steel door, kept that way by Stan's men to keep out vandals and squatters. He bolts the door behind him and awkwardly ascends the narrow staircase to his right with the heavy suitcase, it is not that he lacks in strength only maneuverability. The thirty-eight-year-old Carlton of average build but impeccable dress and good looks, clean shaven with his afro hair shortly cropped, opens the door at the top of the staircase and Stan enters the stark cold room, illuminated by a strong naked electric bulb, with a big grin on his face. His other four pushers: Wigan, Reggae Man, Ace and Tyrone, all of Jamaican decent, are sitting at a large foldable metal table on foldable metal chairs. Stan places the case on the table and takes the vacant chair at the head of it. Carlton seats himself to Stan's right.

"Well my men, the time has come," Stan says as he ceremoniously opens the case and flips the lid back revealing twenty-five cellophane wrapped packages to his relief since he hadn't bothered to check the contents of the cases before due to his uncharacteristic state of mind over the affect Jack had on him. But now, back amongst his loyal cohorts he begins to feel himself and for the first time since leaving Vienna he becomes excited by the thought of how much money he will make.

"Okay, Stan, we've talked about it and decided I'll move ten, Wigan and Reggae Man reckon they can shift five a piece leaving the other five for Ace and Tyrone to get rid of;" Carlton assumes the role of leading pusher, which he is for Stan.

"And how soon can you move it and pay me?" Stan replies.

"Considering what you want for it, Stan, I can move mine in a couple of weeks just in my social circles without using my pushers. They'll bulk buy enough to last them a month or more, plus sell on to their associates I have no contact with," Carlton answers and looks at the other four pushers, who appear uneasy.

"Even though I'm giving it to you at prices you

haven't seen for years if at all and you'll never see them from anyone else again, I don't want you to sell cheap just because we've got so much. Like you say, Carlton, they'll buy in bulk when they get it half-price or whatever. And what will you do when they don't need to buy again for a while?"

"See your point, Stan. Even if I use my pushers I guess Wigan and the rest of us will have saturated the market in Manchester in the short term;" Carlton replies.

"Can't any of you move this gear somewhere else, like Birmingham or London?" Stan asks and scans the five faces in front of him.

"We've all got connections and family all over the place, man, but do we want to put them at risk from the local dealers?" Wigan asks in his deep Jamaican patois.

"Yeah, man, why don't you use your brother in London to get rid of some of this shit if you've got too much for us to sell?" Reggae Man joins in.

"You guys know he's retired. And he may be my brother but if he gets a sniff of what I'm dealing he might think about coming out of retirement then he'll probably take over the whole fucking thing and we'll be left with shit, and I'll be left in the shit with the Russians," Stan explains.

"Exactly, Stan, you're worried about your own brother. The people we have to worry about on different turf sure ain't our brothers," Ace comments, which brings laughter from the others.

"I'm not telling you to compete on their territory. You're getting this coke practically half-price. Why don't you sell to them direct? I know your profit will be only about fifty-per-cent of what you're used to, but it's still profit," Stan explains and looks at their five faces, which are looking at each other in confused contemplation. The magnitude of what he has taken on now dawns on Stan and he realizes that he should have prepared for it long before now.

"I don't need to do business outside the city, I'll just use my pushers to move what I can't but I won't pass it on at such a cheap rate, okay Stan?" Carlton suggests after a long pause.

"Sounds good to me, Carlton. What about the rest of you?"

"My brother deals in Bristol, I was gonna pass some on to him anyway, but I've got to give it to him cheap," Reggae Man puts in.

"That's cool, Bristol is a long way from Manchester and a few k's are not gonna make their way back here. Wigan, you got any ideas?"

"There's always Black Betty…"

"Why you call her Black Betty? That's what her white sucker customers call her," Reggae Man interrupts.

"She was my woman for two years, before she went to London. I can call her what I want. Besides, she wouldn't give a shit, it's her trade name. And she's making a fortune off her trade from the rich white suckers," Wigan answers abruptly.

"She dealin as well?" Stan asks.

"Sure, man. She gives me a call occasionally when her rich white boys want an ounce or more and I take it down to her. Now if I tell her how much I can provide it to her for I'm sure her white boys will come knocking her door down and Betty will be making some nice doe on top of what she gets from her usual business," Wigan explains.

"Sounds good too. Ace, Tyrone?"

"Come on, Stan, we can move five k's easy in two weeks on our streets without dropping the price much. All the more profit for us," Ace answers.

"Now there's more to come after this brothers, that's why I don't want you to flood Manchester with it. We need to push it as fast as we can but not too fast, we can't let the street price drop because it will only cost us. I'll call you all in a couple of weeks when I hope you will have moved the stuff." Stan finishes the business talk and leaves Carlton to divide the contents of the case accordingly, leaves his posse and drives back to the secure storage unit where he parks up to call Roger Facey.

"Yo, Stan, are we ready to go?" Roger answers almost immediately.

"How long will it take you to move twenty-five k's?" Stan comes straight to the point.

"Depends on how much you want for it."

"I can guarantee to undercut anybody else who supplies you but not by a big margin, maybe ten percent. Don't forget this gear is as pure as it comes so you can triple or quadruple it and it will still be quality stuff." Stan considers the only way to stop Roger flooding the market with the merchandise is to make sure Roger does not get it at such a low price to enable him to do so.

"Okay, we can discuss the actual price at the meet. How much can I take on credit?" Roger asks academically so as to appear genuine about the deal.

"Two hundred and fifty grands worth but I need it back within four weeks," Stan replies with a time span that will allow him plenty of leeway if there are any delays.

"Shouldn't be a problem, Stan. Would I be right in

thinking I need to bring along a similar amount in cash?" Roger does some quick calculations compared to what he usually pays per kilo that is not so pure.

"You would be," Stan replies.

"Okay, when and where do we do the transaction?"

"Today, tomorrow, the day after. I'll call you half an hour before we meet so be available in the city until you hear from me and make the cash available, like now." Stan wants to keep Roger in the dark right up until the last moment so to reduce the chance of any kind of set-up being arranged despite the fact he is confident in Roger's fear of him.

"Understood, Stan. I will wait for your call," Roger ends the call before Stan in an attempt to show strength, which has no effect on Stan who is only glad the call is over. He retrieves another case from the secure storage unit and puts it in the trunk of the Fiesta, gets in the car and calls Roger again.

"Stan, did you forget something?" Roger answers quickly again.

"No, I told you it could be today. I wanna do the business in half an hour. Can you get the cash together by then?"

"Jeez, Stan. Can't you give me an hour? I don't have it in a shoe box under the bed, I've got to collect it, man," Roger does have immediate access to the cash but needs time to inform Sergeant Andy Price.

"Okay, but be at the benches by the marina at Cotton Field Park as soon as you can. Sit at the table nearest the water if it is vacant, which it should be at this time of year but if not just sit on the edge of the decking or stand if it's too wet. I'm coming alone and I'll be watching you and you better be alone," Stan instructs and ends the call then sets off to put his plan into action. Roger immediately calls Andy.

"Andy, I just got a call from Stan. He wants to meet me within an hour at Cotton Field Park. He's offered to pass me twenty-five k's but I doubt he'll have it on him since he said he's going to be alone and that I have to be alone also. I think he'll take me somewhere the coke is hidden and do the deal there. I'm supposed to take two hundred and fifty grand in cash for it plus he's giving it me two hundred and fifty on credit."

"Half a million, isn't that a bit steep for such bulk buying?" Andy is used to dealers getting pre-cut cocaine.

"Not if it's pure. It could be turned into seventy-five to a hundred kilos and would still be as good as most of the shit on the streets, so it's really cheap."

"Can't you try and get more time before the meet?"

"I already did, he wanted to see me in half an hour. I told him I couldn't get the cash together at such short notice so he told me to make it an hour, max."

"So you can really get hold of two hundred and fifty grand in cash within an hour?" Andy says unable to disguise the astonishment in his voice.

"Er, yeah. Why?" Roger hates the fact he has to admit he has so much money at his disposal.

"No reason," Andy replies while his mind races to put something together enabling him to confiscate, or better still, steal the cash.

"But do I need to take the money along if you are going to bust him?"

"Of course you've got to take the money with you. If, as you say, he takes you somewhere to pick up the drugs he'll want to see the cash first, and with a bit of luck he'll take you to wherever he is keeping the whole stash of his and we could catch him with the lot."

"You did say something about getting money for the deal. Can you do it?"

"Sorry, Roger, my boss wouldn't sanction it. Besides, Stan has already arranged everything with you. The amount, the cost, the credit and if you can lay your hands on the cash there's no need. We have no time to arrange anything. I need to stake it out. Where exactly are you meeting him?"

"The benches on the marina, you know it?"

"Yeah, of course. It'll be empty there in this weather. I'll have a guy walking his dog around the place to get a visual on you and I'll be with a team in the car-park. We'll use three different cars to tail you with when you leave with Stan to get the coke. Now I've got to shoot to get all this set up," Andy says excitedly and ends the call to make the necessary arrangements.

Stan looks out from under the tarpaulin that covers the two seater speed boat tide up about thirty meters from the benches. He watches Roger clutching what appears to be a small rucksack close to his chest furtively make his way to the empty bench closest to the water. The only other person in the area is a man in a raincoat walking his dog. Stan makes a call to Roger who hurriedly retrieves his mobile from the inside pocket of his leather coat and sees that it is Stan calling.

"Yo, Stan, I'm waiting for you, where are you?"

"Turn and look over your left shoulder," Stan replies quietly.

"And?" Roger asks after he does so.

"Do you see the small yellow speedboat?"

"How could I miss it?"

"Walk around the marina to it staying on the phone with me until you get there."

"Sure, but what's going on, Stan? Don't forget I'm carrying a lot of dough," Roger asks nervously.

"Just do as I say. You can see there's no one around."

"Okay, I'm on my way," Roger replies as he walks around the marina towards the boat and feels a little more secure after spotting the dog walker.

"So you have the cash with you?"

"Yeah, all in fifties and no counterfeits. Well I'm practically at the boat, what next?"

"Get on board, and turn your phone off," Stan shouts as he flings the tarpaulin back and starts the boat's engine.

"What?" Roger answers in disbelief.

"Just get in quick." Roger looks at the dog walker who is now stationary and looking at him from about fifty yards away. Not knowing what he should do Roger gets into the boat in the hope that Andy will be able to follow in some way or other. Stan opens the throttle towards the Rochdale Canal.

"Where we goin, man?" Roger shouts above the engine noise.

"Not far, just chill, Roger;" Stan replies as loudly as he makes a left turn into the canal and opens up the throttle completely leaving a big wake behind them. After about half a mile Stan slows the boat as quickly as possible in a widened part of the canal and pulls up against the canal side and kills the engine.

"Take this, now let's move it," Stan commands Roger

throwing him the rear mooring rope as he jumps onto the tow path with the front mooring rope and secures it. Roger watches and copies Stan's action with the rear rope then retrieves his bag from the boat.

"Follow me," Stan says as he breaks into a fast jog along the tow path in the direction they just came. After fifty yards they come to the end of a dead end street to their left where Carlton is waiting in the rented car.

"Get in," Stan orders as he gets into the rear of the car, Roger joins him by the other rear door. Carlton starts the car and drives away sedately not wanting to draw attention.

"Where we goin now, Stan?" Roger asks in a state of bewilderment. He's lost touch with reality, not sure of what to do, think or say. In a no win situation, Stan gets his money and Andy will probably take the coke plus put him in jail for a very long time and if by some miracle he does not go to jail then Stan will at least cripple him or worse when he cannot pay for the coke given on credit because he will not have it to sell.

"Somewhere safe where you can test the gear and pay me. Now put your head down like me so we can't be seen by anyone outside the car," Stan instructs and puts his head between his legs and Roger very reluctantly and awkwardly, due to his height, follows suit.

"Should be okay by now," Carlton says after five minutes driving. Stan raises his head and Roger does likewise. They drive for a further twenty minutes until they are well out of the city then Carlton pulls off the road onto a farm dirt track and drives down it until they cannot be seen from the road and parks the car well hidden in foliage.

"Let's do it," Stan says as he gets out of the car.

Carlton and Roger join him where he opens the trunk and then the case inside it exposing the twenty-five cellophane wrapped kilo parcels of cocaine.

"Take your pick, Roger," Stan says and stands back to give Roger complete access to the case. Not knowing how far things would go before Andy could step in Roger has prepared himself as though he was going through with the deal, he opens the rucksack and takes out a small vile containing a clear liquid then slits a random package with a long fingernail. He opens the vile, takes a sample of the cocaine on the fingernail and taps it into the vile, closes the vile and shakes it. The liquid turns a deep purple, proof of the highest purity. Stan is perplexed as to why Roger is not enthusiastic on seeing the result of the test.

"Well, is it pure or is it pure?" he asks.

"Sure, it's the real thing," Roger replies nonchalantly in a daze.

"And the cash?" Stan asks. Roger hands over the rucksack, which Stan gives to Carlton who gets into the car and puts the notes through a counting machine and randomly checks there are no counterfeits. Stan closes the case and the trunk.

"Where to now?" Roger asks.

"We'll take you to a taxi rank in the city and then you go wherever you want. But make sure you take good care of the gear until it's sold. Remember I want the balance within four weeks," Stan says threateningly as he pokes Roger in the chest four times for emphasis.

Roger activates his phone after placing the suitcase in the trunk of the taxi then takes a seat in the rear. Within two minutes Andy calls. Roger wishes he had never told him about the deal with Stan and wishes he had never done the deal with Stan but now it was too late. If he lies to Andy then Andy will put him in prison. If he does not lie to Andy then Andy might put him in prison but Andy wants Stan more than him, Roger decides to tell Andy the truth and answers the phone.

"Yeah?" he asks in a dejected tone.

"Where the fuck are you, Roger? What happened?" Andy rants.

"It's difficult. I'm in a taxi," Roger explains.

"Have you got the coke?"

"Yes."

"Can you meet me at your place?" Andy asks more calmly.

"You know where I live now?" Roger had only recently changed address.

"Don't ask silly questions, Roger."

"Twenty, twenty-five minutes," Roger replies morosely.

"I'll be waiting."

Twenty minutes later the taxi pulls up outside the small modern privately owned apartment building in a respectable area where Roger lives with his girlfriend. As Roger retrieves the case Andy, who was waiting in a car across the road, taps him on the shoulder.

"What the…" Roger says as he turns to see it is Andy.

"I told you I'd be waiting."

"Let's go up, I need a drink and a smoke," Roger says as he heaves the case out of the trunk.

"Is your woman home?" Andy asks as they wait for the lift.

"No way. She's too busy earning legal money."

"She's a hairdresser isn't she?"

"Not just. She's got three salons open now. She's kinda cornered the market for ladies with afro hair. The mortgage for this place is in her name although I pay it."

"Guess you couldn't put down 'major drug dealer' as your occupation on the mortgage application form, huh, Rog?"

"Somethin like that," Roger replies as they exit the lift.

"Why do you bother with a mortgage when you can lay your hands on two hundred and fifty grand?"

"It helps my woman out with taxes, and besides I need cash for when opportunities like this one comes up. Though I wish to God I had never taken this opportunity up."

"Okay, tell me everything. Our guy walking the dog said a big black guy, which I guess was Stan, suddenly appeared from beneath the cover of a speedboat while you were talking on your phone and you got in. Then he disappeared down the canal. We found what we believe to be the boat tide up by the end of a street that ends at the canal," Andy states as they enter the apartment.

"It was Stan. Took me completely by surprise. I was hoping you would get involved before I handed the cash over but there was no sign of you. One of his guys picked us up from the boat and we went into the countryside where we did the deal. Then they stuck me in a taxi and you called and here we are."

"Fuck! Fuck! Fuck! Fuck!" was all Andy could say while sitting in a large red cotton upholstered armchair.

"How do you think I feel, man? I'm down two

hundred and fifty k, which is about all I've got. I'm supposed to pay Stan another two fifty and I'm in the shit with you. I've only got prison or a grave to look forward to. Do you want a drink?" Roger asks comically as he opens a bottle of white rum and resigns himself to the prospect of a very bleak future.

"You got a cold beer?"

"Sure," Roger replies and gets a can of Red Stripe from the fridge after taking a generous swig from the bottle of rum.

"Not all is lost, Roger. Do you think you can set up another deal with Stan?" Andy asks and opens the can of beer.

"I dunno, man. Maybe if you let me sell this stuff and I pay him off on time it could be possible," Roger says not believing his luck and rightly thinks that Andy must have some kind of vendetta against Stan to want to bring him down so badly.

"Do you think you can move this stuff in the four weeks?"

"If you give me the opportunity, Andy, I'll move it in three," Roger replies enthusiastically. After believing he was headed for prison or worse less than two minutes ago he is now offered the opportunity to keep his freedom and even make money on the deal.

"How much cash will you make selling this stuff?" Andy asks and Roger sees his profits disappearing.

"The faster I move it, Andy, the less there will be."

"How much, Roger?"

"After my pushers have taken their cut, I dunno, maybe I can make two or three hundred grand, if I'm lucky,"

Roger lies. After cutting the cocaine even if he lets it go at less than he usually pushes it on for he should comfortably make four to five hundred thousand pounds, especially since his girlfriend, whose family are the major suppliers in Brighton and the surrounding area, asked him if he could find some extra supply because they could not satisfy the demand. And Roger knows he has to dangle a carrot for Andy.

"You told me that if Stan has so much he would flood the market and you wouldn't make much if anything."

"That was before my woman asked me if I could supply some pushers down South. She has connections who are major dealers and I could probably move at least half, if not all, of what I've got onto them, but only if the price is right."

"Okay, Roger, here's the deal. I let you keep the coke and sell it. You stay out of jail. You prove to Stan that you're reliable and hopefully set up another deal but the best part of it all is that you give me your profit. Now, is, let's say, two hundred and fifty grand worth staying out of prison for the best part of your life worth it? You can keep anything over that you make," Andy proposes with a smile. The arrest of Stan pales into insignificance compared to the prospect of extorting a quarter of a million pounds from Roger.

"Do I have any choice?" Roger feigns disappointment. He will probably still be close on between one and two hundred thousand pounds better off than if everything had gone to plan as previously arranged whereby the only benefit to Roger would have been staying out of prison and potentially keeping the price of cocaine high in Manchester.

As Sergeant Andy Price drives to the station trying to

concoct a story whereby he can allow Roger to carry on with the drug dealing unimpeded, his superior, Inspector Roy Collins, radios him.

"Why haven't you called in? I thought you would have brought Stan in by now. What's going on?" he growls.

"Sorry, gov, but there's been complications. Shall I tell you back at the station?"

"What bloody complications? Sounds more like a fuck-up, tell me now!"

"Stan basically kidnapped Roger in a speedboat so we couldn't pursue. The boat was ditched and they were picked up by a waiting car and driven out of the city where Roger had no choice but to go through with the deal," Andy slowly explains.

"So have you arrested Roger for possession?" the inspector calms a little.

"No, gov, Roger has been a valuable snitch and we've been after Stan for so long that I thought we could give it another go. Stan only gave Roger twenty-five kilos, which was originally probably only ten at most before Stan cut it. That means Stan still probably has ninety kilos of the pure stuff. If we let Roger sell the stuff he has and pay off Stan then we can send Roger in for another and even bigger deal and this time there will be no fuck-ups. I've discussed it with Roger and he knows he has no option but to go along with it," Andy explains although he knows Roger has uncut cocaine he needs to persuade his boss that Stan will need to use Roger again.

"And what does Roger have to pay Stan?"

"Since you wouldn't authorize any cash for the deal Stan gave it to Roger all on credit, two hundred and fifty thousand. So it was just as well we didn't give him anything," Andy lies once again in order to disguise the purity of the cocaine and therefore its value.

"Why didn't you bring him in so we could have arranged all this at the station?"

"I thought it was better to meet him at his flat where he felt more comfortable and besides, you never know who might see him come and go from the station. If Stan or an acquaintance of his gets wind Roger was visiting the station it would screw up the whole thing."

"Okay, Andy, you can call it a day and go home. See you tomorrow," Inspector Collins replies wearily and ends the call.

20.

After touching base with various friends and associates and the manageresses of his brothels Stan gets home shortly after 03:00 and quietly lets himself in and is shocked to see Lizzy in a similar stance to one he had seen Jack performing, holding the wheel before her but no aura or spinning light.

"Still up, sugar?" Stan asks loudly which alarms Lizzy since she never heard him enter the apartment and was trying her best to be still, keeping her mind unoccupied and as empty as possible.

"Hey, you shocked me. I never heard you come in," Lizzy answers on opening her eyes and lowering her arms, a little embarrassed.

"I thought you would be asleep and didn't want to disturb you. What are you up to? No, don't tell me. I saw Jack doing exactly the same thing but you didn't have the swirling light I saw between Jack's arms. It's Falun Dafa stuff isn't it?"

"This research on Falun Dafa I said I would do for you, I started it in my breaks at work and concentrated on it since I got back. I thought I would be in a position to tell you what nonsense it is but it's kinda got me hooked. You know I'm interested in Buddhism and yoga but this stuff goes much deeper if you believe it, which I guess most people won't but for some reason I don't know I think I do?"

"Don't tell me you're comin on all religious like Jack?"

"It's not like 'church' religious. It's more like 'common sense' religious."

"What! You're really doing it? I thought you thought it was a pile of shit and would tell me that is exactly what you found it to be. I didn't even think you would bother looking at it, just tell me you found out it was a pile of shit. So what did you find out about it?" Stan doesn't hide his intrigue, which surprises Lizzy. She never believed he could be seriously interested in anything beyond the material.

"I wouldn't have bothered but after your crazy dream experience with Jack I thought it was worth taking a look at. A Chinese guy called Li Hongzhi invented it… no, that's wrong. He didn't invent it because you can't invent something that has been in existence ever since things existed and actually caused things to exist and is existence in itself. He revealed it to the masses, which has never been done before, to give us an opportunity to save ourselves. Buddha and Jesus tried to show the way the best they could to the people in a way the people could understand it best. Christianity and Buddhism may have different names as do Judaism, Islam, Hinduism etc. But they all have the same goal - for us to ascend to a better place. Falun Dafa is no different, it shows us a way to ascend and, according to Li Hongzhi, it is the fastest way for someone who is not taught in the secret ways by some master. Now this civilization has advanced so much intellectually people do not follow religion like sheep, well most don't. People look to science as a way to decide on how things will happen and what the expected result will be. But this only limits them to what science has discovered, as far as they are concerned if something cannot be scientifically proven then it isn't true. The most profound thing Buddhism taught me, which is basically common sense and doesn't need proving, is that suffering is caused by desire. You know, just wanting things, being jealous of people who have more than you but Falun Dafa explains it in more depth and goes further…"

"Whoa, woman. Slow down. All I want to know is if it is genuine and not some kind of scam and especially what benefits I will get out of it if I do it," Stan interrupts after taking off his coat and making himself comfortable on the sofa.

"It's no scam. Passing on of Dafa knowledge is absolutely free. As far as benefits go, you won't get any since all you're looking for is to gain something and that is a desire, which will only hold you back," Lizzy replies as she joins Stan on the sofa.

"So if there's nothing to gain, why do people do it?"

"Because they look beyond this materialist world in search of what's beyond it. Probably because, like I do, they want to know the reason for their existence and follow a path that will show them. I guess it's a similar motivation to the one monks and nuns have but they look to God for their salvation. But then again, you could look upon Dafa as God."

"So they 'desire' to know something. Doesn't this 'desire' also stop them?"

"I see you're point, Stan. But I don't think the desire to be truthful, compassionate and tolerant really compares to anything you want, do you?"

"What?"

"Zhen, shan, ren, the nature of the universe. We have ended up here because we have been assholes in previous existences and if we want to get back to the place we fell from, call it heaven, nirvana, paradise, whatever, we need to realign ourselves with the qualities of the universe, which are zhen, shan, ren - truthfulness, compassion and tolerance. Sure, some people try and rubbish it by calling it a cult and saying that Li Hongzhi is a fraud. I can't understand them. Falun Dafa recognizes and respects true religions that guide people on a righteous path but some people, the ones that do blindly follow their faith, run Falun Dafa down because it is not their faith. They're just ignorant twats in my opinion."

"So after just some hours of looking at this stuff you're sold on it?"

"It's been like half a day I've been looking at it and I'm far from sold on it I just feel drawn towards it since, to me, it provides the most feasible reason as to why we are here and where we have come from, no, I mean fell from."

"How can you feel so strongly about something you just read about?"

"I dunno, but like Li Hongzhi says something like the wise will recognize it while the average may take an interest and the foolish will laugh at it. And since I take it seriously I guess I must be wise," Lizzy answers and chuckles at herself.

"So what exactly do you have to do and what exactly does it do for you?" Stan asks, confused by his own fascination.

"There's loads of stuff on the web page to go through. I've only read bits from Zhuan Falun, that's the main book on the subject, and looked at the exercise videos," Lizzy answers as she motions towards her laptop on the coffee table in front of them.

"So what else did you learn?"

"One bit I read about would interest you. The way you're into science fiction and extra-terrestrials, UFO's and all that stuff," Lizzy explains sensing Stan's interest.

"Go on, it's getting late," Stan answers when Lizzy pauses beyond his patience.

"Well, apparently, we have dropped down to this realm, this earth, this reality because of our past sins in higher realms, the ones we need to return to if we don't want to be completely obliterated after committing more sins and growing greater attachments here in this realm. Now the beings from higher realms and dimensions are able to visit us, if they so wish, here on our cesspit planet we call home. And these visitations have been witnessed, as you keep informing me, and are referred to as extra-terrestrials in UFO's. I've read as much but I've only touched on what there is to learn, I think I'm going to carry on learning about it."

"Will you teach me what you learn?" Stan asks with such sincerity Lizzy is quite touched.

"I can tell you, Stan, that even if I try and follow it, which I know is going to be tough, you will never be able to."

"If you can do it, why shouldn't I?"

"I said I don't know if I can because I don't think I can rid myself of the attachments I have. The fundamental thing about succeeding in Falun Dafa is discarding all attachments. And not just attachments like your Porsche. Your very ego, how you think about yourself, the way you put so much into the gym so you look like a body builder. And then there's the way you feel proud about how people fear you. It goes even further; it's not just things you enjoy and desire that you need to rid yourself of but also the fears you hold such as getting old, losing your looks, your power or getting arrested, maybe," Lizzy concludes and looks questioningly at Stan.

"I had the same kind of discussion with Jack in Vienna and in my dream and thought it is not for me but one thing he said stuck in my mind."

"Which was what?"

"He said that because I could see these weird lights around him and appeared to him telepathically I must have a good foundational basis, whatever that means. Do you know what he meant?"

"No. I need more time to study it but if Jack's been doing it for a long time he must know since he will have read everything on it and whatever 'a good foundational basis' is sounds like something positive at least, but I'm at a loss to know why, knowing what you're like, Stan."

"Guess so but the irritating thing is you and Jack tell me I have no chance of doing this stuff but why do I have this good foundation?"

"Like I said, I don't know but I can't believe you would be able to practice, Stan. You would have to become someone you would laugh at. For starters you would have to leave your whole way of life behind and find a legal, decent way of making a living. You would have to change your whole character. You would have to become Stan the Man NOT and all you do is try to nurture and grow that image..."

"Okay, okay. Let's talk about it another time when you read some more. I need to sleep."

21.

It is Sunday evening, almost a week since Stan arrived back in Manchester. Beth is watching television when she sees car headlights trace across her living room window mutes the TV and hears the familiar purr of Jason's Jaguar. She gets up to greet him.

"Hi, Jay, this is a nice surprise. How come you never called?" she asks as Jason approaches the open door.

"Thought I'd give you a surprise," Jason replies just before Beth kisses him in a bear hug.

"Well it's a nice one. Are you hungry?" she asks as Jason eases her away.

"A beer will suffice for now," he replies as he sits at the table in the dining kitchen.

"Not staying?" Beth asks passing him an opened bottle of Budweiser.

"Why do you ask?"

"You haven't taken your colors off."

"Just preoccupied. Here!" Jason says on standing up to take his jacket off and gives it to Beth.

"So, why so serious?" Beth asks quizzically.

"The nigger has been back for nearly a week, the police haven't nicked him and there is no noticeable change in the supply or the price of coke on the streets. I'm beginning to wonder if I underestimate the demand for it or if the nigger is pushing it somewhere else," Jason replies thoughtfully.

"So isn't that a good thing? If the price isn't dropping you guys aren't losing anything. Right?"

"Right. But it's still something I would like to know the answer to."

"Why, Jay?"

"When I'm wrong I always want to know why I'm wrong, that's all. Now, will you call the nigger and find out what's going on?"

"Jeez, Jay, first you make me call and question my brother out of false pretenses and now you want me to call Stan and ask him fucking what after I basically told him to go fuck himself when Jack passed the phone over to him in Vienna, remember?"

"Stan's ego won't allow him to stop bragging about what he's up to, especially as he has already told you about his plans so far. Ask him to come over and give you a taste of his pure imported gear. If he comes you can question him out in your own seductive, subtle way."

"What! Are you fucking crazy?"

"Don't worry, I'll be close at hand. Try him now."

"The things you do for love!" Beth says as she makes a call to Stan.

"Yo, Beth, what's kickin?" Stan answers, surprised by her call.

"Hi, Stan. How's it going?"

"Sweet, just like I told you. But you weren't very interested. You hung-up on me. Why are you callin?"

"To apologize. I've been pretty strung-out lately with various shit and I'm out of my anti-depressants. I was wondering…"

"If you could try my pure stuff?" Stan interrupts.

"Could you, for old time's sake?" Beth feigns sincerity, she has never taken prescribed anti-depressants in her life.

"I'll call round in a couple hours, about ten. You better make it worthwhile for me," Stan replies.

"Great! Thanks, Stan. See you around ten," Stan hangs up before Beth can finish her sentence.

"Now that didn't hurt, did it?" Jason comments with a grin on his face.

"And now?" Beth replies dryly.

"I'll move my car out of sight and then wait upstairs when he gets here."

"I'm sorry, Jay, but you're no physical match for Stan, what if he gets violent with me?"

"I may not be able to handle him but my friend can," Jason replies coolly as he reaches behind his back.

"Who?" Beth asks, shocked.

"Meet Mr. Glock nine millimeter," Stan replies as he holds the pistol up in front of Beth.

"Jesus, Jay! You can get five years just for possessing that."

"Don't act naïve with me, Beth. You know how the Angels operate," Jason says as he replaces the gun down the back of his trousers.

"It was just a bit of a shock. What if Stan's carrying? Are you gonna have a shootout?" Beth says sarcastically.

"Don't be stupid. I'll only come down if I have to.

And if and when I do he's not gonna be expecting it. He ain't gonna pull a gun on you."

"He said that I had better make it worthwhile for him so I guess he wants to fuck me. What are you going to do then?"

"I'll hide in your spare room. If he gets rough with you I'll come in."

"So you don't care if he fucks me?"

"Did you take a naïve pill or something today, Beth? Business is business and this is for the club not us."

"Yeah, the Angels, first the club then the bike and then the old lady," Beth replies with a scowl.

"You knew that before you got mixed-up with me. So don't expect anything different if you want to stay my old lady."

"Yes, boss. Is there any position I should let him fuck me in?"

"Give it a rest, Beth. This is no time to fuck about. I'm gonna move the car. I'm back in five minutes," Jason replies and leaves the door wide open after stepping into the cold evening air.

"Bastard," Beth whispers as she closes the door, ashamed at herself in the knowledge that the way Jason treats her is one of the reasons why she is attracted to him.

Two hours later the roar of Stan's Porsche sends Jason upstairs and Beth to the mirror in the entrance hall where she applies lipstick and perfume.

"Hey, Stan, you're on time," Beth says on opening the door just before Stan can ring the bell.

"Why shouldn't I be?"

"In the old days I was lucky if you turned up, never mind on time."

"I guess you're right but old age must be making me a little more reliable," Stan answers and smiles at Beth as she stands aside to let him in.

"Drink?" Beth asks following Stan into the dining kitchen.

"What you got?" Stan replies making himself comfortable at the table.

"Budweiser or chardonnay. Sorry, out of rum."

"Got any milk?"

"Sure," Beth replies with a look of confusion.

"And a mirror?" Stan asks as he produces a wrap from his inside jacket pocket. Beth pours a glass of milk from the fridge, gives it to Stan then retrieves a small make-up mirror from her handbag and places it on the table.

"Do you need something to chop it?"

"No, this'll do nicely," Stan retorts as he flashes his American Express Platinum card.

"Is it safe to take that stuff when it's so pure?" Beth asks, concerned that she has not snorted for some years and is worried what effects she might experience now her resistance may be low and what Stan might do while she is under the effect.

"Of course, look at these," Stan replies as he chops up two very small lines of cocaine, only a fifth the quantity Beth was used to snorting in the past.

"So little, wow! I guess that can't hurt Beth replies as Stan rolls a twenty pound note for snorting.

"You'll be amazed," Stan says and quickly inhales a line then pushes the mirror towards Beth and hands her the rolled note as she sits down opposite.

"Okay, here goes," she says loudly so that Jason can hear and snorts the line.

"And?" Stan asks as Beth puts her head back.

"Hey, there's no stinging or bad taste. My nose has gone completely numb, and so is my mouth. God this is strong stuff."

"If I cut this into triple the amount it's still the best shit you can get on the streets," Stan boasts as Jason listens from the upstairs landing.

"How strong are you selling this stuff in town? You must be charging a fortune for it," Beth begins her subtle interrogation.

"Nothing like you would think. I've told my guys to cut and sell it at pretty normal quality and price so as not to flood the market here in Manchester."

"You said you were getting a hundred k's. How long will it take you to sell it all the way you are doing it?"

"Not as long as you would think. I've got guys selling it from Birmingham to London as far as Brighton and even down Cornwall way. If I dump it all in Manchester the price will fall through the floor."

"I don't know if it's because I haven't touched gear for ages or is it just the strength of this stuff? I'm flying, Stan," Beth says and glares at Stan, pupils fully dilated. Stan looks at her and smiles. On hearing this Jason grows as concerned about what Beth will do as he is about Stan.

"Probably a bit of both, Beth," Stan replies.

"So how do I make this little visit of yours worthwhile, do you want to go upstairs?"

"What? No, I'm sorry I gave you that idea. No

offence, you still look good, Beth, but I want you to tell me about your brother and this thing he does, you know, this Falun Dafa thing."

"You serious?" Beth asks in astonishment and Jason wonders what Stan is talking about.

"Yeah. At his place, in Vienna, I saw him doing these weird exercises. He was surrounded by a strange beautiful light and at one point he was holding like a circle of light between his arms that turned one way and then the other. It was no trick or anything, he didn't even know I was watching, it was like, magic."

"Wow! Jack's told me many things about what he does, even tried to persuade me to do it, but nothing about circles of light. I never took him that seriously. I put it down to one of his obsessions he gets now and then, his last one was astral projection. But come to think of it, he's been doing this Falun Dafa thing for a long time now."

"He probably didn't tell you about the light because he told me he couldn't see it himself, only feel it. He said that since I could see the light I must have a good foundation, that I must have been a saint or something in a past life. Do you know anything about what that could mean?"

"Are you kidding me, Stan? You a saint!"

"I'm only telling you what he told me. I've got no fucking idea. I was hoping you could fill me in on this shit."

"Sorry, Stan, but I haven't got a clue. Like I said, I thought it was just another fad Jack has. I take the piss out of him over it. I'm sure you would if you hadn't seen the light."

"It's not just what I saw, Beth, it's also the way Jack made me feel when I was with him."

"What do you mean - feel?"

"I kinda felt calm but also really bad about how I've been and how I am. For example, you wouldn't believe how bad I feel about the way I treated you. I'm really sorry for it."

"You said 'feel', does that mean Jack still has an effect on you?"

"Guess so, but not as strongly as when I was with him. And I am almost back to my old self when I'm doing business with my posse. But when I have time to think without distractions I always start thinking about how I felt in Jack's company and the feeling starts to come on again. Basically a feeling of guilt," Stan opens up on the effects of the cocaine and Jason finds it hard to believe what he is hearing.

"Maybe I should start taking Jack and his Falun Dafa more seriously if he is having such an effect on Stan the Man," Beth smiles but her sincerity is tangible.

"I think you should, you might learn something. Like something I was hoping you could tell me about. And what I've told you isn't all that's happened, I saved the best till last. I had a dream the other night. At first it was more like a nightmare and so realistic. I saw myself doing lots of bad shit I've done throughout my life and felt the worst guilt I ever have felt then I met Jack…"

"Met Jack, where?" Beth asks confused.

"I was still dreaming and I actually thought I met him but knew my nightmare was only that, a nightmare. I told him about it and he talked to me about it, but then he told me that he wasn't sure he was talking to me or dreaming himself because he was practicing his Falun Dafa stuff. He said I must have this great foundation thing, you know, like he said I must have been a saint in a past life, since I could contact him in such a way."

"So, it was only a dream, Stan?"

"No. No it wasn't. Before the so-called dream ended Jack told me to call him if I remembered it."

"And did you?"

"Of course. And he knew all about it. We discussed it and he wants me to practice it but that would mean basically giving up this life in the hope of having a better next one but I'm not convinced there is a next one. I was hoping you could tell me more but it seems you know less than me."

"I'm sorry I'm no help, Stan, but Jack did send me a link to the website, which was in about forty different languages. I just took one look at just how much stuff was out there and never looked again, it seemed too much like hard work. Why don't you look at it? I'll send you the link."

"My girlfriend is already doing it. Now she was dead against me getting involved with it because I had changed so much but after she told me she would look into it, which I never believed she would, I got home to find her doing the exercises. So after some hours of reading about the stuff she was sold on it. Now, Lizzy, that's my girlfriend, is an intelligent lady and didn't want me to get involved with Falun Dafa because it kinda makes me not me, so I reckon there must definitely be something real to this stuff. I'll never forget the look on her face when I told her what happened in my dream, or whatever you would call it, with Jack."

"What did she say?" Beth's interest in this unusual conversation is exemplified by the cocaine.

"It was priceless. She thought I was nuts when I told her about my dream so I called Jack and put him on loudspeaker. When he said he was basically expecting my call because of our communication her jaw hit the floor."

"I'm not surprised. No wonder she is into it now. I've gotta take a look at this stuff and ask Jack about it," Beth replies as her mind drifts onto what Falun Dafa is and forgets about questioning Stan anymore on what exactly he is doing with the cocaine. As he listens from the top of the stairs Jason grows very irritated in his confusion, he has learnt all he needs to know about what Stan is doing with the cocaine and does not know or want to know about Falun Dafa, whatever it may be. Since Stan is not interested in bedding Beth, Jason wonders why Beth is still in conversation, but she is animated by the cocaine.

"So I guess I've gotta rely on Lizzy for my info. I just don't have the time to look into it myself," Stan says out of disappointment.

"Sorry, Stan. You definitely know more about this stuff than I do. And you have really made me interested in it."

"Ah, well, it looks like I told you something so my visit wasn't a complete waste of time," Stan says as he gets to his feet.

"You leaving?" Beth asks despondently, she is buzzing and craves more interaction. Jason is angered by her tone.

"Sorry, Beth, but time waits for no man. Here, keep this. There's a couple of grams there, but don't do any more than you just did in any one go, you're already off your head with that," Stan says as he drops the wrap on the table. Beth is bewildered as Stan waves before turning to leave the house.

"What the fuck was all that about?" Jason asks loudly

as he descends the stairs.

"Didn't you hear?"

"Yeah, I heard alright, I just don't believe it. What's this Falun Dafa thing?"

"It's a kind of religion I guess. Something Jack practices. He got into years ago after first going to Tibet and getting into Buddhism. Are you interested?"

"Religion! Are you kidding? I'm an Angel. Being an Angel is my religion. Why do you think we call our Saturday meetings 'church'?" Jason remarks as he seats himself at the table.

"Yeah. Silly me. At least you know what Stan is doing with the coke now. Since it's not affecting your sales and prices are you going to leave him to it?"

"Why? Do you want me to? Do you still fancy the nigger?" Jason does not hide his suspicion or resentment.

"Would it make you jealous if I did, Jay?" Beth asks as she puts two opened bottles of chilled Budweiser on the table and takes the seat opposite Jason.

"I don't touch black meat," Jason replies and flashes Beth a stone look before taking a swig of beer.

"Less than an hour ago you were prepared to let him fuck me."

"That was Angel business. It doesn't count."

"Okay, Jay. Whatever you say," Beth responds before taking a swig herself.

"Well?" Jason pushes.

"Well what?" Beth teases, the cocaine has given her false courage.

"Do you still fancy the nigger?" Jason exclaims slowly and robotically.

"You're the only man for me, Jay. I wouldn't look at another because there is no one like you," Beth gets worried by Jason's ice-cold attitude.

"Good! Now let's see what this stuff is like," Jason says casually as he loosens up and opens the wrap left by Stan on the kitchen table.

"Careful, Jay, that stuff is crazy, and you rarely take it," Beth advises as Jason taps out some of the cocaine onto the mirror.

"I've only got to look at your eyes to see that. Your pupils are so big they make your eyes look black."

"Here," Beth gets up and passes Jason a vegetable knife, which Jason uses to quickly and expertly chop the cocaine on the mirror then forms a neat line not even half the size he would normally do when he samples cocaine he is buying to sell, he believes dealers that use the drug themselves recreationally are just snorting profits. Beth rolls a new twenty-pound note and passes it to him and he snorts the cocaine immediately then sits back in the chair.

"This is the real shit. There's nothing close to it on the streets. The stuff we get can't touch it," Jason says after a few moments.

"But this is the stuff before Stan cuts it, so it's got to be good. You said that there's no better quality stuff on the streets than what you guys are pushing."

"No, there ain't. So although Stan is not moving the stuff quickly he must be making a fortune out of it. He probably turned his hundred k's into at least four. The nigger's not as stupid as I thought he was. And now he wants to get religious? A drug dealing, pimp holy man, that's a new one on me," Jason sits back and takes a swig of beer as he reflects on what he has just learnt.

"If this Dafa stuff has affected him so much there's got to be something to it, Jay," Beth breaks the momentary silence.

"Maybe there is, maybe there isn't. I'm an Angel and there's no room for it in my life. You do what you want with it but leave me out, unless, that is, if you learn how to turn lead into gold," Jason comments, his mind buzzing from the effects of the cocaine.

22.

It has been over three weeks since Stan's return from Europe and Marcus is happily having dinner at home with his wife, Marie, when he gets a call and retrieves his phone from an inside jacket pocket.

"Marcus?" Valentina asks abruptly.

"Valentina, what a pleasant surprise," Marcus replies as he gets to his feet and makes his way into the kitchen so as not to bother his wife or, more importantly, allow her to listen in on the conversation.

"Nikita wants to change the payment arrangements with the black guy in England."

"What! Why? I spoke to Stan a couple of days ago and he said he had already deposited seven-hundred thousand pounds. Isn't he dealing quick enough?" Marcus is alarmed by the fact Stan may have lied to him.

"No, Nikita is happy with the return so far but the money laundering laws they are bringing in affecting offshore companies and banking are going to cause the cash deposits to be scrutinized a lot more closely than we would like them to be so the cash has to be paid directly to us in future," Valentina flippantly informs Marcus.

"And how is that possible?"

"Why am I calling you, Marcus?" Valentina replies dryly.

"Oh, you want me to collect it?" Marcus knows it is not a question worth posing but he tries anyway.

"Find out when your man will have the balance of the two million, let us know then you can collect it, okay?"

"Understood, Valentina. When is the best time to ..." Valentina ends the call before Marcus can finish his sentence. He calls Stan immediately to stop him making anymore bank deposits.

"Yo, what's kickin' Marcus?" Stan answers breathlessly after putting down the weights he is training with in the gym and picking up his phone from the end of the bench.

"What are you doing? Can you talk?" Marcus enquires on hearing Stan panting and the loud techno music playing in the gym.

"Sure, Marcus. I'm just working out but there's no one around me, what's up?"

"The Russians don't want you to deposit any more money into the offshore account. You have to keep it until you have the rest of the amount up to the two million..."

"Then what?" Stan interrupts.

"Then I come over and collect it from you. I know they gave you two months but how soon can you raise the amount, I want this out of my way as soon as possible. Maybe if you don't take any cut from it and leave yours till last you could settle it quicker, what do you think?"

"Why should I do that, Marcus?" Stan grows

suspicious over why Marcus is so eager to get his hands on the money although he doubts Marcus would cross the Russians.

"Because it's the bloody Russians, Stan. I want this deal settled with them as soon as possible. And the sooner you do it the more likely they will be to do it again, okay?" Marcus lies since he does not want to oversee another deal such as this.

"No disrespect meant, Marcus, but tell the Russian chick, Valentina, to call me herself and let me know what she wants," Stan retorts.

"Do you know how hard that'll be? She'll probably laugh at me and turn her phone off, that is if she actually answers me," Marcus replies but thinks it could be a way of connecting the Russians with Stan directly thereby leaving himself happily out of this particularly complicated loop.

"If you want me to hand over more than a million in cash to you I want to know there will be no comebacks from the Russians. I don't believe you're a flight risk, Marcus; especially if the Russians would be after you, but who really knows any man?"

"Okay, Stan. I'll try and get hold of Valentina now. Make sure you're available to answer your phone somewhere quiet soon, just in case she answers my call and then, even more unlikely, calls you."

"Will do, Marcus, and I'll call you back if I hear from her," Stan answers optimistically, he would like to talk to Valentina again.

"What now, Marcus?" Valentina answers impatiently.

"I've just informed Stan of your new requirements and I'm not sure if he believes me," Marcus uncharacteristically admits failure.

"Now, I wonder why that could be, Marcus," Valentina taunts.

"I've no idea, he just said he wanted confirmation from you before he hands over the cash to me."

"Okay, send me his number," Valentina demands as she sits at the bar getting drunk alone in Nikita's dacha on the outskirts of Moscow. She feels neglected by and resentful towards Nikita who always has something more important to do than spend time with her.

"Hello?" Stan answers as he gets into his car not recognizing the country code or number.

"Is that the sexy black man I met in Vienna?" Valentina asks seductively.

"Yo, I mean hi, Valentina, right?"

"And you are Stan?"

"Yeah. So Marcus actually asked you to call me over the payments. I never thought he would. It's not that I don't trust him, I just wanted to be on the safe side. You know it's a lot of dough."

"You're better off not trusting Marcus in any way. Nikita uses him because Marcus knows if he does anything wrong he's as good as dead. It's much more reliable putting your trust in fear than in people."

"I follow the same principal myself, Valentina, but obviously not on the scale Nikita does," Stan tries to sound businesslike and intelligent to Valentina.

"Would you rather give the cash to me in person, Stan?" Valentina asks knowing full well how Stan will answer. She found Stan physically attractive on seeing him in Vienna and would not mind getting to know him more intimately even if it bothered Nikita, which Valentina knows full well it would not.

"What! You mean you come and get it yourself?"

"I don't expect you to come to Moscow, Stan."

"Wow, man! That would be great, when will you come?" Stan enthuses.

"Whenever you've got the money, Stan. Nikita said five or six weeks, what do you say?"

"I could make it in four if you're desperate," Stan is desperate to please Valentina.

"There's no need to rush things, Stan. I'll arrange a shopping trip to London in five weeks. We usually stay at the Savoy in Hyde Park, do you know it?"

"I have never stayed there but I'm sure I can find it, Valentina," Stan replies a little deflated on hearing Valentina say 'we' and she picks up on it immediately.

"I usually go with Nikita but this time I'll only be with my bodyguards, Alexie and Nikolai. You met them before, in Vienna, remember?"

"How could I forget them," Stan remarks before thinking and regrets it immediately since he considers he has just admitted that Alexie and Nikolai are physically superior.

"Yes, they look after me well, Stan. Now, you can meet me with the money at the hotel. I know we said five weeks but, to be sure, call me when you have the full amount and I'll be there in the next day or two, okay?"

"Sure thing, Valentina, how..." Valentina ends the call before Stan can reply fully. He is left a little perplexed over exactly what Valentina may want from him apart from the money when she does not have enough respect for him to even say bye. He makes a call to Marcus.

"Hi, Stan, so she really called?" Marcus answers quickly and goes back into the kitchen.

"Yeah, and you won't believe it," Stan pauses.

"What? Stop playing games," Marcus asks impatiently after Stan pauses.

"She wants me to give her the money personally," Stan answers triumphantly.

"Shit, she must really have the hots for you," Marcus replies and relaxes in the wave of relief that flows over him.

"Do you really think so, Marcus?" Stan asks, desperately wanting to hear what he so desires to be true after Valentina was so dismissive of him at the end of her call.

"What exactly did she say?"

"When I told her it wasn't that I distrust you but I needed to be sure she asked me if I would like to give it to her personally," Stan does not wish to embarrass Marcus by telling him what Valentina said about trusting Marcus.

"Where and when?"

"I told her I could manage it in four weeks but she said there's no rush and she would make a shopping trip to London in five weeks and that I should meet her in the Savoy Hotel to give her the money."

"If it's a shopping trip she will probably have Nikita with her, so don't get your hopes up, Stan," Marcus says fully knowing what Stan hopes for.

"No, she said she'll be with her two bodyguards, she more like pointed out that she would only be with her bodyguards so I thought, maybe she wants some intimate time with me. What do you think?"

"Only time will tell, Stan, only time will tell," Marcus replies unable to disguise a chuckle as he does so, relieved to find himself out of the loop.

"Till next time, my old friend, ciao," Stan ends the call not knowing or caring whether he will speak to Marcus again now he has direct access to Valentina. He sets off for home in a joyous mood. Anticipation of meeting Valentina has dulled his nagging gut feeling that all is not as it should be and that he may be taking a wrong path in life.

"Hi, sugar, what you lookin at, nah, don't tell me, Zhuan Falun?" Stan asks as he enters the apartment to find Lizzy sat at the table, pre-occupied with her laptop. Despite initially setting out to find out what Falun Dafa is all about, Lizzy finds herself becoming ever more fascinated and submerges herself in its teachings.

"You know the Egyptian pyramids?" she asks seriously as she looks up from the screen at Stan.

"And?" Stan replies nonchalantly as he hangs his jacket in the hallway. He does not want to leave the high he is on created by the thought of meeting Valentina and what possibly might happen between them to be replaced by the now almost permanent nagging background realization that he is not living a true existence and must ultimately change his ways and the more he learns of Falun Dafa the stronger the feeling grows only relenting when his ego is massaged and his strongest desires seem obtainable.

"Well, they were not built by man. Maybe man but not men from this civilization. Scientists say they were built by ancient Egyptians and their Hebrew slaves because they have no other answer that could possibly be something they cannot prove, so they feed us this bullshit even though the stones cannot be dated. And do you know they found the remains of a nuclear reactor in Africa that is two billion, get this, billion years old. Scientists excuse is that enriched uranium must have existed then, just more bullshit. They refuse to accept anything they can't prove by their scientific rules and are therefore limited and restricted by them just like some idiots believe we developed from apes. And the complexity of the human body..."

"Whoa, woman, whoa. I just got home and I need some relaxation," Stan interrupts as he sits down on the sofa with a cold bottle of sweet, strong, German beer.

"I thought you wanted to learn about this. I only started to look at it because of you," Lizzy answers dejectedly.

"I'm sorry, sugar, it's just that my head is full of shit from today and I need some peace to process it, besides you're more into this Dafa thing than I think I ever could be," Stan lies as much to himself as to Lizzy, he is drawn by the truth he senses in it but his ego constantly fights against it and the prospect of bedding Valentina is feeding his ego very well.

23.

He waits until his girlfriend has left for work then Roger Facey sits on a sofa at home counting out fifty and twenty pound notes on the coffee table in front of him. After reaching the required amount, fifty-thousand pounds, he stops counting, pushes the uncounted stacks to one side and makes a call to Sergeant Andy Price.

"Roger, are you calling to tell me some good news?" Andy answers just after getting into his car to go to the station.

"Yeah, I've got your final payment. Do you want to

come and collect?" Roger answers emotionless despite the fact he was able to move the drugs faster and at a better profit margin than he initially imagined he could.

"Well done, my man. I'll be there in twenty minutes," Andy answers enthusiastically and Roger ends the call.

During the drive over to Roger, Andy contemplates the implications of what he has pulled off and realizes he cannot spend his windfall as he would like to without bringing unwanted attention to himself from the very establishment he works for and Her Majesty's Customs and Excise - the tax man. Despite this he also contemplates coercing Roger into arranging another deal with Stan, not for the purpose of arresting Stan but for the purpose of extorting Roger's profits once again.

"Come on up," Roger says into the intercom and releases the door to the building for Andy.

"You've got it nice and warm in here," Andy says on entering the apartment to which Roger has left the door ajar.

"Yeah, still not the Caribbean though. But I guess you can afford to take a long holiday there now," Roger replies and nods towards the coffee table as he leans back against the wall, arms folded across his chest. Andy stuffs the five bundles of ten thousand pounds apiece into an empty laptop case and zips it up. He assumes the amount will be correct as it has been on his previous four collections.

"Well, you shifted the gear pretty quick, Roger," Andy tests the water.

"Yeah, because I want this business between us, finished. I got rid of it so quickly I had to take a loss after paying you," Roger lies.

"But I'm afraid it's not finished, Roger."

"What the fuck! I know the fifty grand I've given you, for the fifth time now, ain't goin to a policemen retirement charity. Haven't you made enough out of me?"

"Apart from the cash you had no choice but to give me I said you have to set up another deal with Stan, remember?"

"Yeah, but I thought that was just bullshit about another deal with Stan and that you would leave me alone after I paid you."

"You thought wrong, Roger. Now set up a new deal with Stan, just like the last."

"You don't get it, do you, Andy? Stan sets up the deal if and when he's got too much stuff to push himself. And he ain't made any kinda suggestions that he does or will do."

"Have you paid him all you owe?"

"Of course I've paid him. I paid him before I paid you. You might put me in jail but Stan would put me in the ground. You dig?"

"Contact him anyway. Tell him you can move another twenty-five kilos…"

"Are you on somethin, Andy? Stan ain't gonna have another twenty-five k's left himself, I'm sure," Roger interrupts incredulously.

"How do you know he doesn't have another trip to Vienna planned?"

"Vienna? You talkin about Vienna, Austria?" Roger asks, confused

"That's where Stan collected a hundred kilos of coke from the Russian Mafia, so we believe."

"Whoa! Stan's dealing with Russian Mafia! He must be feeling brave."

"Stupid, more like. We believe some of them have connections right to the top, like Putin, even," Andy comments.

"If you have such good information why didn't you just arrest him when he entered the country with the coke?"

"Don't you think we would have done if we knew where and when he was coming in?"

"Yeah, Stan's a real sly one. Look what he did to me with the speed boat."

"Exactly, that's why you have to set up another deal with him."

"You mean you actually want to arrest him?"

"I would like nothing better, that is, apart from making another two hundred and fifty grand," Andy decides to tell Roger what he is intending.

"If you're not gonna arrest Stan and you want to earn money out of his coke, that makes you basically a dealer yourself, but you're using me to do all the dealing and take all the risks," Roger says indignantly.

"Okay, Roger. This is what I'll do with you. Instead of taking the two fifty off you I'll only take one fifty. Therefore you get to make a profit too. Or would you rather me arrest Stan and confiscate the coke. I won't bother arresting you I'll just let Stan know that you set him up for the arrest and you told me yourself how vengeful Stan's brother would be. So which do you prefer, Roger, making some money or looking over your shoulder until Stan's brother catches up with you?" Andy asks knowing it is not really a question.

"Like I said, the problem is not me moving the gear, it's Stan supplying it. He only contacted me on this occasion because he had more than he could move himself. I can't make him deal with me when he doesn't have to, I wished I could now that you're gonna let me take a cut," Roger plays along.

"We won't know until you ask him, so give him a call."

"Now?"

"Yes, now. And put him on loudspeaker so I can hear what his answer is," Andy replies scornfully and Roger makes a call to Stan.

"Yo, Roger, what's up? I thought our business was finished," Stan answers while Lizzy massages his shoulders and back as he lies face down on the bed at home.

"Yeah, it is but your gear went so well I was just wondering…"

"If I've got anymore," Stan cuts in.

"Obviously."

"No, afraid not my man. It's all been assigned," Stan replies in a relaxed tone.

"Is there any chance you'll get anymore?" Roger makes the enquiry more for Andy's benefit than his own.

"You know better than to ask such questions, Roger. How do I know you're not trying to set me up? Why do you think I took so many precautions when we did the deal last time when I transferred you the gear?"

"You approached me first, Stan."

"Yeah, sure I did. And I'll approach you again if ever I have a surplus, okay?" Stan ends the call.

"Told you, Andy. Stan calls the shots when he's the supplier."

"Ah, shit!" Andy growls.

"Can't you find out if and when Stan might make another pick-up in Vienna from whatever source you found out about his last visit?" Roger is intrigued by the fact Stan obtained a supply in Vienna, albeit through the Russian Mafia but still one of the last places he could imagine a major drug deal going down. He is also curious about the chances of Stan taking on more than he can move again since he would be more than happy to help out Stan in moving the cocaine again but next time without Andy taking any of the profits.

"No chance to ask since we have no idea who the snitch who told our snitch is. We don't know why he gave the information. The only reasons that come to mind is a vendetta with Stan, or possibly they were dealers themselves and didn't want Stan to flood the market. Since we haven't nicked Stan I don't think whoever they are, are going to give us any more info on Stan and anymore deals he might have come up, that's why I got you to call him," Andy answers and exhales deeply.

"Looks like we're fucked, then," Roger, not regrettably, wants to draw a closing line under the situation with Andy.

"For now, Roger, just for now. Let me know the first thing you hear about Stan and another surplus he might have to move, understand?" Andy says as he goes to leave.

"You'll be the first to know; Andy, you have my word, ciao," Roger answers with a surprisingly skilled performance of sincerity as he lets Andy out of the apartment. After closing and locking the door he goes to the small bedroom that he uses as an office, but usually surfs internet porn in it. He is jubilant to see the spy-cam and sound recorder have captured his meeting with Andy in every detail perfectly as it did on the four previous occasions when Andy picked up money from Roger. Now he has the ammunition, if needed, to keep Andy off his back for the foreseeable future. Although it may have been possible to blackmail Andy with the first recording and therefore possibly not give him anymore payments Roger considers it the best course of action to stay on amenable terms with the policeman since he is unsure how Andy would react if confronted with the recordings and has come to the conclusion that they should only be used in the event of serious developments, such as a strong possibility of going to prison.

Stan drops the phone on the mattress and turns over to face Lizzy.

"Roger must be short on supplies," he says as he pulls her down towards him and kisses her passionately.

"Are you going to get anymore?" Lizzy asks as she releases herself from Stan's embrace and sits upright on the edge of the bed.

"I don't know if they'll offer another consignment. I guess I'll find out when I pay them off in London," Stan casually answers.

"I thought you had to deposit the money into some offshore bank account for them."

"I did but they changed it over a week ago. I have to give them the balance of the two mill personally when I've got it, which will be in about a month," Stan retains his casual manner not wanting to alarm Lizzy or provoke her interest in his visit to London.

"And if they do offer you more?"

"Well things are going pretty good so far, Roger is eager for more and my posse is moving it fast, if I do another shipment I could buy something really fancy for us to live in," Stan encourages Lizzy to encourage him into doing another deal if one comes up, which he is not confident of after the change the Russians have called for in the payment method but hopes he might convince Valentina when they meet, but uppermost on his mind is what might happen between him and Valentina when they meet. With all the money he is taking and the anticipation of meeting Valentina, Stan's ego is not struggling too hard against feelings of guilt and wrongdoing although they have not disappeared.

"Not so long ago you were feeling bad, even guilty about what you're doing and now you want to carry on?" Lizzy asks unable to hide her dismay. She has become enthralled by Falun Dafa after reading Zhuan Falun and carrying out the exercises daily. The sensation of the turning of the wheel in her abdomen after such a short time of practicing is enough solid proof for her to believe in the practice. Initially keen to learn from her she senses that Stan is increasingly suppressing his enthusiasm for learning about Dafa. She correctly believes he is afraid to submerge himself in something that may well change his whole attitude towards life and the way he leads it because he believes that things could not be much better than they are panning out at the moment and he is far too attached to the crest of this particular wave to lend his attention to anything else.

"Yeah, I know, Lizzy, but I feel that I have got to look after the here and now. I mean, what are we, our relationship? It's the here and now, should I forget about it, forget about how I feel about you, to follow something that might, and it's a big 'might', benefit me in some afterlife? Okay, it might make me healthier and live longer but why would I want to live in a way I would have to, to practice Falun Dafa and basically give up everything I enjoy?" Stan tries to find the words that might excuse his denial of something he finds difficult to deny and also threaten Lizzy into leaving the subject alone. This is difficult for him since the proof of witnessing the light when Jack was practicing, the telepathic contact with Jack in what at first appeared to be a dream and now Lizzy's experiences as a new practitioner all stack up against what he wants to pursue and only lend the occasional nagging gut feeling he has more credence. From what he has learnt from Lizzy he realizes that everything he lives for would have to go if he were to seriously follow Falun Dafa and although he does believe it is something that has a real effect on practitioners he does not want to live a life he considers practically monastic and wait until he dies to realize the full potential benefits as described in Zhuan Falun if, in fact, they do transpire.

"Does this mean you don't want me to teach you anything more about what I learn?"

"There's no point, Lizzy. You go ahead with it but I don't have the time or inclination. I've got to concentrate on building something good for us in this here and now material world. Or has Falun Dafa got to you so much that you don't want a nice house, nice car, clothes, exotic holidays?" Stan is surprised by himself for genuinely wanting to provide Lizzy with the better things in life as he considers them, his focus not completely on himself anymore, is it love or another expression of the effect Dafa has on him? He is not sure.

"It has gotten to me enough to say that I wished I didn't long for those things but don't forget, I'm only a beginner," Lizzy answers forlornly.

"So in the meantime I'll build something for the two of us and you just let me know when you don't want anymore," Stan answers and taps Lizzy on the nose with a forefinger.

"Don't patronize me, Stan," Lizzy angrily pushes his hand away from her face, which takes on an expression of stone as she looks him in the eyes.

"Whoa, Lizzy. I didn't mean to, seriously," Stan replies in a shocked tone.

"I'm sorry. It's just that I hoped we could go on this spiritual journey into something I feel is so true together," Lizzy says apologetically.

"Look, Lizzy, I love you, I love my life and where it's going and it's all part of the whole thing. My reputation, my power, my money and my lifestyle, all are increasing. Don't try and stop me now because before I give it up for some kind of religion I'll give up you. I respect your opinion and what you do is your prerogative and I'll let you get on with it but don't interfere with what I do. Don't tell me anymore about Dafa. If it makes you feel any better, I believe there is something to it, the problem is that my belief is not strong enough to make me leave everything behind. If it were, what should I do? Get a job as a fitness trainer - no offence meant - a security guard maybe, or a garbage collector? You know I couldn't exist like that," Stan says and looks questioningly into Lizzy's eyes.

"Okay, Stan, I guess I was living in a fantasy world to even consider you might practice but I feel I have to carry on.

And that could mean that one day I might have to leave you," Lizzy replies with equal gravity.

"Que sera, sera, Lizzy," Stan conveys his understanding of the situation.

24.

My inner vision witnesses such colors of dazzlingly beautiful lights as I seem to be flying at a tremendous velocity through some huge ethereal tunnel, all sense of my physical body abandoned in this orgy of visual overload, even the sensation of the throbbing of the wheel between my arms has abated. Where am I going? Could I be journeying deeper into my inner eye or third eye as some cultures refer to it? The acceleration is so intense, as I believe I can travel no faster so I do, unrelentingly. My exhilaration is such that I am unable to comprehend the fact that I am merely practicing. Although the seat of the third eye resides in the pineal gland located deep in the brain and is the size of a pea it may be the equivalent of several thousand miles across in another dimension, could I be travelling deeper into it?

"Jack! Jack! Snap out of it," Nora aggressively interrupts the exercise by shouting and roughly shaking my arm.

"Hey, calm down, I'm only doing an exercise. What's the panic, is there a fire in the house or something?" I am bewildered as Nora appears to be on opening my eyes and lowering my arms.

"I got home after dropping Tasha at kindergarten over an hour ago. You never replied when I told you I was back but then I saw you in that position and I decided to leave you to it even though I've never known you hold that position for so long..."

"So why interrupt me now?" I interrupt Nora.

"Beth's on the phone, well she was, I don't know if she hung up or not. I have been trying to get through to you for ages! You were more gone than when I found you on the terrace the other morning. What on earth is happening to you, Jack?" I am already lifting the handset as Nora finishes her sentence.

"Hi, Beth, you still there?"

"Of course. How could I hang up when I heard Nora doing all that shouting, what's going on? Are you okay?" Beth asks out of surprised concern.

"Yeah, I'm fine. Just got a bit carried away doing my Dafa. What's up? You need me to harbor another drug dealer?" I cannot resist reminding Beth that she was not completely truthful when telling me about Stan's real reason for visiting me.

"Hey, you know I'm really sorry about that but I had no choice," Beth replies apologetically.

"Okay, Beth, forget about it. So what do I owe this honor? You must have called me more in the last month than you did the previous year," I exaggerate but not that much.

"I had a visit from Stan recently..."

"What?" I cut in.

"Yeah, I actually asked him to. I was feeling low and had run out of my anti-depressants and since he had mentioned that I could try his gear before, I thought why not?" Beth has to unwillingly keep up her pretense of taking anti-depressants in case Stan mentions it to her brother.

"You're taking anti-depressants?" I know Beth has used many drugs in her life but all recreational and none of them legal.

"Like I told you, I haven't touched the gear for years but when I get low I use anti-depressants. My doctor reckons I've got an imbalance among neurotransmitters or something like that and gives me a prescription."

"You never cease to surprise. I would have thought that the doctor would be the last person you would turn to for depression, maybe a bottle of scotch but never a doctor."

"Yeah, I guess I must be getting old."

"So you called me to let me know you have seen Stan again?" I am a little confused as to the reason for Beth's call.

"It was what Stan told me about your Falun Dafa thing. Is it true?"

"Maybe if you tell me what he told you I could let you know if it is true or not, Beth," I want her to say in her own words what Stan witnessed and experienced. My anticipation in savoring the payback of all the years of her ridiculing Falun Dafa is hard to disguise.

"He said that you told him he must have been a saint or something in a past life and I find it hard to believe you said it."

"Yes, I said it," I play with Beth and wait for her next utterance.

"Why on earth would you say that?"

"Because that's what I believe."

"Okay, Stan told me that he had some kind of dream whereby he communicated with you, is it true?"

"Yes, it's true."

"So how does that make him a saint?"

"Is that all he told you?" I want Beth to ask about the lights Stan saw while I was practicing."

"No, he also mentioned something about a light around you when he saw you doing your Dafa stuff."

"And that coupled with his telepathic ability is why I think he must have been of very good character in a previous life." I am finding this moment quite enjoyable.

"How so?"

"If you had listened to me in the past and at least learnt a little about Falun Dafa you wouldn't need to ask. If someone has paranormal capabilities that come naturally it is probably because they haven't departed from their true self as much as the great majority of us here on earth have. And the closer you are to your true nature the less black karma you have created, I say black karma but Falun Dafa refers to all karma as black and the opposite, what might be referred to as good or white karma is called virtue. The karma encases our true selves, our virtue, and restricts what we call supernatural abilities although they are perfectly natural to our true selves. Stan retains more capabilities than the great majority of us, even I can't see the light and I've been practicing for some years, which means that he hasn't created as much karma as the great majority of us. And for him not to have created this karma indicates that he must have been of excellent character in a past life, especially considering how bad a character he is in this one," I answer trying to camouflage my 'I told you so' attitude.

"I see, I think. But if he was such a good character before this life why is he so bad in this one?"

"I can't answer that, Beth. Nearly all of us get worse rather than better as we journey through life after life conditioned by humanity - now there's a funny word 'humanity'," I pause and wait for her to ask.

"Why is it funny?"

"Because when we think about humanity and being human we automatically class ourselves as civilized and caring when in fact we are human because we have been cast down from our true divine status time after time from one level down to the next accruing more and more karma for wrongful deeds and thoughts until we finally reach here, earth, the last stop before complete annihilation."

"What do you mean by 'last stop' and 'annihilation', Jack?"

"Exactly what I said. We all come from a divine place, every living thing that exists on this planet does. Because we never aligned ourselves with zhen, shan, ren, which translates into truthfulness, compassion, tolerance, the very nature of existence, the universe at its most fundamental level, we have descended until we reached here and there is no lower realm than this unless you consider being reborn as an animal, insect, plant, whatever, they still all reside on this planet. And it's only due to the great compassion of some divine beings that this place exists, created by them to give us one last chance at redemption. When I read Zhuan Falun it all makes complete sense to me, it's just very hard not to be an everyday human being, and the harder it is means the more karma you have to cleanse yourself of. People with immense karma do not even try to cleanse it because they don't believe in such things as cultivation and karma. They are so gone in this materialistic mirage and cut off by their karma that they laugh about such things. They have been and carry on to be so blind to what they do that they consider the following of religion and the practicing of cultivation methods such as Falun Dafa to be something carried out by fringe lunatics and fanatics. They can only see as far as what the next benefit may bring such as a pay rise, a lottery win, a new car they long for, etc. I've tried to explain it to you before, Beth, but you were never interested so I reasoned you were not ready yet, like this is your first time here, as I think it could be Stan's, or you are too far gone down the path of no return because your karma is too dense to let you see any way out and so you laugh at it because your past deeds are too many and too severe to allow you to see anything outside of what you desire or hate. In which case, people like you, who make up the large majority, I pity, despite the fact you laugh at people like me. But in truth, the ones that laugh at such beliefs of ours are the ones to be laughed at if we were to belittle ourselves to be such base human beings as to laugh at such things. It is far more noble to feel compassion towards such lost souls."

"So Stan really met you in a dream?"

"It wasn't a dream, it was telepathic communication, just as real as we are speaking now. I believe something deep within Stan wants me to help him because of what he has witnessed and how I make him feel because I practice Falun Dafa. I've read that spending time with a practitioner can have an effect on an everyday person by healing and putting right what is wrong and after spending time with me in Vienna, Stan told me I made him feel calm but also guilty for what he's done and how he lives. I believe I have that effect on him because I'm a practitioner. Falun Dafa influences things, including people, to become more in tune with zhen, shan, ren even if you don't practice yourself but are in close proximity to someone who does."

"You never had any sort of effect like that on me

when I visited."

"That was a long time ago, Beth. I think and hope that I've developed a lot since then. Besides, you had already closed your mind to Falun Dafa and thought it was a joke whereas Stan never had any kind of a notion about it, and having a notion can blind you to many things. No disrespect meant, Beth, but adding to that you were pretty blind to a lot of things due to the amount of alcohol you put away when you last visited me."

"Yeah, I know but I was pretty strung out about my ex leaving me, that's why I came over to see you, remember?"

"How could I forget, you were on a right downer and tried to escape through the bottom of a bottle. That's why I'm surprised you turn to anti-depressants now."

"So now you have my attention and I want to learn more about this Falun Dafa thing you do," Beth says in an obvious attempt to change the subject but I am not concerned as to why.

"I told you a long time ago, Beth, I am trying to find a way back to myself, my true self. When you are born here, apart from a tiny amount of reported cases, you have no recollection of past lives whether they were here or somewhere else but your fate is already mapped out for you. I was fated to find and follow Falun Dafa and I thought you were not, but who knows, you may be changing your mind," I test Beth's interest level.

"Why would Stan want you to help him and why would you?"

"Because it's only natural to help a soul that genuinely wants to cultivate to higher realms. Stan can only relate to what he knows to be true here, such as power and money but buried under the karma he carries is the knowledge of something divine and it's not buried so deep as to be obliterated from his subconscious and his subconscious is trying to tell me I'm on the right path, I think, but Stan's consciousness is telling him that he lives in the here and now and his ego demands to be satiated with power, money and celebrity. You know Stan better than I do but underneath all his macho machismo and aptitude for violence I sense a kind of naïve innocence, which makes me believe it's his first time here. It's just the circumstances he was born into that have shaped what he is, he knows nothing different."

"Yeah, I guess there were some moments with him that I thought he had kind of fell out of character and even seemed vulnerable but they were very few and far between moments. But when he came to see me to let me try his stuff he actually apologized for the way he had treated me in the past. I was gob-smacked to say the least. That's why I'm calling you, Jack, this effect you have on Stan means there must be something to your daffering, sorry, I mean you practicing Falun Dafa. When I called him to ask him round he said that I better make it worth his while, so, knowing Stan as I do I thought he wanted to fuck me in exchange for the coke, but no, he just wanted me to tell him what I know about Falun Dafa, which, as you know is not much. In fact Stan told me more about it than I know. I did look at the link you sent me but there's just so much stuff out there and I was wondering if you could point me in the right direction."

"Sure, Beth, who knows, maybe you are actually ready for it, fated for it. I started by reading Zhuan Falun and then Zhuan Falun volume two and watched video presentations of the exercises to learn how to do them, which are pretty simple. Then I read the Great Way of Spiritual Perfection, which details the exercises in depth, their exact purposes and how to perform them. I read them constantly and discover something new in them each time I read them. I only hope you find it as enlightening for the soul as I do."

"Are you going to get in touch with Stan about Falun Dafa again?"

"No, he's welcome to call me but I don't think he will. Even though he has witnessed and experienced a great deal of proof that there is something to Falun Dafa he is too attached to his existence to risk giving it up for something he cannot see immediate benefits from. It's a great shame but maybe on his next time around he will be born into an existence more conducive to spiritual practice, whether it be Falun Dafa or something else, even Christianity, let's hope for his soul's sake he finds a real purpose to his next life."

"So why do you say he needs your help?"

"I said or meant deep in his subconscious he senses I can help but his conscious mind and especially his ego fight against accepting that there is a far more deeper meaning to his existence other than notoriety, power and money. I believe he is a fledgling human at the very beginning of what could be many appearances on earth depending on how he conducts himself in future lives. Will he shed his karma or increase it, only he can find the answer to the question during his reincarnations."

"Okay, Jack, I'm full for now but I promise you I will start to research Falun Dafa and begin the exercises."

"You have no reason to promise me anything, Beth, I can only inform you of the benefits of practicing Falun Dafa.

Whether you take it up is your decision and in your fate but if you do, it would make me happy to have been the one fated to have passed on the knowledge of its existence to you."

"There you go again, Jack. I told you I'm full. I'll give you a call once I feel I'm qualified enough to speak to you about Falun Dafa. But I don't know how long that's gonna take me."

"Okay, Beth. Hope to hear from you in the not too distant future, ciao," I end the call.

"That sounded pretty heavy, what was it all about?" Nora asks from the kitchen, which surprises me since she never wants to talk about anything related to Falun Dafa.

"Beth had a strange conversation with Stan and wanted to know if what he told her was true."

"Yes, I gathered as much from what you said but what actually happened between you and him when he was here?" I had never talked about Stan's visit to Nora and she never asked. I was only too happy to see the end of the subject of Stan's visit since it had been such a traumatic event in Nora's eyes.

"Not a lot, really. I took him to the triangle and the next day he left to do his business. I made it clear to him that he couldn't come again and he accepted it. On the Sunday morning he saw me practicing unawares to.me. He saw my aura and the wheel rotating between my arms. I was more surprised than he was."

"What do mean, Jack?" Nora asks with a seriousness I find quite alien since it is in connection with Falun Dafa.

"You know of auras, we all have them but Stan could actually see mine while I practiced and he saw the light of the wheel I've told you about that I can feel spinning between my arms while I was doing the same exercise as the one you just interrupted when Beth called."

"So does Stan believe in this Falun Dafa thing you do?"

"Not enough to give up his lifestyle I'm afraid, despite the fact he has so much proof of its existence."

"But the light could have been caused by some other inexplicable phenomena, why should he believe it's caused by your practicing?"

"Because I told him in detail the morning you found me practicing in the snow on the terrace, as you've just mentioned I was in a trance like state then."

"Okay, so how exactly did you talk to him?"

"Telepathically: He thought he was dreaming and I wasn't sure if I was too although I knew I was practicing. But he called me the next day conventionally and we discussed what we had discussed during our telepathic communication."

"Why didn't you tell me about it? It's amazing!"

"It's not all that happened to me practicing on the terrace that night, Nora. Before coming into contact with Stan while I was practicing in the lotus position I levitated until I saw well over the terrace wall despite the fact my eyes were closed," I divulge not knowing if I'm doing the right thing in doing so by the laws of Falun Dafa, but she is my wife and I am being truthful.

"But, Jack, this is incredible. Why don't you create a blog on it or write a book?"

"Because as soon as I showcase any supernatural abilities they will be taken from me, besides I am nothing compared to more serious practitioners not only of Falun

Dafa but other cultivation methods too. Look at the miracles Jesus performed, and there are still individuals alive today capable of such feats but you would never hear of them because that is not their purpose in life it's just a byproduct of their cultivation or religion if you like." Since Nora shows such an interest I know by mentioning Jesus she may well want to engage further and perhaps become more accepting of Falun Dafa.

"But Jesus showed his abilities by performing those miracles."

"Jesus was on the level of a Buddha. He was enlightened and able to perform miracles where and whenever he wanted. To direct people onto a path towards their own enlightenment, heaven, as you Christians call it, he performed miracles for all to see. Jesus was so karma free that he was able to take the burden of all humanity and cleanse it to a certain extent and he died in doing so. And that I learnt from Falun Dafa, not the Bible."

"And what about saints that perform miracles?"

"Going on what I've learnt I guess it's the same scenario. They are so karma-free that they are closer to their natural selves and therefore retain supernatural abilities. We, on the other hand, are so encased by the karma we have created over many lifetimes in different realms that we are blinded to reality and consider anything really real to be supernatural. We are enslaved by this material world because all we do is fear and grasp at things we can see feel and touch, whether it be a cancerous growth showing up in an x-ray or winning a huge lottery prize. They may be at the two extremes of what we don't and do want to experience but they are just an example of the duality we form in our minds here on earth. This duality represents attachments, desires and aversions. I know it's crazy to think it is possible to rid ourselves of them because they are exactly what make us human, but being human is not such a good thing since it's been our wrongdoings that have made us human."

"Well, Jack, for the first time I begin to see what you see in Falun Dafa. I'm sorry I have been so closed to it in the past and made fun of you for practicing it. It doesn't give us much of an optimistic outlook on this life but you've always been a pessimist anyway, so I guess it suits you. I appreciate the fact that you, or Falun Dafa, recognize Christianity, which can only strengthen my belief in it although it doesn't need to be strengthened. So no more put-downs or ridiculing of your practice from me anymore."

"Thanks, Nora. I appreciate it. I should celebrate! You and Beth have decided to take my practice seriously and even on the same day."

"But, still. I don't want you to indoctrinate Tasha, okay?"

"Of course I won't. But when she gets to the age whereby she can make her own decisions. I hope you don't do the same with her and the Catholic Church, especially if she shows an interest in Falun Dafa, okay?"

"Okay, Jack, she'll be allowed to make up her own mind," Nora replies but I am far from sure she will be able to stick with her words in the years to come.

25.

Theresa Hogan hugs her son, Rory, as he enters the large dining kitchen on the morning of his twenty-fifth birthday and hands him a BMW key-fob.

"Happy birthday, Rory. It's on the driveway," she says as Rory's face lights up and he hurriedly leaves the kitchen and runs down the corridor to the entrance hall of the imposing country mansion set on the outskirts of Dublin. He hurriedly opens the front door of the house. The new red BMW four wheel drive has been parked at the bottom of the stone staircase that leads up to the house entrance. Rory descends the steps and enters the car. After a few moments of examining the interior he looks out to see his mother standing at the top of the steps smiling down on him. He gets out, runs up the steps and gives her a kiss on each cheek.

"Mother, this is the best present I've ever had. I can't believe it. Let's take it for a drive now," Rory enthuses.

"It's not just a birthday present, I thought you deserved something special for doing so well in getting your law degree. Let me get my coat," Theresa answers and disappears into the house as Rory goes back down the stairs to the car. She soon returns and joins Rory who has already started the engine and made himself familiar with the rudimentary functions of the car.

Theresa ultimately sacrificed what she considered to be her future when she decided to go ahead with the pregnancy. It was nine months of torture not knowing what color the baby would be. Although her father was furious at the news he respected her for not aborting the child in secret and her mother was very sympathetic. She had told her parents that the child she was expecting was the result of a short relationship and drunken night with one of her fellow students at Manchester University and that the student in question had demanded she have an abortion because he had no intention of being tied down for the foreseeable future.

This, her father understood and decided to provide for Theresa and her child so long as she lived in the family home and led a virtuous and respectable life to which Theresa agreed and upheld bringing Rory up in a traditional Catholic manner. She knew her parents, especially her father, would never consider or accept the fact she had slept with a black man and gambled the child would be Jack's and if not then she would have to admit that her short term boyfriend at the university was not white. Fortunately Rory was born with the pale skin, dark hair and blue eyes of his father. Theresa had never experienced such relief in her life as she did when her newborn was put into her arms by the midwife.

Rory was a healthy, athletic, intelligent and congenial child, which made it easier for his mother to come to terms with her sacrifice. From the very beginning she pushed him to learn how to read and write, do math and take an interest in science to the point he was always the most advanced from kindergarten right through to grammar school when his knowledge of what he decided to study far surpassed his mother's.

Although Theresa did not encourage Rory's relationships with the opposite sex she never discouraged them either until her father died three years ago leaving his substantial construction and property business to Theresa and her mother. Due to his good looks and privileged background Rory was never short of interest from female students. He dated several of them but never became so serious as to live with any of them. When his grandfather died Theresa made it clear to Rory that his first duty was to maintain the family legacy. Rory realized that with his knowledge of company law and the sound foundations the company his mother controlled he had potentially a very bright future ahead of him and decided to concentrate the majority of his effort into learning the family business and law and so put his own immediate desires on hold, until now.

"So, are you happy with the car, Rory?" Theresa asks as Rory takes the BMW at speed but sensibly through a winding lane from the family home and has not spoken.

"Of course, Mother. How could I not be?"

"It's just that you seem a little reticent, Son."

"Do you remember my twenty-first?"

"Rory, how could I not? You are my son," Theresa replies as a feeling of dread envelops her.

"When you gave me Jake, you asked if I was happy with my horse and of course I was but I asked you, since it was my twenty-first, to tell me about my father. You told me that at the time it was difficult but you would tell me sometime in the future. Well, we're another four years into the future, Mother, so how about it?" Rory slows the car a little in order to concentrate on his mother's response.

"The reason I didn't tell was because I lied to your grandfather, my father, about the exact circumstances of my pregnancy. I told him I had a short term steady boyfriend at Manchester University and that I accidentally got pregnant but my boyfriend was nowhere near ready to have a family and told me to abort you and this I couldn't do. Your grandfather respected me for that and so took us in and I eventually became the CEO of the company since I have no brothers or sisters and my father, your grandfather, wanted the company to stay in the hands of the family and for you to eventually take over," Theresa explains as she feels her stomach sink.

"So why did you lie? Who was my father? What did he do?"

"Slow down, Rory," Theresa interrupts, "one at a time, please."

"Sorry, Mother."

"Your father's name was Jack Jones, a man about town. Good looking, you take after him in your looks but thankfully not his character, flash car and plenty of money and plenty of women. I had known him for quite a long time but he was never a steady boyfriend. I didn't want a steady boyfriend. The only reason I was in Manchester was to get my degree then come back to Dublin and work for our company. Don't get me wrong, I wasn't promiscuous, I just drank too much one night and found your father hard to resist, I had fancied him for some time," Theresa reflects and feels nauseous at the thought of Rory ever knowing that Jack was not the only one she slept with on the night of his conception.

"Does he know about me? Does he know I exist?" Rory asks with a little desperation evident in his voice.

"No, Rory, he doesn't. There really was no point in telling him, he would have run a mile from that type of responsibility. His family owned clubs and betting shops and he enjoyed his work getting to know the ladies in the clubs far too much to let himself get tied down.

"Do you think he would want to see me if he knew of my existence?" Rory's question wrenches at Theresa's heart and she has to fight to hold the tears back.

"I don't know, Rory, I really don't know. As he was when I knew him, I would doubt it very much. He wasn't much older than I and he was promiscuous, very promiscuous and had no shortage of admirers. But since that time I have changed a lot, I have grown up. I had to pretty quickly when you came along. Maybe, after all these years Jack has grown up too," Theresa answers as she reflects further on Jack.

"Do you know how to contact him, Mother?"

"No. I haven't been in touch with anyone who knew Jack since I left Manchester when I found out I was pregnant. I don't think he was the type to take to social media but there's no harm in looking on Facebook, Twitter, whatever. If he is still in the family business you might find him in some club or gambling company," Theresa replies in the hope that Jack cannot be traced and if he can then by some miracle he will have become respectable and responsible and show Rory kindness and sympathy if ever they were to meet.

"Thanks, Mother," Rory says as he slows the car and turns into a field gateway.

"What are you doing, Son?"

"I'm going to look for my father," he answers enthusiastically as he reverses the car back out of the field opening and then pulls back onto the lane facing the opposite direction to go home. Theresa resigns herself to the fact that she is unable and has no right to try and stop her son searching for his father.

On entering the house Rory goes straight to his room and turns on his computer. After over three hours of trawling the web's social media platforms and people search sites he decides to call it a day and joins his mother who is busy at the stove in the dining kitchen.

"Any luck?" Theresa asks apprehensively as Rory takes a seat at the generously proportioned dining-table.

"I'm afraid not, Mother. I cannot find a thing on Jack, John or Johnathan Jones involving the nightclub or betting business and it's a pretty a common name in Manchester and the rest of the UK. Did he have a second Name?"

"I don't know, Son. Like I said, he was more like an acquaintance, not someone I was that close to," Theresa answers as she relaxes in the wave of relief that rolls over her.

"He can't have just disappeared!"

"Rory, if you want to pursue your father until the end you must prepare yourself for what you might find at the end. He was living a pretty volatile existence when I knew him," Theresa tries to prepare Rory for the worst scenario.

"What do you mean, volatile?"

"Being involved with the nightclubs and the scene that goes with them, he was obviously mixing with the kind of people I would rather you didn't."

"What are you trying to say, Mother?" Rory asks as Theresa turns from the stove to face him.

"Rory, you are a disciplined, sensible and serious young man but I know you are not a naïve one. Drug dealers, bouncers and pimps, and perhaps even worse were part of your father's life. What I'm saying is that if he is dead, which he could well be if you can find no trace of him, it may not have been through natural causes," Theresa explains and takes a seat next to Rory feeling great shame at not telling him about Stan who might be traceable and know what happened to Jack but she knows her shame would be all the greater if ever Rory were to learn from Stan that his father was not the only person she slept with on that night. A night at first she considered ruinous but her love for Rory soon extinguished any regret.

"I do not want to believe that, Mother. Is there nothing else you can tell me about him or a close friend of his, perhaps?" Rory's question only serves to intensify Theresa's shame.

"Rory, he had many friends and associates, he was working in the nightclub business but I don't remember their Christian names never mind their surnames. The name of the best night club he and his family ran was called the Hacienda and it was in a district called Deansgate but nightclubs have a short lifespan so I'm sure it no longer exists but you can check it out. It's online," Theresa says motioning to her laptop on the table. Rory pulls it towards him and goes to work on searching for the Hacienda in Manchester.

"There's some stuff from people who went there a long time ago, but nothing about the owners," Rory remarks after a few minutes.

"Rory, don't you think it's better to get on with your life and not be distracted by something that will probably only bring you grief?"

"Grief and, perhaps sorrow, I need to know, Mother."

"I don't think anyone, including myself, has the right to stop you."

"I guess my last resort is a private detective."

"You had better look for one in Manchester, they may well have heard about him from times gone by," Theresa relents to the fact her son is determined to go as far as he can in finding his father.

"Okay, Mother. I'm going back upstairs to search for one," Rory says getting to his feet to leave the table.

"Don't be too long. I'm cooking us beef bourguignon.

It will ready within the hour."

"Great! I'll be down for it."

"Hello, Invisible Investigations. Can I help you?" a young woman's voice answers the second call Rory makes, he hung up on the first when got a recorded message asking to call back the following day.

"I hope so. My name is Rory Hogan and I'm looking for a missing person."

"Hi Rory, my name is Stacy and I'm responsible for your case placement. Could you please give me all the details you have on the person and the reason you want to trace them, such as debt recovery, inheritance, etc. so I can pass it to the most suitable investigator?"

"Sure. I'm looking for my father."

"Oh, really. I can see you're calling from Ireland, did your father come to Manchester?"

"No. My mother got pregnant with me by him in Manchester when she was at university there. I have never met him but would like to. After getting pregnant my mother came back home to Dublin. It's an irrelevant story but she has only just given me details about him now on my twenty-fifth birthday."

"Happy birthday, Rory. So what can you give me?"

"Oh, thanks. His name is Jack Jones and he is in his mid to late fifties and some twenty-five years ago he worked in his family business, which was bookmaking and nightclubs, based in Manchester. One of the nightclubs he ran was called the Hacienda in Deansgate."

"Well, that's certainly no longer there. Our office is not far from Deansgate and I often socialize there."

"Yes, I know it doesn't exist. I tried googling it and

found nothing but stuff from years ago. I've also tried to find my father on the net but came up empty handed. This is why I'm calling you."

"We have an investigator with us called Peter Tomlinson. He's almost sixty and has lived in Manchester all his life. He was a police detective before he joined us and I think he's the right guy for your case. He may have even visited your father's club, if not I'm sure he will have heard of it and maybe your father too. I'll pass on what you have told me and you should expect a call from him within the week."

"Thanks, Stacy, I look forward to his call."

"Have a pleasant, what's left of the day, Rory, bye."

"Thank you; Stacy, I will," Rory ends the call.

26.

Stan is wearing his favorite black Armani suit and cashmere overcoat as he saunters into the reception hall of the London Savoy with a bulging black and white Nike sports bag.

"I am expected by a Miss Valentina Petrov," Stan asks the immaculately dressed, effeminate looking slim middle-aged man at the reception desk.

"Your name, please, sir?" the receptionist asks in a voice which matches his appearance as he picks up a desk telephone and looks Stan up and down in a manner Stan does not appreciate, especially since he finds male gays abhorrent.

"Just tell her it's Stan from Vienna, she'll confirm," Stan replies with an overly obvious false smile.

"There's a, er, gentleman at the desk in reception, ma'am, who says you are expecting him. He says he is Stan from Vienna. Should I show him up? Thank you, ma'am,"

The receptionist replaces the receiver and looks at Stan for a long moment as though loathing to communicate.

"Well?" Stan asks without hiding his irritation.

"Third floor, suite 316. Would you like someone to take your bag, sir," the receptionist asks but Stan ignores him, turns his back and heads towards the lifts. He nervously knocks on the door of 316.

"My sexy Englishman has finally arrived, come in, please," Valentina remarks on opening the door wearing little more than a smile and the flimsy see-through negligée leaves very little to the imagination.

"Sorry I'm late but finding somewhere to park took me almost as long as it did to get to London," Stan replies taking in the magnificent view of the Thames and the London Eye on the opposite bank as he enters the suite, thankful of the distraction.

"Would you like some champagne and caviar?" Valentina asks as she takes an open bottle of Dom Pérignon from an ice bucket on the bar and sits on one of the high bar stools as she replenishes her glass.

"Um. Yeah, sure, Valentina," Stan answers and holds up the sports bag.

"Just leave it on the floor there, take off your coat and sit next to me," she replies and pats the stool next to her. Before Stan seats himself there is a knock at the door.

"Should I get it?" he asks.

"Yes, it's only Alexie. He's here to check your delivery. Just give him the bag."

"Okay, Valentina," Stan obeys as he picks up his sports bag and opens the door. Alexie gives him a smile, takes the bag and leaves. "Is he not staying in your suite?"

"No. Sometimes I need privacy, especially when I have special guests," Valentina explains and raises her glass. Stan sits next to her and does likewise.

"Cheers or should I say 'Nastroyeniye?'" Stan says lifting his glass.

"I don't care what you say, my sexy Englishman, I'm not interested in your voice," Valentina replies before emptying the champagne flute in a single gulp then places her hand on Stan's crotch, which makes him feel intimidated, he has never experienced such an approach from a woman before, especially not from such a powerful and untouchable one. He empties his glass and refills it, embarrassed that he cannot manage an erection.

"Would you like some more, Valentina?" is all he can think of saying.

"Well, it feels like you can't do anything else with me apart from offer me a drink, and I thought you black guys were real studs," Valentina goads when she feels no change in Stan's flaccid manhood, which only serves to make Stan ever more so.

"Sorry, Valentina, but I never quite expected this, it's a little fast, even for me," Stan attempts to excuse himself.

"Drink some more and come to the bedroom with me, perhaps you can relax more there," Valentina suggests.

"Let me take a draw first, that's what really relaxes me," Stan answers as he retrieves a perfectly rolled joint from his inside jacket pocket, "would you like to try?"

"I feel horny already, but I know it can make you feel very horny though I haven't smoked it for years," Valentia answers and returns to the bar stool next to Stan as he lights the joint.

"This is real good shit," he remarks before taking a lung full, "as good a draw as the gear you supplied me is a snort. Your turn," he chuckles after holding his exhalation sometime before passing the joint to Valentina who inhales on it deeply as Stan downs another glass.

"Come, now, my sexy Englishman," Valentina beckons on getting off the stool, champagne and joint consumed. Feeling more than relaxed, Stan gets off his stool and follows Valentina into the bedroom.

"Whoa! What's this?" he exclaims on entering the room to see the king size four-poster bed has been equipped with leather arm and leg restraints attached to the posts.

"Don't you like bondage, Stan?" Valentina replies as she discards her negligée and stands naked by the side of the bed.

"Whatever turns you on, Valentina," Stan mumbles as he starts to quickly undress.

"Now, that's more like it!" Valentina says with a big grin on seeing the huge erection Stan is now sporting.

"A good spliff always does the job for me. Now, how tight do you like to be tied up?"

"I've never thought about it for myself but I like my man to be tied up really, really tight," Valentina explains with a mischievous grin and Stan gulps.

"You serious?"

"I'm always serious, my sexy Englishman. Come and get on the bed I'll take care of the straps." Stan has never been the submissive one in the bedroom before but finds the situation quite a turn-on especially under the influence of the cannabis. "No, no, turn over, I like it doggy-style," Valentina instructs when Stan lies on his back.

"How do we do this?"

"Don't worry, just get on your hands and knees, I'll do the rest," Valentina replies and Stan does as she says.

"Whoa, please!" Stan exclaims when the ankle straps are tightened to the extreme.

"Don't be a baby, I'll get under you now," Valentina replies and fondles Stan to keep him hard before climbing underneath him and then fixing the wrist straps as tightly as she can. Then she raises her buttocks into Stan's crotch, which for Stan, has the desired effect, hardening his erection further and he enters slowly with the help of her guiding hand. Valentina sighs and Stan starts to vigorously thrust into her as she comes up to meet him on each thrust, she begins to scream in ecstasy, a testament to Stan's virility and performance, so he believes until he feels the stern grip of hands on his hips followed by something hard against his anus. He stops thrusting as he feels the penetration first gradual, Valentina raises her rear as far as she can so there is no escape for Stan but then a sharp thrust so deep he worries about internal injuries and cries out in agony. He tries to look back and sees Alexei approaching him with a piece of duct tape between his hands. Someone firmly takes hold of his head, presumably Nikolai, from the other side of the bed and Alexei covers Stan's mouth with the tape. Valentina retains her position high and rigid and the pain Stan is experiencing leaves no room for any thought or reasoning as to what is happening and who is raping him, the pain obliterates all.

When it finally ends Stan hears a very harsh but female voice that is not Valentina's, who remains rigid and silent beneath him, speaking in Russian. He sees Alexei who has been leaning against the wall, arms folded and smiling during the ordeal, nod, unfold his arms and start to undo his trousers as he walks around towards the rear of Stan and hopes beyond hope that Alexei is not going to do what he thinks he is going to do. His hopes are soon dashed as he feels Alexei penetrate him, although not painful compared to the initial rape Stan has the luxury of being able to digest the fact he is being raped by a man and feels such shame and remorse at leading a life that has culminated in this situation that he would do or give anything to turn back time. Is this the result of black karma? He wonders. As Alexei pumps away another figure enters Stan's vision. He sees the back of a tall slim female dressed in a skin tight black latex cat-suit and wearing six-inch stilettos, her straight black hair falling to her waist. As she turns to take the place at the wall where Alexei stood Stan is horrified further at the sight of the thick twelve-inch black dildo she is wearing, blood still dripping from the tip of it. She looks like something out of a kinky horror film with her large dark eyes and deep red lipstick. Stan does not know which is worse, the sheer physical pain the dominatrix inflicted on him or the utter humiliation and degradation of being raped by a man.

"Did Nikita satisfy you as much as she satisfies me, Stan?" Valentina says loudly and laughs a maniacal laugh.

"I think he's too preoccupied enjoying Alexei to answer you, my lovely," Nikita says casually with a smile and folds her arms as she leans against the wall in the same way Alexei had done. "Nikolai," she calls across the room and he is at her side in a few seconds. They speak in Russian and Nikolai laughs and shakes his head. Alexei squeezes Stan's hips as he ejaculates into him then dismounts and fastens his trousers.

"Did you enjoy your present from Alexei, my sexy Englishman?" Valentina says as she climbs from beneath Stan who has tears rolling down his cheeks then she violently tears the tape away from his mouth.

"Why? Why? What have I done to deserve this? I've done everything you asked," Stan sobs.as he looks at Valentina who joins Nikita, who still has the dildo strapped on, standing at the wall with Alexei and Nikolai. They mutter to each other in Russian and Stan fears for his life. They could easily get away with his murder. Give him a lethal dose of whatever and say he did it himself.

"I was bored, nigger and since I will not require your services in future I thought I would take this opportunity to sample some black meat. Now if you don't shut up I'll have to persuade Nikolai here to give you a good servicing too, despite the fact he prefers to use his massive manhood on ladies," Nikita castigates and Stan buries his head in the pillow. After quietly conversing further in Russian the four leave the room. Stan hears a shower turn on and then giggling from Nikita and Valentina. Half an hour later the shower is turned off and Stan can hear Nikita and Valentina talking in Russian and wonders if they are arranging his demise. After about another half-an-hour, Stan is finding it difficult to judge time, Nikita and Valentina enter the bedroom, laugh at Stan when he looks at them and leave.

"Rodney, I'm afraid we have left rather a mess in the suite. You may well enjoy the scene so please see to it personally and bill me in the usual way," Nikita says to the effeminate receptionist before she leaves the hotel foyer with Valentina on her arm and Alexei and Nikolai following behind with the luggage. Rodney, who has looked after

Nikita on many occasions over some years, immediately places a subordinate in charge of the desk and hurries to suite 316 in eager anticipation of what he might find. In the past he has witnessed and joined in orgies with gays and lesbians, but sometimes he has had to have drunken, drugged and occasionally naked unconscious people of either sex discreetly removed and often paid off.

"What do we have here?" Rodney says on entering the bedroom and seeing Stan fastened to the bed and spread-eagled face down, a large patch of blood between his upper legs. Rodney takes out his phone and starts filming Stan from behind. He films closely between Stan's thighs and then gradually along his torso up to his face. Stan strains his neck to see who has entered the room although he is confident of to whom the effeminate voice belongs.

"Oh, Jeez, stop fucking filming me," he demands. Although relieved the Russians have not returned he hates to be seen in his predicament by a homosexual, especially one who is filming him in all his degradation.

"Now, that's not a very polite way to greet your savior," Rodney says, overemphasizing his effeminate speech and positioning his phone directly in front of Stan's face.

"Can you please stop filming?" Stan realizes that he is in no position to demand anything.

"I don't know about that. Perhaps the press would be interested, especially the gutter press. It might be worth some money to me. I can see the headlines now, 'Black Boy Buggered in Five Star Hotel', or maybe, 'Silly Boy Sodomized', or perhaps, if you are musically inclined, how about 'Rapper Raped'? No, I have it, 'Negro Nancified'."

"You're not serious?"

"Why? Would it be bad for your reputation? You look like you can handle yourself. I bet you have quite a name as a man not to cross, a man to be feared, where ever it is you come from. If your homies see you like this you'll never live it down…"

"Will you please undo the straps?" Stan interrupts.

"Well now, since management would not be happy with me if this got out and my job and reputation are worth more to me than a handout from some newspaper I suppose I better let you go and get this place cleaned up, unless, of course you want to call the police," Rodney answers confident in his belief that calling the police would be the last thing Stan wants.

"The police! Are you kidding me?" Stan answers.

"Okay, I'll just put this in safe keeping before I attend to you," Rodney answers then saves the video and places his phone in the safe of the suite.

"What are you going to do with the video of me?" Stan asks on Rodney's return to the bed.

"Don't worry, black boy, I'll only use it to amuse myself when my boyfriend is away. Now let's set you free. Do you feel okay? You have lost a lot of blood, Nikita is not usually so brutal. You better get to hospital casualty when you leave here," Rodney says with genuine concern on realizing just how serious Stan's injuries appear as he unfastens the straps binding him.

"You know her?"

"Of course I know her, I have done for years. Why do you think I'm here now and not the regular hotel cleaners?"

"I guess it figures. So you never considered going to the papers or calling the police?"

"Of course not, I was just playing with you."

"Don't worry about the blood, it just looks a lot but it's not really," Stan replies from his knowledge of blood-letting of other people as he turns to sit up, which he finds extremely painful.

"You can use the shower while I try and make it less obvious what happened here," Rodney offers.

"Thanks, what's your name?"

"Rodney, and you are Stan from Vienna. Though I have never met anyone less Viennese than you are, Stan."

"It was where I first met Valentina and her bodyguards, a business transaction."

"I won't ask what that transaction was but I'm sure it wasn't something strictly above board."

"I appreciate your help and discretion, Rodney."

"Come on, Stan, you know I have to do it for Nikita. Now, unless you want a blow job, please shower and make yourself scarce," Rodney says and winks at Stan who immediately gets to his feet and makes his way to the bathroom.

27.

"Your father was quite a well-known face amongst the nightlife of Manchester when I was a policeman, but that was about a quarter of a century ago. Things change faster in that industry than they do in most. Clubs, bars and pubs come and go, close and change as do the owners and customers," the bespectacled, balding but otherwise fit looking Peter Tomlinson says to Rory inside the modern office of the private detection agency he works for.

"Why did he leave Manchester?" Rory asks.

"Well over twenty years ago, within a matter of weeks all the entertainment venues and betting shops closed down. The family business, which your father was a major part of, went bankrupt. I think your grandfather salvaged something but he had remarried after the death of his wife, your grandmother, and he has since died over ten years ago. Your father ended up broke and left the city for a location somewhere cheaper to live since he was unemployed. Knowing the image he had I wouldn't be surprised if embarrassment had something to do with his disappearance from the Manchester scene. He was very flash and egotistical, many guys were jealous of him because of his position and his looks, of which you have been lucky enough to inherit."

"So my mother tells me," Rory replies and coughs in an effort to hide his embarrassment.

"I've exhausted my usual means and the latest I could find out about him was that he worked for a mail order catalogue company in Bolton as a computer programmer, but that was well over ten years ago. He resigned from there and basically disappeared."

"A computer programmer?"

"Yes, the government offered extra benefits for the unemployed if they took part in some further education and your father enrolled in a government sponsored programming course. It took him a while but he did finally get a job as a programmer."

"So he must have found another job as a programmer, why can't you find him?"

"He never gave a reason to the last company he worked for, he just resigned and disappeared."

"So that's it. You can't find him?"

"Hang on, Rory, I haven't finished. Like I said, I have a big advantage over most dicks you could hire. I know or knew of some of the people your father mixed with, he also had a sister but she moved away some time ago and I can't get anything on her. I have spoken to all the people I could trace and they know nothing of where your father went but I still need to find the one I think could help."

"And who might that be," Rory replies while wondering if Peter is being completely honest and not just trying to prolong his investigations in order to inflate his charges.

"A black guy called Stan, Stan the Man as he was known and still probably is."

"If he's still around why haven't you contacted him?"

"Stan was pretty close to your father. He used to be a kind of body guard, about six foot four and full of muscle. I believe he also supplied your father with drugs and probably many more things. I saw him with your father many times. No one would dare cross Stan, as they still don't I believe. He was and still is involved in drug dealing, prostitution and protection but it's difficult for me to approach him directly."

"But if you know all this why can't you get hold of him?"

"Because I shouldn't know all of this. I only know it through old associates from the police force. I can't go banging on his door because if I do and Stan starts squealing about data protection and the like, it's not like he's on the electoral roll, and wants to know the source from which I got my knowledge of his living accommodation he could screw up my relationship with the police who are priceless to me for information."

"So what is your next step?"

"I'm sorry, Rory, but I'll need to put some hours into visiting the places I know he uses and try and make a direct contact with him by coincidence so to speak. Tell him I want some coke and then ask about your father. That's my plan, roughly put. I don't know how long it will take and how many hours I have to put in but I need you to trust me if you want me to go ahead."

"Okay, Peter. If you haven' got anything within a week call me so I can reassess the situation," Rory says getting to his feet and shaking Peter's hand.

That night, Peter, uncharacteristically scruffily attired, visits The Moon Under Water, which is surprisingly quiet even for a Tuesday night. He orders himself a large scotch and water and slouches at the bar observing the dozen or so customers. A table of after work office drinkers, a couple at a small table who seem to have a grievance with each other and three guys standing at the other end of the long bar in jovial conversation. Finishing his drink Peter is about to leave when a very tall dreadlocked Negro wearing a long black leather coat enters the bar. Peter knows him to be Roger Facey, a known drug dealer and pimp.

"Roger?" Peter asks as Roger approaches the bar.

"Who wants to know?" Roger replies defensively and looks Peter up and down having no idea who Peter is.

"Could I have a quiet word?" Peter replies and nods towards a small table away from any customers.

"Sure, a Bacardi and coke, a large one," Roger replies and saunters over to the table in the belief Peter wants to score some drugs. Peter orders the drink and another scotch for himself.

"Large enough, I hope, I made it a triple," Peter says placing the drinks on the table and sitting himself opposite Roger.

"So are you looking to score?" Roger asks just above a whisper.

"No, Roger, I just want some information."

"What! Are you a cop?" Roger asks at normal volume.

"No, my name is Peter Tomlinson, I'm a private investigator," Peter replies and shows Roger his ID.

"So what do ya wanna know and what's in it for me?"

"I only want to contact Stan, Roger. I thought I might see him in here. Can you tell me where I can get hold of him?"

"What's in it for me?"

"I don't know what your relationship with Stan is but it might be beneficial to him. If you do him a favor he's going to owe you one," Peter says the first thing that comes into his head that might encourage Roger.

"It's strange you should ask about Stan now because he has disappeared from the scene this past week. You're not the first to ask me where he is. I've tried calling him to ask what's going on but he is not answering his phone or to the messages I've left. If you do find him maybe you could let me know where he is," Roger answers since several of Stan's regular customers have been coming to Roger because they cannot get hold of Stan. Although happy to supply them he is fascinated by what has happened to Stan. If Stan is dead then he will be able to massively increase his market without repercussions from Stan.

"Shit! I guess I better look somewhere else," Peter says to himself aloud, finishes his scotch and gets to his feet."

"Sorry I'm no help, man. But it is strange Stan has disappeared. I wonder what's happened to him."

"No worries, Roger. Enjoy your evening. If I do find him I'll tell him you were looking;" Peter answers and leaves the pub. Left with no alternative he goes to Stan's apartment.

"Yes, who is this?" Lizzy abruptly answers the building entrance intercom.

"I have some important information for Stan," Peter talks into the speaker.

"What about?" Stan, who has been listening and petrified it might be someone from the Russians, takes the handset from Lizzy.

"It's about Jack Jones," Peter answers casually.

"Okay, come on up, fourth floor, if you didn't know," Stan says feeling relieved on hearing the name of the only person who seems to bring him some sort of comfort in an inexplicable way when he dwells on him while going through such inner turmoil. Peter eagerly enters the apartment building not knowing why but happy none the less that Stan has agreed to see him without even asking him his name. He concludes Stan must be in some sort of crisis.

"So who are you?" Stan asks filling his open doorway with his muscular torso exemplified by the tight vest he wears as Peter exits the lift.

"Peter Tomlinson, pleased to meet you," Peter extends his hand on approaching Stan, which Stan shakes.

"Okay, Peter, what's this about Jack?" Stan replies as he walks into the living room and Peter follows. Under

Stan's instruction Lizzy has made herself scarce and huddled herself away in the bedroom.

"Please, Stan, if I may ask first. Why are you hiding? I just spoke with Roger Facey and he tells me that he can't get you and several people have asked him what's happened to you. To be honest I'm glad to find you still alive and okay."

"Take a seat, Peter. Do you want a drink?" Stan asks as he loosens up.

"Sure, what do you have?" Peter asks not knowing if Stan means a drink in the form of a coffee or a scotch.

"Well, I got beer, I got rum and I got brandy," Stan answers to Peter's satisfaction.

"Could I have a brandy, if that's okay?"

"Sure," Stan replies as he opens a cupboard and retrieves a bottle of Remy Martin V.S.O.P.

"The reason I'm here is because Jack has a son that he probably doesn't even know exists. To be honest he doesn't know he exists."

"Whoa! How old is this guy?" Stan asks as he gives Peter the drink and motions him to take a seat.

"Twenty-five. Jack would still have been here in Manchester when he was conceived," Peter replies taking the drink and sitting down.in the armchair close to the coffee table. Stan pours himself a cognac and sits on the sofa on the opposite side of the coffee table from Peter.

"Do you know Jack?" Stan asks since Peter knows Jack lived in Manchester.

"No, not personally but I used to see him around all those years ago. I remember seeing you too, Stan, Stan the Man they used to call you but you had hair then."

"Those were the days before I started going gray but I'm still known as the Man," Stan chuckles.

"Do you know where Jack is?"

"Yeah, but tell me who the mother of this son is," Stan is curious to learn if he knows the mother.

"Theresa Hogan. She's out of a wealthy family in Dublin. From what Rory, he's the son, tells me, she never had a serious relationship with Jack. I'm not surprised knowing the image Jack had at the time," Peter reflects.

"Shit, man! Are you sure Rory's not kinda coffee colored?" Stan asks on remembering the night he and Jack slept with Theresa. It had stuck in his mind due to Jack's uncharacteristic disappointment at not being able to contact Theresa again after she went back to Dublin.

"No, Stan. Rory looks very much like his father, Jack, and is a qualified lawyer working for the family business," Peter replies as he digests the fact that Stan probably also slept with Theresa.

"I remember the night, Jack and I stayed at her place after partying. Jack was pretty pissed-off that he couldn't contact her again afterwards. He must have really been into her. She disappeared back to Ireland and that was the last he heard about her."

"It must have been when she found out she was pregnant, poor woman. No disrespect, Stan, but she must have gone through hell not knowing who the father was."

"No worries, Peter. Jack lives in Vienna now, has done for years. He went out there for some high paying programming contract. He's married to an Austrian professor he has a kid with. Don't think he'll ever be comin back."

"How do you know all this, Stan?"

236

"I tracked down his sister, Beth, since I hadn't spoken to Jack for over twenty years and got the information from her. Why haven't you tried her before me?"

"Because I remembered Jack and you from the old days and it just seemed convenient to get hold of you in Manchester. Beth moved away and I didn't put that much effort into finding her."

"She wasn't too hard to find, but I guess I know the right people to ask. Anyway, I went to see Jack about a couple of months ago..."

"What! You actually met him so recently?" Peter interrupts.

"Sure."

"In Vienna?"

"I just told you he lives there, man. I stayed at his place for a night because it was convenient for me."

"So what was your reason to see him after such a long time?

"Peter, you say you used to know what we were like over twenty years ago. And I'm guessing you're not so naïve as to think that at least I, if not Jack, haven't changed much over that time, so why do you think I wanted to meet up with someone I hadn't seen for decades?"

"Business?"

"Bingo!" Stan exemplifies and holds his hands up as he mentally relives his pain and degradation at the hands of Nikita and Alexei.

"Okay, Stan, I'm not going to ask you what business you went to see Jack about. I just want a contact method for his son to follow up."

"I'll take him to meet his father," Stan answers in a

decisive tone.

"You what?" Peter sounds perplexed.

"Listen, Peter, you asked me why I was hiding. I'll tell you why. You know what I was, what I am still. I thought this was the only kind of life open for me to progress. To cut a long story short I had some experiences in Vienna when I was with Jack that made me reconsider who I am and what I do. I was able to push it to the back of my mind most of the time until something terrible happened to me that really made me realize I was on some fucked-up path to destruction. Jack tried to sort of council me on my future, tried to encourage me to lead a clean law abiding life, but I didn't want to know. I need to talk to him again and be in his presence, just being close to him made me feel like I was being healed, from what, I don't know but I felt it."

"But you said you were doing business with Jack, which I'm sure wasn't legal, so why would he try and persuade you to go on the straight and narrow, Stan?"

"You've got it wrong, man. I kinda coerced him into letting me stay at his place, he wasn't involved in what I was doing. I could tell he was pissed off about me being there. I had a deal going down with some Russians in Vienna and I couldn't stay at any hotel because of registration so I basically forced Jack into letting me stay at his place. I did promise him I wouldn't show up again."

"So if he didn't want you around, why do you think he'll let you visit him again, especially with a son he never knew he had?"

"His son is probably a reason why he would let me see him. You see Jack is not the Jack you or I remember him as. He's turned kinda religious."

"Austria is a very Roman Catholic country. Has his wife got him into it?" Peter's question makes Stan laugh.

"No, no way. He's not religious in that way. He follows something called Falun Dafa."

"Falun what?"

"It's a practice within the Buddhist school but it goes further than Buddhism. Do you know anything about Buddhism, Peter?"

"No more than the next guy in Manchester I guess."

"What about karma?"

"Bad karma - bad luck. Good karma - good luck?" Peter looks at Stan quizzically and wonders what the hell is going on having a conversation with a drug dealing gangster about Buddhism.

"No, that's totally wrong. Now what Falun Dafa tells us, or better still, shows us is that all karma is bad and we create it for ourselves. The opposite is virtue, which is a matter that consists of infinitely minute particles so small that we couldn't comprehend; forget protons, neutrons and quarks. It is created by the Fa and our true selves are made of it, which means that the Fa, or God if you prefer that expression, created us. Now us being us: selfish, arrogant, greedy, jealous, you name it, have created karma through these negative traits. Since we have created karma and not the Fa it is nowhere near as fine or divine as the virtue created by the Fa so it has no way of penetrating it and turning it foul. Our only hope of redemption comes by removing all the layers of karma we have covered our virtue with over countless lifetimes. This means that we are all virtuous beings under the layers of karma we have created, which has caused us to be here on earth, the last stop or dustbin if you like, before total obliteration. Now if we don't want to be completely destroyed we have to find a way back to our virtuous selves, and this ain't easy, especially for someone like me. You see the main objective to getting back is relinquishing all attachments to this existence..."

"Hold on, Stan, hold on," Peter interrupts in an effort to slow down the overload of information.

"Sorry, I just got carried away because I'm so excited about it. I was drawn to it as soon as I learned of it from Jack but fought it until that something terrible happened to me to make me look at it deeper. My girlfriend, Lizzy, has really got into it after I asked her to take a look. She practices it herself and has been teaching me about it these past days since whatever happened to me happened. Hey, Lizzy, come out here!" Stan shouts and Lizzy, who has been listening, comes into the lounge.

"Peter, nice to meet you," Peter says as he gets to his feet and extends his hand out to Lizzy, surprised by her natural beauty and elegant but casual appearance as she approaches him. He did not know what to expect Stan's girlfriend to look like but he never thought she would look anything like this.

"I'm pleased to meet you, Peter. As you now know, I'm Lizzy," Lizzy responds and takes Peter's hand. Peter is further surprised by her perfect speech and fights the blush he feels coming on as she gently but firmly shakes his hand.

"The pleasure is all mine, I assure you," Peter verges on the obsequious, which makes Stan laugh.

"Do you really want to know about Falun Dafa, Peter?" Lizzy asks giving Peter a piercing look as she seats herself next to Stan on the sofa and Peter sits back down in the chair.

"No offence meant, Lizzy, Falun Dafa sounds fascinating, but something a little above me. The only reason I'm here is to ask Stan if he knows how I can contact Jack."

"Yes, I know, about an unknown son Jack has, I was listening, and from my lover's inference this son may well have been his," Lizzy says and squeezes Stan's knee as she throws him a mock grimace.

"Hey, sugar, I was young and carefree, not to mention, off my head," Stan responds in his defense.

"Please, the last thing I want is to cause any problems between you, I just want to find Jack," Peter intervenes obviously concerned.

"Cool it, Peter, Lizzy's just fuckin with us, ain't you, sugar?" Stan looks at Lizzy who just chuckles.

"So, are you really serious about taking Rory to see Jack?" Peter regains his composure.

"Sure, Peter, I don't know of a better excuse to get to see Jack again. The first, which was also the last time I visited him I promised it would be the last. I understood the fact that he doesn't want a black drug dealing pimp around his family. Now the fact that someone doesn't want me around would never bother me usually, if I wanted to be around, for whatever reason, I would be around without taking anybody's feeling into account, even Jack's and we go back a long way. But I saw Jack doing the Falun Dafa exercises, though I didn't know what they were at the time, and he had a beautiful aura around him and I saw like a disc of light spinning between his arms. It wasn't just this that made me feel differently about Jack, the longer I was in his company the more I felt respect for him and I ain't never felt respect for anyone, that and the healing thing I've already mentioned."

"How can you be sure Jack will see Rory?" Peter asks as he wonders if Rory will even go with Stan

"I can't be certain but I'm pretty sure. Like I said, Jack is a different person from how we knew of him, I'm sure he'll feel some sort of responsibility towards Rory. On top of that, when I tell him I have decided to take up Falun Dafa and change my lifestyle he can't stop me from visiting on the account I'm a drug dealing gangster."

"Okay, Stan, I'll put it to Rory, what you want, and get back to you with his answer."

"Don't go to the trouble Peter, just tell Rory my offer and give him my number."

28.

Out of curiosity and the possibility of expanding his market Roger Facey calls the only person he has not yet tried who might know what has happened to Stan.

"Yeah, Andy Price here, who is this?" the sergeant answers sardonically.

"Hi, Andy, this is Roger."

"Yo, Roger, tell me you've got another deal set up with Stan," Andy's tone grows optimistic on hearing Roger's voice and assuming Stan has another shipment coming in.

"No such luck, Andy."

"So why are you calling me at ten at night? Got some info for me?" Andy asks a little deflated.

"I was hoping you could give me some."

"What the fuck are you talking about, Roger?" Andy becomes agitated.

"Lots of Stan's customers have been coming to me for about a week now because they can't contact Stan. I've tried but he never answers his phone. No one has seen his face around town, and I even had a private detective ask me about his whereabouts yesterday. I thought that maybe you had taken him in or know if something worse has happened to him?"

"What did the detective want?" Andy's intrigue is piqued.

"Didn't say, just wanted to contact Stan," Roger replies flatly.

"Shit, Roger. I guess I better pay him a visit."

"You know where to get him?"

"Roger, I'm drugs squad and Stan is the major dealer in town!"

"Hey, I would appreciate it if you let me know what's happened to Stan."

"Why would that be, Roger? Are you concerned about his welfare? Or are you hoping to increase your market exposure if Stan is permanently gone?"

"Back off, Andy, I just wanna know so I can pass it on to all that keep asking. That's all."

"Okay, Roger, I'll let you know what happened to Stan if it's worth knowing," Andy replies and ends the call.

"Who the fuck can that be? Did you order anything, sugar?" Stan, who is lying on the sofa watching TV, asks Lizzy when the intercom to the flat sounds.

"No, I would have asked you if I was getting food. Don't get up, I'll get it," Lizzy answers as she gets up from the table where she has been researching Falun Dafa on her laptop and goes to the intercom handset by the entrance to the apartment. Stan follows her to listen who it is.

"Who is this?" Lizzy asks pointedly.

"I'm really sorry to bother you, miss, but I've been sent by friends to see if Stan is okay since he's not answering any calls..." before Andy can finish his sentence he is interrupted.

"And who are these friends?" Stan asks abrasively after taking the handset from Lizzy.

"Just customers who want to know when they can score," Andy gambles.

"Customers? What fucking customers? I think you've called at the wrong place, man, now fuck off," Stan replies aggressively and replaces the handset.

"Who was that, honey?" Lizzy asks perplexed.

"I dunno, and don't want to know. I've told you, I'm through with the life I led. Could have been anyone but it wasn't one of my clients. Only the big spenders know my address and if it was one of them they would have identified themselves. I've told my posse I'm out but it might have been another dealer or even the law wanting to know why I'm no longer on the scene. I don't know and don't care. I just hope this Rory kid of Jack's will agree to go to Vienna with me."

"Why is going to see Jack so important? We can both learn about Falun Dafa without Jack's help," Lizzy asks despondently. After learning of his ordeal at the hands of the Russians in London, which necessitated anal stitching, and the paranoia Stan exhibits since it happened she is beginning to worry about his mental state and what he might do in Vienna without her holding him up.

"If it wasn't for Jack and what you have taught me

further about Falun Dafa I think I would have topped myself or at least had a nervous breakdown. You know I'm still a nervous wreck, I think if I see him he'll have a calming effect on me and help me consolidate my faith in Dafa," Stan replies and gives Lizzy a forlorn look.

"We can only hope so, my love."

After being rebuked by Stan, once in his car Sergeant Andy Price makes a call to Roger Facey.

"Hi, Andy, have you got any news on Stan?" Roger eagerly answers.

"He's at home and he sounds pretty pissed off, told me to fuck off. Is there nothing on the streets about him?"

"I just got a call from Reggae Man, he deals for Stan…"

"Yeah, I know who he is, what did he say?" Andy impatiently interrupts.

"He said Stan is out of the game. Told his whole posse to get their own suppliers or better still, get religious. No one knows why, he just said Stan was talking very strangely about how he regrets doing what he's done and wants to turn things around in his life," Roger answers questioningly.

"And did Reggae Man want you to be his supplier?"

"Yeah, he did ask if I could push something his way, Andy. But after moving the surplus Stan pushed me as quickly as I could so I could pay you I'm pretty low on supplies myself," Roger lies since he told Reggae Man he would get him whatever he wanted. He is able to offer this after forming an unlikely alliance with the Hells Angels who have agreed to supply Roger, at an agreeable price, with as much cocaine he can sell.

"Have you got any idea why Stan is behaving this way? He's a bit young for Alzheimer's," Andy asks out of genuine interest.

"If I had any idea about what Stan is up to I wouldn't have bothered you, Andy."

"Okay, Roger. Keep me up to date with anything you hear," Andy replies and ends the call.

29.

The extreme nausea abates and the subtle pressure of the rolling sensation against my ears and the palms of my hands subsides as I finish the last position in the standing stance of holding the wheels at either side of my head. It is a great relief despite the intensity of my migraine, which has persisted for over a week now, while I stand, hands overlapping but not in contact just below my navel. I commence the next exercise, my third, penetrating the cosmic extremes sending energy out from the bottoms of my feet and the crown of my head as my hands glide up and down in opposite directions. The tingling at the crown becomes so intense that it is easy for me to imagine it splitting open in another dimension, which I presume and hope that it is despite the fact I should not hope for anything. Even this attachment to desiring enlightenment will hold me back. At the final repetition my right hand stays suspended as far as possible above my head palm down while my left hand raises into a similar but opposite position and I proceed with the double handed body stroke. Again I experience travelling at immense velocity through some dazzling multi-colored spectrum, which appears to only consist of intense hues of different colored beautiful light. A tremendous cracking sound or feeling, it is hard to define and distinguish, reverberates through my head and my migraine instantaneously disappears. My mind is now empty and completely clear, just the vision of light apparent, no thoughts or notions just serenity. I have no choice since there is no decision, direction or desire only cognizance, nothing more. I am completely at peace, time dissolves. Please no, I beg of I know not what on visualizing the image of a young man dressed in a business suit and nailed to a cross. Could it be myself in times long gone by? The young man looks directly at me with a pleading expression, tears rolling, but a plea for what? Is it myself communicating from another dimension and time that I am on the wrong path and should turn to Christianity? Why else would I be on a cross?

"Please let yourself find me, before I die on this cross," the young man asks and the vision evaporates just as quickly as it manifest. My hands automatically stop held high for a moment at the end of the last repetition. I consciously and slowly bring them down until my palms are facing and are about two inches from my abdomen below my navel. I spin the wheel four times to retrieve energy that was expended during the initial phases of the exercise. As I conjoin my hands the lights fade and I'm left with nothing but darkness. I am too intrigued and confused to commence the fourth excise, the Falun Heavenly Circuit, and so sit down to ponder my experience. This vision was obviously not myself since he basically asked to be released from Christianity and I never have been opposed to it. If anything Falun Dafa has made me appreciate it and understand more about who Jesus actually was since Christianity is a form of Buddhism. Who was this person who tried to communicate with me?

30.

Rory is woken by his mother just after eight the morning after getting back from Manchester and his meeting with Peter Tomlinson.

"Morning, Mother, did I oversleep?" Rory asks yawning on rousing and Theresa stops shaking his shoulder.

"No, I wanted to let you sleep since you didn't get back until the early hours, but that private detective you went to see yesterday is on the phone and said it was important. Should I tell him to call back later?"

"Really? No, no I'll speak to him now," Rory replies getting out of bed."

"Here," Theresa passes him his dressing gown, "I left the phone off in the kitchen."

"Thanks, Mother," Rory replies hurriedly slipping into his house shoes and putting the dressing gown on.

"Hello, Peter, are you still there?"

"Rory, hope I didn't wake you but I was able to contact Stan last night and thought you would want to know what he said as soon as possible."

"What, so soon already!"

"Yes, I sensed you were not exactly comfortable with the fact that it might take me some time so I went out to find him last night. It was just as well I did since he has disappeared from the scene recently. I had to use my highest level intelligence source, which I hate doing but I had no choice."

"I appreciate it, Peter, and please reflect it in your expenses. So how did you get him? Phone, email, how?"

"I know where he lives but I'm unable to divulge that information due to its source. I was extremely apprehensive about turning up at his residence but took the gamble due to his apparent disappearance. As luck would have it he was there and let me in and even gave me a drink."

"I'm confused, Peter, why the cloak and dagger story, why did Stan vanish from the scene?"

"On my part, like I said, I can't divulge how I know where he lives and I don't know why Stan is lying low, he just said something terrible happened to him but didn't say what and I wasn't going to push my luck. I was amazed that he even spoke to me."

"Okay, Peter. So what exactly did you talk about with him and does he know where my father is?"

"Now this is the weirdest thing about my meeting with Stan. He says he'll put you in contact with your father, who lives in Vienna, on condition he takes you to see him. He visited him there not long ago."

"What! My father lives in Vienna?"

"Yes, has done for some time after getting some high paying IT contract there. He's married to an Austrian professor and has a child with her. He is living a very respectable life. I've done all the searches I know for him in Vienna and come up with nothing and if he's still contracting he'll probably be hired under a company name and not personally."

"Does he have a boy or a girl?"

"I didn't ask, Rory, but he or she will still be very young."

"So is Stan still a good friend of my father's, does he see him much?"

"It's a little bit complicated, Rory, but to give you the basics Stan still is or was until very recently, the same gangster I've always known him to be. He hadn't seen your father for over twenty years. Then Stan had some kind of business deal with Russians come up in Vienna. He couldn't let his whereabouts be known so couldn't stay in a hotel. He got your father's contact details from your father's sister, your aunt. Stan then basically told your father that he was going to stay at his place in Vienna while the deal with the Russians was done."

"And my father allowed it?"

"Knowing of Stan's reputation I don't think he had much choice, Rory."

"And this Stan wants to take me to Vienna after threatening my father?"

"This is where it really gets complicated, Rory. You see your father has become sort of religious in a funny sort of way."

"Religious and funny don't really mix, Peter," Rory answers as his mind turns to the Roman Catholic Church and its strict authoritarian character, which he feels so constricted and straightjacketed by. Although he believes in a God he does not believe the Catholic Church portrays him truthfully but has kept his feelings to himself for fear of upsetting his mother.

"Let me try and explain. Your father practices something called Falun Dafa. I've looked at it on the net and some call it a cult but it seems pretty innocent to me from the brief look I had at it last night. Stan had some experience and learnt of its existence from your father while he was in Vienna. Now something, which I think was pretty traumatic and related to his lifestyle, happened to Stan. I think Stan wants to change his ways but needs your father to guide him but your father made it clear to Stan he doesn't want him visiting again. Stan basically wants to use you as a ticket to get to see your father. He has asked me to give you his number to arrange things. Do you want it?"

"I don't think I have any choice if I want to see my father soon, Peter."

"Okay, Rory, whatever you ask. It's been a pleasure getting to know you but I guess you will no longer need my services," Peter replies and gives Rory Stan's number before ending the call.

"Did he find him?" Theresa cannot withhold her curiosity as she leans against a kitchen work surface.

"Not my father, Mother. But he found someone who knows where he is. A black gangster from Manchester..."

"Stan the Man," Theresa says barely above a whisper as her look darkens.

"Did you know him?" Rory asks out of shocked intrigue compounded by the expression on his mother's face. A dilemma Theresa considered dead and buried raises its ugly head again. Should she tell Rory how well she knew Stan but leave out the fact she slept with him. If she does Stan might tell Rory himself if there is contact between them and this would be even worse than if she tells Rory herself. Although not overtly a racist one Rory has been brought up in a strict white Roman Catholic environment and he has had no involvement with black people.

"He was a friend of your father's, also his kind of bodyguard too, his minder if you like," Theresa decides not to lie but only give the information Rory asks for in the hope he does not ask for much, especially how well she knew Stan. "He had a feared reputation and known to be violent when necessary. Did he say where your father is now?" Theresa tries to keep the conversation away from herself.

"Not exactly his address, but he did say he would personally take me to see him."

"Is he still in Manchester then?"

"No, my father lives in Vienna now," Rory answers indifferently since he does not know how to feel about the fact.

"Vienna! Do you know what he's doing there?" Theresa exclaims out of genuine surprise but she is also relieved that Stan is less of the topic now.

"Yes, according to Stan he's been there for some time. He initially went to work as an IT contractor but married an Austrian professor and has a child there now."

"Really, I would never have thought your father would become something so conventional as an IT worker," Theresa remarks.

"Yes, apparently he's been doing it for some time."

"And he's still in touch with Stan?" Theresa asks tentatively for fear of bringing Stan back into focus.

"No, they haven't been in contact with each other for many years until recently, Mother. Peter tells me this is why Stan wants or insists on taking me to see my father himself. Apparently Stan had some dodgy deal going down with some Russians in Vienna quite recently and forced my father to let him stay at his place after all the years of no contact with him, what a cheeky bastard. Anyway, while he was staying at my father's he found out about Falun Dafa."

"What on earth is Falun Dafa?"

"It's some kind of religion which my father practices from what Peter tells me and it had a very profound effect on Stan. From what I gather Peter says Stan has had some bad experience and wants to turn to this religion and needs my father's guidance but my father has told Stan not to visit again so Stan wants to use me as a way of getting access to my father," Rory explains and exhales deeply.

"I've very worried about all of this, Rory, what are you going to do?" the severity of Rory's revelation blindsides Theresa.

"What else can I do if I want to meet my father as soon as possible?"

"Why don't you try and look him up in Vienna on the internet before trusting Stan?" Theresa makes a last attempt to stop Rory contacting Stan.

"Peter has already tried and come up with nothing and I'm sure he does a better job with searches than I do since it is part of his job."

31.

Nikita appears naked with a huge freakishly weird green scaly erection, her long raven hair tumbling over her full breasts. She parts her scarlet lips to display shark like teeth and cackles as she takes Stan by the shoulders and turns him, forcing his head down as she does so.

"Now enjoy, as you enjoyed my Valentina," she says before viciously penetrating Stan.

"Wake up, wake up, you're having a nightmare," Lizzy says as she tries to bring Stan to consciousness.

"No more, please, I beg, no more..." Stan mumbles as he comes out of his troubled sleep.

"Was it her again?" Lizzy asks and Stan nods as he sits up in bed, face bathed in sweat.

"When will I get over this?"

"It's only a matter of time, my love. It's still fresh in your mind, besides, it's only karma you are paying off. Why don't you go and do some exercises? That always calms you down," Lizzy puts her arms around Stan and hugs him in an attempt to comfort him but his body is tense. He looks at the clock and feels that even though it is only 03:00 he will not sleep due to his distressed state and so removes her arms and goes into the living room to practice, leaving Lizzy in bed.

He spends half-an-hour on the first four exercises, which for him is quite a long time and he feels good about it. The trauma of his nightmare having faded somewhat since the exercises require that the mind be as free from direction or intention as possible. Despite his physical fitness and strength Stan finds it impossible to get into the lotus position for the fifth exercise to strengthen supernatural powers, the sheer size of his thigh muscles make it a seemingly unachievable task.

"Hey, Stan, you just need to do the exercises more frequently to train your legs that I showed you and you will get there, I promise. You've stopped going to the gym and your appetite is non-existent so your legs will get thinner, which will also help," Lizzy suggests on seeing Stan struggling to get into position as she enters the living room to see how he is.

"I'm gonna have to do it sitting on the stool again, can you get it for me, please?" Stan learnt from Lizzy that it was acceptable to initially practice the fifth exercise on the edge of a seat if the full or even half-lotus position was not possible.

"Sure," Lizzy replies and goes into the kitchen to retrieve a low stool she usually uses to stand on to access the higher shelves in the kitchen cupboards.

"Thanks, sugar. Can you leave me for twenty minutes or so?" Stan asks as Lizzy passes him the stool.

"Are you serious, I don't work until lunch so I'll sleep until ten," Lizzy answers in an effort to make light of the situation and goes back to bed. Stan seats himself, straightens his back and empties his mind. Performing the mudras is already becoming natural for him and he does them quickly but gracefully. After sitting for some minutes, eyes closed, hands extended on either side, about a foot from his torso at waist level, palms down for the first time he feels an electric like tingling in them and then an invisible subtle force pushing them upwards. He has to concentrate to keep them stationary and as he does so he feels the crown of his head tingling also for the first time, something Lizzy told him would happen as he progresses. After what Stan estimates is seven or eight minutes he changes hand positions so that his left hand is positioned just under his chin, palm down and his right hand is positioned under his navel palm up. After another seven or eight minutes he reverses hand position as he begins to feel waves of nausea overcome him. Less than a minute later he has to stop for fear of vomiting, Lizzy has not told him about this side effect if she knows about it or if it even is one. Not wanting to disturb Lizzy he lies down on the sofa and the nausea subsides almost immediately. He falls into a deep sleep, his nightmare all but forgotten.

At 09:00 Lizzy is woken by Stan's mobile, which he left on the bedside table. She lets it ring since she never answers his phone and especially now since Stan rarely does either. She stays in bed. It is loud enough to be heard in the living room and when Stan does not come in to retrieve it to at least see who is calling she grows concerned and gets up to take the phone into the living room. Stan is still soundly asleep, snoring rhythmically and just as she goes to shake him the phone stops ringing but Stan wakes anyway.

"Morning Lizzy, what are you doing with my phone?"

"It was ringing and I was just about to wake you…"

"Here, quickly," Stan snaps and Lizzy gives him the phone. He immediately looks at the display of the missed call and is happy to see a number with an Irish international dialing code; he looked it up after speaking with Peter in the hope Rory would call since he wanted to make sure that he did not pick up to the Russians and most people who would call him from the UK. He selects the callback button.

"Hello, is this Stan?" Rory answers in his slight Dublin accent on seeing the caller's number is the one he has just dialed but got no answer.

"Yes, and you are Rory?" Stan answers trying to disguise his black Mancunian accent.

"That's right. Peter Tomlinson told me that you want to accompany me to see my father, Jack Jones, is that correct?"

"You got it, Rory."

"Why would you want to come with me?"

"Didn't Peter tell you?"

"The way I see what Peter told me, Stan, is that you want to blackmail me into giving you access to my father," Rory replies tersely, surprising his mother who has taken a seat at the table opposite Rory.

"I don't mean to be so underhand, Rory, I don't want to upset you and I especially don't want to upset Jack. I guess Peter told you the kind of guy that I am;" Stan waits for a response.

"Yes, you're a feared black gangster in Manchester. And in my view someone to stay away from so why would I want to cross a road with you not to speak of joining you on a trip across Europe?" Rory does not soften his tone.

"Rory, I can't deny what I've been, but please believe me, I am a totally different person now. Your father did actually ask me to call him if I ever changed the way I feel about leading my life. Did Peter tell you about Falun Dafa, the thing your father practices?"

"Yes he did but not much."

"Okay, I never heard of it before I met your father. I probably would never have heard of it and if I had I would never have taken it seriously even after I met him and he had told me about it. But one morning when I was at his apartment I woke up earlier than your father expected. I went up the stairs of his apartment and saw him standing with his eyes closed and moving his arms in a strange pattern then he held them in a kind of circular shape in front of him. He was surrounded by a beautiful light and there was a kind of wheel of light spinning between his arms. He changed the positions of his arms after a while and each time the circling light stayed between them spinning one way then the other. When he opened his eyes and saw me, I could tell he wasn't happy that I was watching him but he never said as much. And it wasn't just this light thing that I saw that had a strange effect on me. Just being with your father made me feel good and bad."

"Good and bad, in what way?" Rory's tone becomes more conciliatory

"He made me feel bad for what I am - well I hope I can say 'for what I was' - you know, basically a bad person. Being in your father's presence made me actually feel guilty about the things I've done. Without actually saying anything he made me question how I lead my life."

"And good?"

"That's harder to explain. When I was with him I felt like I was in a bubble of acceptance and forgiveness, that all was not lost. I am completely honest with you, Rory. I made your father let me stay at his place because I needed somewhere to stay untraced in Vienna. I was making a major drug transaction with Russian Mafia people. I was told by them that I was not to stay in a hotel or anywhere my location could be recorded in any way so your father seemed the perfect answer. Due to the business I was conducting I had to suppress the way your father was making me feel, and hoped I would get back to my bad old self once I left him."

"So why exactly do you want to see him now?" Rory asks genuinely interested.

"Although I still had kind of relapses into feeling how your father made me feel, the business I was doing and the money I was making helped me push the thoughts and feelings to the back of my mind. That was until the day, not so long ago, that I had to settle with the Russians. Let me just say that I have never felt such physical pain or experienced such humiliation and degradation as I did that day I met the Russians. This episode makes me question everything and makes me feel just like I did in your father's presence but only the bad side. I need to see him again just to stabilize myself with the comfort he also made me feel."

"So why don't you just call him and tell him what you have just told me?"

"Because although he said I could call him if I ever wanted to follow Falun Dafa he also made it clear, very clear, that I could not visit him again."

"And you think that you can use me to blackmail him into seeing you?" Rory's tone harshens once again.

"Do you have to keep using that word, Rory?" Stan pleads.

"I'll tell you what I will allow you to do, okay?" Rory lets Stan know exactly who is in charge.

"Whatever you say, Rory," Stan accepts his subjugation.

"You call my father and tell him about me and that I would very much like to meet him. Tell him that I have wanted to all my life but, for very good reason, my mother kept his identity a secret until now. Give him my number and tell him to call me if he would like to see me. You can tell him you would like to take me to see him and give whatever reasons you want as long as they are truthful. If he calls me to say he would like to meet me and tells me it is okay to bring you along then I'll accept it and go with you," Rory explains forthrightly, which is not what Stan wants to hear.

"And what if he wants to see you without me?"

"Then you're out, Stan."

"Shit, man. Sorry, Rory, thinking out loud."

"Look, Stan. I now know he's living in Vienna and I have the time and the money to track him down myself. I'm only giving you this opportunity because I want to meet him as soon as possible and I guess I feel a little sorry for you. Take it or leave it," Rory explains dispassionately.

"You give me no choice, Rory."

"You don't deserve one, now are you going to do as I say or should I commence my own inquiries into how I should contact my father?"

"How strange life is, Rory. I called you with an ultimatum and you give me one. I have no choice but to go along with your wishes, such is life," Stan answers despondently.

"And such it is, Stan. When will you call my father?"

"I can do it now, if you like."

"Okay, Stan. After you speak to him call me straight away and let me know his reaction."

"Will do, Rory," Stan answers meekly and Rory ends the call.

32.

I rise at 05:00 in order to practice before Nora and Tasha awake, which would make it impossible in the rented accommodation we are staying in for a few week days in a small ski resort high in the Austrian Alps where Nora initially learned to ski as a three-year-old. We are staying in the only Gasthaus to serve the three slopes, which predominantly locals use; a far cry from the glamorous and glitzy ski havens such as Kitzbühel frequented by the rich and famous and this is reflected by the relatively few skiers, especially in week days, and low prices and for this I am grateful. I stand at the foot of the bed with my back to it and begin to open my chakras by performing Buddha Stretching a Thousand Arms. All phenomena I have grown used to manifests except the sensation of the spinning of the wheel in my lower abdomen. This, Zhuan Falun states, would subside after some time. The eerie outline of my arms and hands provided by my inner eye becomes ever clearer as time goes by. The light ones stay longer, my head is alive with the electric tingling sensation and the nausea begins to bubble away. I doubt if I will be able to complete the exercises in the room since I feel the usual warmth envelop me and intensify as the exercise progresses.

After I complete the third repetition of the exercise, my pajamas moist from perspiration, I quietly venture out onto the balcony to the side of the bedroom and leave the door slightly ajar as not to disturb Nora and Tasha by closing it too. I find the subzero chill of the air and the snow on my bare feet refreshing as I take up the standing stance. The nausea now receded immediately grows again as I stand holding the wheel before me. I am determined to tolerate it and try to banish all thought from my mind and reside in a state of wu wei but it is so difficult to be effortless and thought free when I need to make such an effort to sustain the stance and ignore the nausea. The wheel so palpable within my arms throbs and pulsates, it feels like it is life itself, nothing transcends it, I feel so privileged and unbelievably grateful to have discovered this practice. If saved souls were a measure of divinity Li Hongzhi is rubbing shoulders with Buddha and Jesus Christ of that I am sure. Stop! I should not be thinking anything. It is such an effort to be effortless and thought free.

"Papa! Papa!" Tasha, pulling at my elbow, brings me out of my empty contemplation as I perform the fifth and final exercise in the lotus position. I open my eyes to see the sun has risen and the snow around me has melted.

"Good morning my little one. Did I tell you I love you already today?"

"No. Papa."

"Then, I love you. Is Mama awake?"

"Yes, she is in the bathroom getting ready for breakfast I think."

"Come on, let's get you inside, your hands are freezing," I say getting to my feet then leading Tasha back into the bedroom.

"Did she come out to you?" Nora asks coming into the bedroom from the adjoining bathroom wrapped in a towel.

"She sure did but I had basically finished practicing so it didn't matter apart from the fact she is so cold."

"Sorry, but she was asleep when I went to the bathroom. I saw you practicing outside and knew that you wouldn't be happy if I disturbed you. Give her to me, I'll put her under the shower to warm her up," Nora says taking Tasha's hand and leading her into the bathroom. I lie on the bed and think about things, it feels like a privilege to do so after retaining an almost blank mind for so long. I recollect the dream I had about the young man on the cross and still do not understand what it meant. I let my mind drift and for no apparent reason or trigger my thoughts take me to Cairo and the great pyramid in Giza. Before and since visiting it over ten years ago I found it impossible to believe that people from this earthly civilization were capable of erecting such a monolithic giant structure with such precision engineering so long ago although science cannot date them specifically. But Zhuan Falun has now provided an answer to that as well as to many more questions mankind is faced with. Questions science cannot answer so science ignores them. Man did create the pyramids but not man from this civilization. Man from a civilization that roamed the earth a long time before Darwin determined we are the end product of some ape, which is an insult to the human race despite the fact we are close to the bottom of the pile of existences we are still at the top of the rubbish heap. Why are not the discoveries of pre-civilization giant human skeletons publicized? Why are ghosts and similar phenomena laughed at despite proof of their existence? But truth cannot be denied and slowly but surely science is having to admit that things exist that it cannot explain, which ultimately means science is flawed, is not completely true. This fact is now bared out by governments admitting to the existence of UFOs. Vehicles that have even been observed by military flight personnel who claim the vehicles defied the laws of physics in the way and the speed at which they maneuvered. The feats can only be described as miracles since they cannot be explained by natural or scientific laws. Should they be explained as divine intervention or merely the activities of beings far closer to their true selves than we are? I believe both explanations are true since the beings, compared to us, are surely divine.

"Are you coming down to breakfast?" Nora asks as she bundles Tasha onto the bed next to me wrapped in a bath towel.

"Since it's included in the rates I may as well, there's nothing else to take advantage of. No wifi, you can't even get a signal for the phones up here," I answer as I dry Tasha.

"That's a plus as far as I'm concerned. I'm totally free from students who think I should be available at any time or day they have a question. Besides, you rarely call anyone anyway, why are you complaining?"

"I'm not complaining, I just miss the internet, that's all."

"We're here to ski and to teach Tasha to ski. Why can't you just enjoy these few days practicing your dafa and skiing?"

"Whatever you say, Nora," I resign myself to a very boring few days. I only learnt to ski a few years before Tasha was born and only quite badly under Nora's coercion and do not really enjoy it.

33.

Out of desperation Stan calls Beth when he cannot contact Jack.

"Hi, Beth, do you know what's happened to Jack?" he asks nervously as soon as Beth answers.

"Stan, what do you mean what's happened to Jack?" Beth replies, confused.

"I just tried calling his landline and there's no answer and I get some message in German and then one in English telling me his number is unavailable when I try his mobile. Do you know where he is or how I can contact him?" Stan asks, the urgency in his voice obvious.

"Hey, Stan, what's the problem? You never spoke to him for years until recently, why so desperate to get him now? Have you got another drug deal going down in Vienna?"

"No way, I'm finished with all that shit. It's a long story but I think you could see that I've changed when we met last. I need to contact Jack because, Beth, you have been

Auntie Beth for the last twenty-five years."

"What the fuck?"

"Yeah, Jack has a twenty-five-year-old son called Rory who lives in Dublin."

"He never mentioned him to me," Beth replies still confused.

"That's because he doesn't know Rory exists. That's why I need to talk to Jack. Rory wants to meet him and I'm a sort of go between."

"So what's in it for you, Stan, why are you needed to contact Jack, why don't you just give Rory his number?" Beth asks as she contemplates informing Jack of Rory's existence herself since she does not trust Stan.

"In a word, no two, Falun Dafa. Jack told me never to visit him again only to call him if I changed my ways and wanted to follow it," Stan explains.

"I'm confused, Stan. What has telling Jack about Rory have to do with Falun Dafa?"

"Do you remember, I told you Jack has a calming effect on me when I'm in his presence?"

"And?"

"Well I need to be in his presence again. I'm hoping that if I tell Jack that I've changed and what changed me he might allow me to take Rory to see him."

"So what did change you, Stan?"

"An experience so painful and degrading that it gives me nightmares and I believe the suffering it has put me through has cleansed a lot of my karma. Believing this I do not want to accumulate anymore karma. I'm too humiliated to give you the details but I'll tell Jack if he asks, which I'm sure he won't."

"Sorry, but I can't help, Stan. I don't know where he is right now and you have the same contact details as I do for him," Beth answers, the concern evident in her voice.

"Shit, man. I guess I'll just have to keep trying his numbers. Thanks anyway, Beth. Let me know if you hear from him."

"Yes, I will. I'll try him myself later today. Will you give me this Rory's number so I can pass it on if I get him?"

"Please leave that to me, Beth. It's the only card I've got to play," Stan asks pitifully, which makes Beth feel compassion towards him.

"Okay, Stan. Good luck and let me know if and when you get him."

"Will do, Beth. Ciao," Stan ends the call wondering what to say to Rory that will not set him off on his own independent search for his father. He decides not to call Rory until the following day if he still has not been able to contact Jack.

"So what was all that about? What does the nigger want now? I thought he might have been put out of action," Jason, who is sat at the kitchen table drinking coffee, asks as Beth finishes speaking.

"I wish you wouldn't use that word, it died decades ago. He's been trying to get hold of Jack but there's no answer to his landline and no access to his mobile. Why did you think Stan was put out of action?" Beth answers thoughtfully, in contemplation as to what might have happened to her brother.

"The demand on the street has gone up and we're getting new customers who used to buy from his dealers. Even other pushers who used Stan are coming to us."

"Stan said he's done with dealing and wants to contact Jack because something very traumatic has happened to him, something he was too embarrassed to tell me about. He said being with Jack makes him feel better. It's all to do with Falun Dafa. I know you don't even like me mentioning it but I find it very calming when I do the exercises and I get a very strange feeling in my lower stomach, which I think is the turning of the wheel."

"What fucking wheel?" Jason mutters.

"I'm not going to waste my time with you on it, Jay. You'll only ridicule it and insult me for practicing it."

"Fair enough, woman. I've got things to do," Jason replies curtly as he gets to his feet to leave.

"Bye, lover. Have a nice day," Beth replies in a similar tone and Jason leaves. After he has gone Beth tries calling Jack on his landline and mobile but gets the same results as Stan.

After Lizzy leaves for work Stan tries calling Jack for the fourth time to no avail. As he lies on the bed staring up at the ceiling and wondering what his next move should be his mobile rings. On seeing that Rory is calling he is thrown into a predicament: Should he answer and tell Rory that he is unable to contact Jack? If he does Rory might proceed with his own search for his father, but if he does not answer then Rory will probably do that anyway.

"Hi, Rory," Stan decides that it is best to hear from Rory what he is going to do rather than sit and wait to see what he might do.

"Stan, why haven't you called me back? I told you to straight after you called my father and that was hours ago.

Doesn't he want you to take me to see him or doesn't he want to see me?" Rory sounds lost.

"No, Rory, neither of those. I'm sorry, but I haven't been able to contact your father yet. Please give me another couple of days before you start anything yourself," Stan begs.

"You've got twenty-four hours, okay, Stan?" Rory replies and ends the call leaving Stan more perplexed.

"Why is it so imperative you contact your father as soon as possible after all these years, Rory? You are better off taking more time and finding him yourself. I'm your mother and I really don't want you fraternizing with such characters as Stan," Theresa asks Rory at the kitchen table where they had just finished lunch before Rory made the call. Although she is against her son being involved with characters such as Stan as any caring mother would be, her own ulterior motives to stop Rory meeting Stan take precedence.

"I'm not really that bothered over the amount of time it will take Stan to put me in touch with my father compared with how long it will take me to find him myself, Mother. Stan knew my father well, as you have told me. Therefore I would like to ask Stan about my father. Ask him things that, perhaps, my father would feel ill at ease to answer. Things like what they got up to? What did Stan really think of my father? How did the community in which they were part of consider and look upon them? If my father wants to see me I would like to know more about him before we meet," Rory explains to his mother's dismay. She dreads Rory becoming so familiar with Stan due to what Stan might divulge to Rory.

"Rory, I was part of the community they mixed in and I've told you what they were like, what more do you need to know?"

"You also told me that my father was not your boyfriend so you obviously didn't know everything about him. You said Stan was his minder so he must know things about my father that you don't. If my father is okay with it then I would actually prefer to go with Stan than I would on my own, just to learn more about my father on the way to see him," Rory's answer leaves Theresa in a state of utter distress, which she disguises well.

"I guess I can't argue with what you say, Rory, but if it happens and you do meet Stan please be careful, Son," is all Theresa can think of saying.

"Mother, I'm twenty-five and people will be around if and when I meet Stan so stop worrying."

34.

I am driving down the autobahn back home when my phone, which I placed in a cup holder on the center console, rings out.

"Should I get that?" Nora asks.

"Please, and tell whoever it is that I'll call them back when we get home," I answer not having a clue or caring who it could be.

"Should I put them on loudspeaker?" Nora asks as she picks up the phone.

"No, it's useless with the noise of driving in the car."

"Hello, who is this, please?" Nora politely asks on answering.

"No, you can't he's driving. Can I give him a message or should he call you back when he can?" she then says in a very brusque and cold tone.

"Who is it?" I ask on hearing the annoyance in Nora's voice.

"That drug dealing pimp from England who made me and Tasha leave our home because he had to visit," Nora says loudly and partly into the phone.

"Stan, I'll call you back in an hour or so but if this call is about you coming to see me again the answer is no before you even ask," I say as Nora holds the phone to my head with an expression on her face as if she wishes it were a gun. She ends the call and places the phone back in the cup holder.

"So, what do you think he wants now?" Nora demands.

"You just heard as much as I did. And you heard me tell him he can't come, I said it for your benefit as much as his," I respond with similar annoyance since I feel I am being treated unfairly. Then I have to remind myself that I am only paying off my karma as I do every day throughout the day at one point or usually many.

"Just don't bother calling him back, you've told him he can't come to us and if that was the reason he called he won't bother calling back if he has any decency;" comes Nora's curt response.

"Now 'decent' was never something you would ever say in relation to Stan, what changed your mind?" I cannot resist retaliating against Nora's automatic derogatory rejection of Stan's call.

"Decent is the last thing he is so he might still bother you. So what will you say if he does?"

"Give it a rest, Nora. I'm going to call him when we get back. I said I would and if I said it, then it's only decent of me to do so," I reply in an effort to make a point and close the subject.

"Have it your way but there is no way he comes to our home. Okay?"

"Jeez, Nora. You heard what I just told him. I've promised you he will never come again. What else can I do?" I reply but Nora does not answer and we make the rest of the drive home mainly listening to the radio occasionally interrupted by Tasha's requests for food and drink while she sits in the rear child seat.

We arrive home late in the afternoon just as it is getting dark. It's a chore in itself to unload and carry the ski equipment and other luggage up to the apartment, especially with a little girl in tow. I leave everything I am carrying on the living room floor for Nora to organize, not to be lazy but I never place things where she wants them anyway, something always needs to be cleaned or washed before being put away. I retreat to my PC room upstairs and reluctantly make the call to Stan.

"Yo, Jack!" he almost immediately answers.

"Hi, Stan. What's up?" is my fatigued response.

"I'm really sorry to trouble you, Jack. Was that your woman who answered before? Wow! Was she pleased to hear me, or was she pleased to hear me," Stan tries to make light of Nora's previous reaction to his call by accentuating it.

"What do you expect, Stan? You heard what she said. Now what is it you want?"

"You told me to only ever call you if I decided to practice Falun Dafa," Stan says and waits for a reply.

"If you called because you want to practice Falun Dafa I find that very hard to believe, Stan."

"That's not all, Jack. Remember that I told you how you made me feel different. Especially how I felt kinda guilty for what I am and what I do?"

"Where's this going, Stan? I haven't got all day."

"Okay, at first I did get Lizzy, my woman to look into Falun Dafa for me. She got into it straight away and started practicing herself. Although I found it interesting and Lizzy tried to encourage me I would basically have had to drop everything I was doing and I was earning some big money so I tried to block Falun Dafa and you from my mind." Stan is taking a strange way to get to the point and this makes me suspicious.

"What have I got to do with this?"

"The way you make me feel when I'm in your presence. Although you make me feel guilty you also make me feel kind of safe and secure, like all is not lost no matter how bad I've been…"

"Well, I wish I could help you, Stan, but my life is in Vienna with my family," I interrupt since I do not like the sound of where this could be going.

"Just let me finish, there's more, lots more. Something terrible happened to me, Jack, which was carried out by the Russians. It was physical and mental torture, I still have nightmares about it and I desperately want to see you because I think you can help me get over it. Now I know you told me I can never visit you but maybe if I brought someone over to see you, someone very special, you might let me do it," Stan pauses.

"And who is this very special person, Stan?" I answer

impartially since I do not believe Stan knows anyone who I would be interested in meeting and I have no intention of letting him visit under any circumstances.

"It's your son," Stan answers and my mind races. Is someone trying to frame me in some way? If it's true the mother can only be from my hell raising partying days of many years gone by. The days I used to mix with Stan.

"How do you know for sure he's my son?" After a long pause I respond in a whisper, I do not want Nora to hear anything about this until I have the facts and only then if she needs to know.

"Is your wife at home?" Stan catches on.

"Yes," I answer at normal volume.

"Okay, I'll do all the talking. A private detective got in touch with me a couple of days ago. He was a copper on the scene in Manchester when we were out and about together over twenty years ago. A twenty-five-year-old man named Rory Hogan from Dublin had contacted him in the search for you, his father," Stan pauses for my reaction. He knows I will remember Theresa.

"Theresa," I revert back to whispering.

"You got it, Jack. Even I remember that night. At first I wondered, you see I haven't met Rory, but apparently he looks just like you did at twenty five according to the detective.

"Scheiße," is all I can muster. I picture Theresa on the last day I saw her and now realize why she was so distraught that we never used any contraceptives that night. And I now know why she never returned to Manchester despite not taking her degree.

"Now this is the bit that I don't want to tell you but I

must," Stan says reticently.

"Go on," I reply in shell shock.

"I've spoken to Rory over the phone and put it to him that I could take him to see you. He's a clever kid and a pretty tough cookie. He said that firstly I should ask you if you want to see him and I know he's desperate to see you, he has been most of his life. Theresa kept your identity a secret from him until now but she could only give him your name, where you were from and what you used to do, that's why he hired a detective because you disappeared. He told me to give you his number if you want contact. He also said that I could take him to see you on condition you allow it, if not he'll meet you alone if you want to see him," Stan finishes and exhales deeply leaving me stupefied in such a cocktail of emotion I am at a loss as to what to say.

"I don't know what to say, Stan. Of course I'll see my boy but I've got to straighten things with Nora first. Give me his number and tell him I'll call as soon as I can, let's say tomorrow morning at the earliest if things go okay with Nora?" I talk at normal volume since Nora has started vacuum cleaning downstairs.

"Um, Jack, what about me?"

"Does Rory want you with him?"

"I don't know, Jack, he never said either way," Stan reluctantly replies in a fashion that raises my suspicion.

"I'll tell you what I'll do, Stan, I'll ask Rory if he wants you to tag along, if he does then you're welcome to come too. I don't expect Nora to take this very calmly, not so much you although you alone are bad enough, but the existence of Rory, so I would like Rory to stay at a hotel where you will also stay if he wants you to join him," I say envisaging Nora's fury, "I will also ask Rory if he would prefer me to visit him in Dublin or wherever he wants, in which case you probably wouldn't get to see me," I add in the hope this second scenario plays out, which would allow me to get to know Rory without simultaneously having to ride-out the inevitable storm at home with Nora.

"Okay, Jack, I'll call him now and text you with his number," Stan replies despondently. After finishing the call I sit and mull over what I have just learnt. Then I deliberate how I should break this news to Nora.

"Did you call that Stan back?" she asks caustically on entering the room with a coffee for me.

"Yeah, I just finished talking to him."

"And?" she asks placing the coffee on the desk

"He had some pretty startling news for me and probably for you too."

"Which was?"

"I've got a twenty-five-year-old son in Ireland," I state unemotionally in a pointless effort to suppress the enormity of the revelation and Nora drops herself into the large bean bag on the floor by my chair.

"What?"

"Yeah, first a detective that my son had hired contacted Stan only a couple of days ago. Then Stan spoke to Rory, that's my son, and Rory told Stan that he would very much like to meet me."

"Jack, how can you be sure he's your son and why has he taken so long to try and meet you?" Nora asks, the uncertainty of not knowing how to react discernable in her voice.

"He's my son, you don't need to know the details but

he is my son. The reason he's taken so long to try and contact me is because his mother wouldn't allow it. And I think I know why. I told you what my life used to be like, what I used to be like before the business went bust. Well Theresa, that's Rory's mother, came from a wealthy respectable Catholic family. She disappeared back to Dublin not long after I spent a night with her and I never saw her again."

"Why didn't you tell me about her?"

"There was nothing to tell. We had a one night stand then she disappeared." After saying Theresa came from a respectable Catholic family I did not feel mentioning the fact that Stan was also there would be helpful, to say the least, in my endeavor to meet Rory.

"So what do you plan to do now, Jack?" Nora asks and I sense the vulnerability in her voice. This was a reaction I never expected.

"What would you do, Nora? You know I have no choice, I must meet my son."

"How will you do it, would you like to invite him here?" she asks in a way which makes me believe that she actually wants to meet him.

"Are you sure?"

"He is Tasha's brother, where else would you want to meet him?"

"Wow! I didn't know how you would take it but I never expected you to take it like that," I answer incredulously.

"He's your family, which makes him Tasha's, how else should I be?"

"Okay, I'll call him in the morning," I answer a little bemused but mostly relieved.

As soon as the call is ended with Jack, Stan calls Rory.

"So did you contact him, Stan?" Rory asks on answering the call.

"Yes, just…"

"And what did he say, does he want to see me?" Rory interrupts excitedly.

"Yes, Rory, he wants to see you, I mean, what decent father wouldn't? But first he needs to explain it all to his wife so I guess depending on her reaction, he said he will call you tomorrow as soon as he can, so I guess in the morning."

"Excellent! Thank you, Stan. And will you be going along with me or not?"

"Well, that depends on you, Rory, so I doubt it."

"Why so?"

"I told your father exactly what you told me to say. He said that I could join you if you wish, and I guess you don't wish, do you?" Stan answers forlornly.

"Were you a good friend of my father's, Stan?"

"As good as he had at the time I guess, why?

"I would like to know more about him before I meet up with him. If I take you along, maybe you can tell me what he was like when he was my age, tell me what you used to get up to with him?"

"Up to a point, Rory, but there's stuff that I don't think it would be in your best interests to know, stuff that I will not divulge," Stan answers as he reflects on sleeping with Theresa.

"Fair enough, Stan. I'll call you after my father calls me and we will discuss it further, have a nice evening," Rory ends the call and Stan calls Beth to let her know he has contacted Jack.

35.

Nora and I are discussing how and what I should say to Rory when the landline rings. Before answering I look at the display and see that Beth is calling.

"Hello, Beth, you're calling as frequently as a member of my own family would, how are you?" I cannot resist the goad.

"Your wit knows no boundaries, does it, Jack?" Beth retaliates.

"And to what do I owe the honor of this call?"

"Stan, I guess. He has called you to let you know about your son, he just called me to let me know he's told you."

"So you know about Rory?"

"Yes, Stan told me and asked me to let him tell you, which I agreed to because he thought it might help in getting you to allow him to bring Rory to see you."

"That's about it, Beth," as I speak I realize that I have not told Nora about the possibility that Stan might accompany Rory to Vienna.

"How do you know he is your son, Jack?"

"Didn't Stan tell you?" I ask presuming that Stan would have given Beth every sordid little detail.

"No, nothing. He was just focusing on seeing you. How does he know that Rory is your son?"

"It's a pretty unsavory story, and one which you don't need to know. Let's just say that Rory is definitely my offspring," I answer in the belief Beth will not question further.

"Casanova had nothing on you in your early days, do you know who the mother is?" Beth does not leave it.

"Yes, I do, Beth now let's just leave it at that, okay?"

"Sure, Jack, I was just curious. Have you told Nora yet?"

"We were just talking about the situation when you called."

"And is she okay with it?"

"Yeah, Nora's very okay with it. As far as she is concerned Rory is a member of the family who we didn't know about until now," I explain without emotion.

"Jesus, you're shitting me!" Beth cannot hide her astonishment.

"No, I was pretty shocked too, but when you think about it and take out the jealousy and anxiety all that is left is that Rory is my son as Tasha is my daughter and I am so thankful that Nora sees it this way," I elucidate and give Nora, who is sitting next to me on the sofa, a smile, which she reciprocates.

"I'm practicing Falun Dafa everyday now, Jack."

"That's good to hear. How are you finding it?"

"Zhuan Falun is fascinating and really makes me question everything but trying to free myself of attachments seems like an impossible task."

"Beth, I've been practicing for years and it still seems like an impossible task to me, especially cutting the attachment I feel towards my family. But believe me, as you keep practicing and reading Zhuan Falun the attachments will gradually fall away as they are replaced by zhen, shan, ren. I stopped smoking without trying, the same goes for drinking and I don't even enjoy a steak anymore. The most subtle one to go was my prolific use of profanities…"

"Now you mention it I have noticed it. You never use bad language during our calls anymore," Beth interrupts.

"Yes, I only noticed it because Nora stopped reprimanding me for the use of it. I know they were only mild attachments I had but you have to start at the beginning. And the loss of these attachments was not the only benefit I experienced after beginning my practice. I may have already told you, I don't remember, but my health has also improved. I had a problem with my digestion and took laxatives at least once a week, now I don't need them. I also suffered from heartburn almost every day and that has completely subsided. A more worrying symptom I noticed was that I was increasingly finding it harder to take a piss, you know, prostate cancer, and now I have no problems in that area anymore," I try and encourage Beth. I want to also mention sex as another attachment that I have relinquished but do not want to bring it up in front of Nora.

"The exercises are easy in a physical sense, my yoga comes in handy with the full lotus, but I find it so hard to keep my mind in a state of wu wei. I start off okay but then I wonder what shopping I have to do or what should I cook for dinner. I even start thinking about my boyfriend, Jason, in erotic ways, if you get my drift," Beth explains and I have to subdue my chuckle.

"Beth, I had exactly the same problems when I started, I couldn't even get into the lotus position for months. My mind still wanders occasionally but nowhere near as much as it did when I started. You just need to apply yourself. If it was easy it would mean you have little karma to cleanse and therefore wouldn't be here on this planet in this realm."

"At least I can follow what you're talking about now since I'm reading Zhuan Falun."

"I think it's great that you're doing it. You know I've had other more dramatic experiences, which since you're now practicing, will realize I won't divulge."

"You don't have to, Jack. What Stan told me about his experiences with you was enough to persuade me there is something profound in Falun Dafa."

"I did try and tell you about it many times, Beth, but you never took it seriously."

"Yeah, I guess it took Stan to make me see the light. I reckoned if someone so egotistical and bad through and through can be so transformed by something he can't touch or explain then there must be something to it. I'm sorry I never took you or Falun Dafa seriously in the first place."

"I don't think the years you ignored it are going to make much difference in the grand scale of things, just so long as you put some dedication into it."

"Hope you're right, Jack. Part of my reason for calling is to forewarn you."

"Of what, sis?"

"That there's a good chance that Rory is going to agree to bring Stan with him."

"How come?"

"Stan told me that you said he could come over with Rory to see you if Rory agrees and Rory didn't exactly say as much but spoke in a way that Stan would be going along depending on the call you make to Rory. Stan must feel like a ping pong ball. I could never pity Stan but Falun Dafa states that compassion is a big part of our true selves and I guess I feel it for him. So what will you have to say about Stan joining Rory, Jack?"

"I don't know. Nora will not be happy but I need to know exactly how Rory feels about it."

"When will you call him?"

"In the morning, after I've slept on this bombshell."

"Okay, Jack. Sleep well and I'll speak to you soon," Beth says before ending the call.

"Nora won't be happy about what, Jack?" she asks wearing an expression that would make a lemon taste sweet.

"It sounds like Rory wants to come to Vienna with Stan," I disclose in the full knowledge that the unexpected and welcome reaction Nora had on learning of Rory's existence is about to implode.

"You mustn't allow it. You have to tell Rory what Stan is like, what Stan is. How can you let your own son get involved with such a character?" Nora demands.

"Nora, it was Stan who told Rory where I am. Stan has got involved with Rory before I have even spoken to him, before I even knew Rory existed. Now if Rory wants to come with Stan I'm not going to stop it. The alternative and probably the most comfortable thing for me to do is to go to Dublin alone and see Rory there," I coldly state, which seems to have a restraining effect on Nora's tyrannical demeanor. I do believe that she is happily excited about meeting Rory.

"There's no way he's staying here. Rory can and should but I don't want to set eyes on this Stan character," she says after a long pause.

"Okay, if Stan comes he stays in a hotel. If Rory prefers it I will see him in Dublin. I'll ask what he wants when I call him in the morning."

36.

At three minutes past six in the morning Lizzy is woken by Stan's crying and mumbled begging. She is grateful that it is so late, his nightmares usually wake her much earlier. She shakes him out of his torture.

"Wake up my love, you're just having a bad dream again," she says soothingly into his ear.

"Sorry, Lizzy, what time is it?"

"Just gone six. Try and go back to sleep."

"There's no chance of that. Jack's gonna call Rory this morning. I won't rest until I know what they arrange together. Rory said he will call me after Jack has called him."

"Well that's not going to happen for at least another three to four hours, Stan, so stay in bed with me," Lizzy tries to persuade Stan.

"You go back to sleep while I do some Dafa exercises," he answers as he gets out of bed and affectionately rubs Lizzy's head.

After being unable to sleep most of the night due to the eager anticipation of speaking to his father Rory is awoken at 08:00 by the alarm clock on his bedside-table. He presumes and hopes his father may call early since the clocks are an hour ahead in Europe. He gets out of bed and goes to the ensuite bathroom. While taking a shower he gives thought to what he will say to his father and also wonders if his father will be adverse to Stan going with him to Vienna.

"Would you like breakfast, Son," Theresa asks as Rory enters the dining kitchen.

"No thanks, Mother, just a coffee would be fine," he

replies as he sits himself at the large dining table.

"Nervous about your father calling?"

"I don't know if nervous is the right word, but I do feel strange and certainly not hungry. What time do you think he will call?"

"I have no idea, Rory, if he said he'll call in the morning it could be any time up until midday."

I awake feeling strangely empty considering I will be speaking to my, unbeknown to me until recently, twenty-five-year-old son this day. It is a few minutes before five and Nora is sleeping soundly. I silently get out of bed and look in on Tasha, who also looks peaceful, before descending the stairs to carry out my exercises. Although it is a little cooler down here I open the lounge windows wide in preparation for the inevitable heat that will quickly envelop me once I commence the exercises. The cold air initially refreshes me but is soon so chilling as to be on the uncomfortable side since I am wearing flimsy cotton pajamas. I take up the stance in preparation to perform the initial stretching exercise of Buddha Stretching a Thousand Arms, to open my energy channels and chakras in preparation for the following exercises. Almost immediately I feel the warmth generate through my body as I stretch my arms high.to the utmost extreme I can and hold for a few seconds before abruptly relaxing everything in readiness to make the next stretching movement. About ten minutes later, after completing Buddha Stretching a Thousand Arms three times, I am soaked in sweat and grateful for the chilling breeze coming in through the open windows. I give myself half a minute to cool down a little before performing the Falun standing stance of holding the wheel. It makes its presence felt stronger than ever before in my experience. My shoulders begin to reverberate from the pulsating turning of the wheel. It feels like my arms are in danger of being wrenched from my shoulders but I am calm in the knowledge that this is happening in another dimension, one where the laws of our physics have no rule. I stand contented that I am in no physical danger in this realm and the laws of our physics are not recognized in others. I feel utterly detached from the reality we know as reality. I do not see, feel, hear or smell Stan, but I know he is here with me, through which sense I do not know I can only assume he or an entity of him is with me or an entity of me in another dimension. He is beseeching me to understand him and begs me for help. I feel great compassion towards him and then he is gone and my mind is again empty.

I perform the third exercise, Penetrating the Cosmic Extremes, and the fourth, Falun Cosmic Orbit, without added normal drama. I am able to stay in a temporary state of wu wei just aware that I am practicing and experience the usual nausea, heat and intense tingling at the crown of my head also my visions are quite vivid. Points of brilliant white light appear here and there interspersed by images of beings from I know not where. They are various and I have never seen the same one twice throughout my practice. Some appear beautiful and serene while others grotesque and fearsome and many in between but none quite human. I remain in quiet observation and appreciation of what Dafa enables me to see.

The inferno within dissipates as I settle into the lotus position and perform the mudras of Reinforcing Supernatural Powers. As I finish them and become stationary with my hands palms down about a foot from my waist my state of wu wei is interrupted by the familiar vision of the young man on a cross I thought may have been myself but now doubt that my first assumption was correct. Could it be my son? Who else could it be? I push my confusion aside and manage to return to a state of wu wei.

"Good morning, Jack," Nora greets as she descends the stairs. She knows I will have ended or be ending my usual practice since it is 08:00 and time for Tasha to be getting ready for kindergarten for which I have to be available in order to prepare her snack and drink for the morning.

"Morning, Dear. I'll get Tasha's food sorted," I respond and go through the usual ritual of preparing her breakfast and a snack and as I do so I contemplate what I should say to or ask Rory, my son. Although I find it hard to grasp the fact I have a son who is now well into adult life and who I have never met I still feel a bond with him and great anticipation of meeting him.

"What time will you make the call to Rory?" Nora asks unable to disguise her curiosity. I should be grateful for it since she shows genuine interest in Rory, my son by another woman.

"I don't know. It might be considered rude to call him before nine his time, which is an hour behind us, so I guess I'll call him at ten."

"What will you say?"

"I have no idea. I guess I'll start off by asking how he is and what he's done with his life up until now. And, I would imagine, he has many questions himself," I pause and then add, "and, of course, I will ask him if he would prefer to see me in Dublin," in an advanced attempt to suppress Nora's display of anger if Rory chooses to come to Vienna with Stan.

"Oh, okay," she replies submissively, which makes me believe that she would rather be able to meet Rory with Stan in tow than not meet Rory at all.

Nora leaves with Tasha at 8:30 and I read Zhuan Falun for an hour and a half before calling Rory. Almost as the ringing tone begins he answers.

"Father?" his voice is deep and authoritative, which impresses me.

"Rory, or do you prefer Son?" I say expectantly.

"Whichever you prefer, you are my father."

"Okay, Son, where and when would you like to meet?"

"I thought I would come over to see you, to see where you live. I know you are married with a young child so I don't expect you to come to Dublin. Besides, I would like to see Vienna," Rory answers decisively, which makes me think he has set his mind on coming over to me so I decide not to suggest going to meet him in Dublin.

"Okay, Son. When would you like to come over?"

"Whenever it suites you best, Father. I could visit in two weeks or so. Come for a long weekend because I have a lot of work on my plate with the company so I couldn't make it much longer."

"What do you do exactly?" I ask despite the fact I know Theresa comes from a very wealthy family and presume Rory is cosseted by it.

"I work with my mother. We control a construction

and property business and I'm a qualified lawyer."

"How is your mother? Is she married?" I ask as I reminisce about how attractive I found Theresa.

"No, when she became pregnant with me she went back home to Dublin and put her time into bringing me up and working for her father, who died a few years ago. What are you doing for a living now? I was told you became a computer programmer after your family business went bust."

"Yes, that's what brought me to Vienna. I got a contract here but that finished a while ago so I haven't been doing much lately. Nora, my wife, is a university professor so I spend a lot of my time looking after Tasha, that's our four-year-old daughter," I answer and hope Rory does not feel too alienated by me mentioning my family.in Vienna.

"How should we arrange my visit?"

"However you want, Son. I presume you'll fly in and I can collect you from the airport. You can stay here with us unless you prefer to take a hotel."

"And what if I come over with Stan?"

"Ah, Stan. I had actually forgotten about him with the anticipation of talking to you for the first time. If you want to come over with him that's no problem but he knows he's not welcome to stay in my apartment, Nora forbids it and you can't really blame her. I guess you know what Stan is and I was not so different over twenty odd years ago."

"I know a little about you and Stan from the private detective I used. He actually knew the two of you by sight when you used to go out in Manchester. Stan has also told me a little about how you were but that you have changed a lot since then and by the way he spoke I think he wants to change too."

"Did he tell you about Falun Dafa?" I ask hesitantly.

"Yes, that's the reason he wants to see you and I would like to learn more about it when we meet. It sounds interesting from what Stan says," Rory comments and I am pleasantly surprised since I expected him to be a strict Roman Catholic.

"If you google it you can find the web page easily, falundafa.org," I suggest.

"I will, so we can discuss it when we meet in greater detail than if I was completely ignorant of it. I need to make some business calls now, Father, and I will call you when I have made arrangements to visit."

"I look forward to hearing from you. Do you need my number?"

"No, I have it stored now. Will call in the next few days. Bye, Father."

"Bye, Son," I end the call.

37.

Before booking a flight to Vienna Rory calls Stan.

"Hi, Rory, did you get to speak to Jack?" Stan anxiously asks on answering.

"Yes I did, Stan, yesterday and he has agreed to you going to Vienna with me," Rory answers dispassionately.

"Fantastic! Thanks so much, Rory," Stan is ecstatic on hearing Jack has agreed he can accompany Rory.

"So how do you want to do this, Stan?"

"What do you mean?"

"You are in Manchester and I am in Dublin, I presume you want to arrive in Vienna with me, my father will pick us up from the airport so you'll get to meet him as soon as you get there. You better make the most of it because you won't be staying at my father's, you'll have to stay in a hotel."

"Okay, I see what you mean. Can I meet you at Dublin airport where we can take the same flight to Vienna?" Stan's mind races as to find a way how to get as much contact with Jack as possible.

"That's what I had in mind. I'll book a flight to Vienna scheduled two weeks from now and send you the details so you can book it too. How will you get to Dublin?"

"I guess I'll take a flight there. Depending on what you book to Vienna I'll get there the day of the flight or night before and stay in a hotel if we have to leave early to Vienna."

"Okay, Stan I'll send you a photo of me, can you do the same so we recognize each other in departures?"

"Sure thing, Rory. See you in a couple of weeks…" Rory ends the call as Stan speaks.

Nora is working and Tasha is at kindergarten when Rory calls to let me know when he and Stan are due to arrive at Vienna airport. I arrange to pick them up, drop Stan off at a hotel and take Rory home with me. He tells me how fascinating he finds Falun Dafa but cannot talk for long due to business and I inform him that he will learn of all my experiences when we meet.

Although Rory was told by the detective, Peter Tomlinson, that Stan was a big man he never expected him to be quite as big as he looks in the photo he received. When Rory sets eyes on Stan, who is sat at a small table in the departure lounge, he is further surprised. Stan has taken off his jacket and is wearing a white, lightweight cotton polo-neck, which is so tight fitting as to clearly define the hard bulging muscles of an obvious steroid taking body builder.

"So good to meet you," Stan says as he gets to his feet and extends his hand to Rory.

"Have you been here long?" Rory asks as he shakes hands with Stan.

"My flight from Manchester got in about three hours ago. Do you fancy a drink?"

"Guess you could do with one if you've been hanging around for me for so long and it's half-an-hour to boarding," Rory replies and Stan puts his jacket over his arm and picks up his Versace cabin luggage. They go to the nearby bar and order pints of Guinness and stand at the bar while the brew settles.

"How was your flight from Manchester?" Rory asks out of politeness.

"Terrible, it only took about an hour but it was an hour of hell. I've never been on such a turbulent flight. When we landed the wind was so strong I thought the wing was going to hit the runway," Stan explains, the anxiety in his voice evident.

"Let's hope it's calmer on the way to Vienna."

"I'll drink to that," Stan says and takes a large gulp from his glass and Rory follows suit.

I alternate between exploring ways of income and checking the status of Rory's flight while sat at my PC. As I am looking at the screen the flight departs on time and is due to land in Vienna at 20:35, which gives me about two and a half hours before I have to leave to collect my son and Stan from the airport. Nora is bathing Tasha. She does not usually do that on a Friday evening but I can tell she needs to occupy herself because she is nervous over meeting Rory. I leave my PC to prepare a goulash since Rory says it is one of his favorite dishes. After I finish with the ingredients I leave it to simmer and return to my PC.

"That's strange," I say as Nora comes down the stairs after putting Tasha to bed.

"What is?"

"I checked on Rory's flight about an hour ago and saw it had departed and was due in Vienna at about half-eight. Now it says it's delayed. What's going on?" I ask myself.

"Check it again later," Nora replies casually.

I try calling the airline but get a message all lines are busy and to call back later. I bring up the BBC and to my horror the breaking news is: 'Plane crash on takeoff at Dublin airport, few survivors'. I sit in stunned silence, my stomach so heavy with dread that I need to vomit. I rush to our downstairs toilet and throw up into it.

"Please no," Nora gasps on seeing the news on my screen as I clean my face.

"Maybe it's not his flight, maybe he's a survivor," I say as I put my arm around Nora who is stood motionless staring at the screen. I do not have the emotional fortitude to think as Falun Dafa asserts. Who is repaying their karma now? Is it me, Rory or Stan or all of us and everybody else on that plane and their loved ones? I am in too much of an emotional mess to think straight.

Since they checked in separately Stan and Rory are not seated together but Rory is able to swap seats with the passenger sitting next to Stan in a window seat, much to the passenger's relief due to the width of Stan, as boarding is completed.

"This is the best part," Stan says as the plane accelerates down the runway. Rory remains silent since he hates any part of flying accept disembarking the aircraft. On takeoff there is a deafening boom and the plane lurches to the right as it crashes back down onto the end of the runway. This causes Rory's head to hit the interior side of the plane so violently as to render him unconscious. The emergency lights are activated and Stan can see that Rory is slumped forward. Amid the pandemonium of screaming passengers acrid smoke begins to fill the cabin. Stan undoes his belt and tries to shake Rory into consciousness to no avail. Up ahead an emergency exit is opened and people start clamoring to get out. Stan releases Rory's belt and pulls him from his seat. He waits until everyone behind him able to passes to get to the exit then carries Rory towards it. Standing at the exit he can see forward that the plane's fuselage is damaged to the extent that he feels the wind blowing in. As he gently places Rory on the emergency chute he hears a woman cry out up ahead where the plane is most damaged. He releases Rory down the chute and hopes someone will receive him and take him to safety then shakily makes his way in the direction of the crying woman. He passes several bodies to his right where the plane's fuselage is destroyed. He discovers the woman on the left of the plane in an aisle seat.

"Please help me, I can't move my legs," she begs as Stan reaches her and sees her legs are trapped underneath the mangled seat in front. Stan releases her belt.

"Put your arms around my neck and I'll try and pull you out," he says calmly. As he tries to gently but firmly extract her there is an explosion and the interior of the fuselage is engulfed in flames leaving no possibility of any survivors still onboard.

38.

It is a cold and frosty morning in Manchester as I stand shoulder to shoulder with my son watching Stan's coffin being lowered into its grave. We have no idea or care who the hundred or so, predominantly black, other attendees are.

"Do you think he is at peace, Father"?" Rory asks.

"I know he is, Son. He came and told me so last night."

Printed in Great Britain
by Amazon